Chapter One

Spokane

With an odd mixture of rage and foreboding, Archer eyed his disguise in the men's room mirror after his plane landed. The confrontation he'd planned with Brian Wade was risky. He didn't want anyone to know for sure that he was still alive. But a face-to-face meeting was the only way to judge Wade's reactions to the accidents. With this disguise added to his changed appearance, he should be able to protect his new identity.

A light brown wig with a big bald spot covered his short black hair. Thick horn-rimmed glasses hid his blue eyes and dark eyebrows. A fine film of white powder turned his emerging beard to a sandy color and gave him a careless, unkempt look. By stooping slightly to camouflage his six-feet height and adding a seedy gray overcoat, Archer guessed he looked twenty years older than his actual thirty-one. If he could only keep his cool, he'd be okay.

From the airport, Archer took a cab to Grand, and walked to a side street a block away from the Cathedral of St. John where Wade had agreed to meet him.

Then he waited in the freezing January wind, hands shoved in his pockets, until he saw Wade's green Buick park between piles of snow on E Street.

Wade, a fringe of red hair showing beneath his uniform hat, buttoned his overcoat as he locked his vehicle and started across the street toward the cathedral. Feeling his anger, Archer forced himself to subdue it.

What would his old buddy say when he heard two of Albright's accusers had been killed in accidents? Though the deaths occurred in other cities, Wade might have heard of them. Would he suspect Don Albright was responsible—in retribution for last year's murder conviction?

As far as Archer could determine, nobody was following Wade.

Still, he watched for a full ten minutes before leaving his hiding place behind a parked car. It was quiet on the street. On this frigid holiday afternoon, few pedestrians were willing to brave the biting wind and hard-packed snow on the sidewalks.

It was time to go. Archer sucked in his breath and concentrated on keeping his expression carefully neutral. Wade mustn't see his festering rage. Stooping, he assumed a limp and moved slowly down the side street and across Grand. Wade glanced toward him but didn't move from his position on the sidewalk in front of the cathedral.

Archer saw no recognition in Wade's eyes as he approached.

"Captain Wade?" Archer asked.

"Yes. Are you Mr. Dillon?" While speaking, Wade

turned his head sideways so he wouldn't be facing into the biting wind.

Archer pulled his hand out of his pocket and shoved it toward Wade. "I'm Glenn Dillon, Captain Wade." It was a false name to protect his new identity.

Wade shook Archer's hand without removing his glove. His round face was tinged with crimson in the bitter cold.

"Just who the hell are you, Dillon?" Wade spit out the question in his raspy tenor voice. "What's your interest in this case?"

"It's to your advantage to talk to me," Archer shot back. "That's all you need to know." He affected the same accent he'd used yesterday on the telephone when he made the appointment.

"Let's hear your big news, Dillon." Lifting his glove, Wade glanced down at his watch. "This better not take long. My wife and I have plans for the evening."

"It won't take long, Captain." Archer pictured Susan Wade in his mind from the photographs he'd studied. Long gold-blond hair, brown eyes, sturdy frame. Mrs. Wade, an air force lieutenant, was the intelligence officer in Wade's squadron. Though Archer had never met her, he'd known who she was when she answered the phone yesterday. They'd married only four months ago.

Poor woman, Archer had thought at first, aware of Wade's many affairs. But then Archer had learned they'd known each other only five or six weeks before they married. If she was that impulsive, maybe they deserved each other.

"Well?" Wade asked, obviously irritated at Archer's silence.

"The matter concerns two of the men who were witnesses to Captain Albright's murder of your squadron commander last year—" Archer spoke slowly, dragging out the suspense. "The two who were transferred from Spokane to San Antonio and Colorado Springs."

"What about them?" Wade asked tersely. Ignoring the wind, he leaned toward Archer, his eyes narrow.

"Did you know they both died in accidents recently?"

Wade muffled his quick intake of breath. Archer sensed rather than heard it.

"The police say the deaths were accidental, but I don't believe it." He paused, enjoying the momentary look of fright on Wade's loathsome face. "How about you, Captain? Don't you think that's too much of a coincidence?"

Archer felt Wade staring at him, and deliberately turned away so the other man wouldn't see the hatred in his eyes.

"What's it to you, Dillon?" Wade asked, his eyes accusing. "You're starting to sound like a nosy private detective. Who the hell are you working for?"

"Nobody you know," Archer returned, expecting the question. "I'm sure you're not surprised that the case has attracted high-level attention."

Wade's face was carefully devoid of expression. "You think the accidents were arranged—that those men were killed—because of what happened last year?" His answer was cold, noncommittal, in the tone of a man used to hiding his emotions. But in spite of the keening wind, Archer heard a tiny tremor in his voice. Whether Wade had known about the accidents or not, Archer suspected that talking about them made him nervous.

"Damned right they were arranged," Archer said.

"Then you must suspect that Captain Albright—the man convicted last year—didn't commit suicide. That he had a hand in these deaths, too." Wade was studying Archer's face the way a hawk eyes a field mouse.

"Maybe," Archer said, trying to sound thoughtful. "From what I read in the papers, Albright had a strong motive, and there's some doubt about his suicide."

A fierce gust of wind swallowed his words.

"What did you say?" Wade asked.

Nodding in the direction of the cathedral, Archer started toward the arched entry to the building's west-facing wing where they'd have some protection from the wind. After a moment's hesitation, Wade followed. The stairs had been cleared of snow, and they reached the vaulted entrance with no difficulty.

Masking his rage, Archer turned to face Wade. "I was talking about motives." It was getting harder to keep his emotions hidden. In spite of the piercing cold, his face burned and his armpits were wet with perspiration. Wade's face blurred before his eyes. He blinked, struggling to clear his vision.

Then he heard a cracking sound above the howling wind. Unbelieving, Archer watched Brian Wade's big body topple forward, his crimson blood oozing onto the entryway's white sandstone floor.

THE TELEPHONE was ringing when Susan Wade walked into her well-ordered office at Fairchild Air Force Base. She frowned, glancing at her watch. Six-thirty. And this was a holiday. The caller had to be Brian. He was going to be late again. She just knew it.

Oh, he'd have a good excuse. He always did. She was beginning to think Brian put her at the bottom of his priority list. He was never late for anything or anybody else.

The telephone rang again. She picked up the receiver. "Lieutenant Wade."

"I'm glad I caught you, Susan." It was her commanding officer, Major Savage. "I tried to reach you at home but got no answer."

She tensed. The major never called anybody by their first name. Something must be wrong.

"Yes, sir," she said automatically, conscious of her pounding heart.

"Would you stay in your office, please? I'll be down to talk to you right away." His usual authoritarian tone was gone. Instead, she heard a faint quiver in his voice, as though some emotion had touched him. The sound sent anxious tremors jolting through her. Could he have stumbled onto her covert mission at Fairchild? Heaven knows she'd spent enough time out on the flight line snooping around the C-130s. But nobody knew about her assignment except the military brass at the Pentagon Intelligence Agency. Not even the FBI or the treasury people had been informed about it.

"I'm not in uniform, sir." She heard herself, weak

and tremulous, and struggled to put more confidence in her voice. "Brian's picking me up here as soon as he runs over the check-list with the ground crew for tomorrow morning's flight. We're going to dinner, then the reception at the club."

"Civilian clothes will be fine, Lieutenant." The major's voice was still gentle, but a measure of his usual command authority was back. His changed tone made Susan feel better. Maybe it was nothing after all. Maybe he just wanted to discuss tomorrow morning's briefing.

"This won't take long," he went on, "but it's vital that I see you right away."

A few minutes later he appeared in her open doorway, a somber expression on his hawklike face. Behind him was a heavyset colonel Susan recognized as the senior base chaplain. Standing to greet them, she felt the blood drain from her face. Why was the chaplain here? Had somebody died?

Major Savage, whose beak of a nose and sharpsighted eyes matched his wiry appearance, took the empty seat beside her desk. The chaplain pulled one of her spare chairs near her desk and settled himself on it.

"Colonel Ratigan, this is Lieutenant Susan Wade," Major Savage said.

The colonel reached out and clasped her hand between both of his. "I'm one of the chaplains here at Fairchild."

"I know," she blurted, scarcely aware of her own voice. "What's happened?"

"Please sit down," the colonel said.

Numbly, Susan sat.

The chaplain eyed her, his brow furrowed. "There's been an...accident, Susan."

"My husband?" She could hardly force the words out.

"I'm sorry to have to tell you this," Major Savage began, "but Brian's been shot."

She jumped to her feet. "Is he in the base hospital?"

"No, he's not." The chaplain rose and put his hand on her arm. "Captain Wade—well—he's no longer with us."

"You mean he's dead? That's impossible." For a moment Susan wasn't sure she'd heard correctly. Shaking her head, she sank back into her chair. "You've made a mistake. Brian had an inspection scheduled for his ground crew this afternoon." She heard her voice rising and knew she was on the verge of losing control. But she couldn't help herself.

The major leaned toward her, lines of worry between his sharp-sighted blue eyes. "He must have left the base after his inspection, Susan."

You're wrong, she wanted to scream. *He had a date with me. Why would he leave the base?* Instead, she looked down at her hands twisted nervously in her lap. "It wasn't him," she said. "It couldn't be. Someone's made a terrible mistake."

The chaplain shook his head. "There was no mistake, Susan. His ID card and driver's license were in his wallet. The man they found was Brian."

Waves of disbelief swept over her, and she struggled to keep from screaming. "I want to see the body."

"Of course," the chaplain said, glancing at Major Savage. He nodded slightly.

The room swam around her as tears blinded her eyes and choked her voice. Until now Susan had been able to fight this awful lie. But she couldn't any longer. Unable to see clearly, she fumbled in her purse for a tissue. In front of her, a clean linen handkerchief appeared in the chaplain's hand.

"Take it," he urged gently.

He and Major Savage got up, and the two men turned away while she wiped her cheeks dry and blew her nose. Thank God they knew enough to give her some privacy. She heard the low murmur of their voices as from a great distance, though they were only a few feet away.

Finally she gained a measure of control over herself. But even then she couldn't seem to function properly. When she tried to stand, her knees buckled. Leaning on her desk, she sank back to her seat.

An instant later, the chaplain pulled his chair closer and sat down. "Are you certain you're up to seeing Brian right now, Susan?"

She nodded, swallowing her sobs.

"Come with us," Major Savage said.

THE MORGUE WAS COLD and silent. An attendant ushered them into the sterile white room where the identification would be made.

Please let it be someone else, Susan prayed as she approached the gurney where the body lay. Holding her breath, she watched the attendant fold back the sheet. Brian's face stared up at her, still and white.

All the breath seemed to leave her as she stood there rooted to the floor. Stepping closer, she touched his face with her fingertips. His skin felt cool and smooth, like old silk. Though he hadn't lived up to her expectations, she couldn't bear to see him like this. Standing there beside his body, she felt tears slipping down her cheeks.

"It's him," she said, unable to speak above a whisper. "It *is* Brian." Finally the chaplain took her arm and eased her away from the table.

Shivering, she hugged her wool coat around herself. Though still inside the building, she felt cold, so terribly cold. Would she ever be warm again?

Not until she was in the car with Major Savage and Colonel Ratigan, headed back to the base, did she think to ask who fired the shot that killed him.

"Do the police know what happened?"

"They've already identified a person of interest," Major Savage announced, glancing at her beside him in the front seat. "A taxi driver described a bald, middle-aged man who was in that area about the same time your husband got there."

"An eyewitness?" Her mind was still too full of the horror of Brian's cold, pallid face to digest the importance of what she was hearing. "Do the police know who he is?" She heard herself ask the question, but it was as if she were on autopilot and her intelligence training had kicked in.

"No, but they're trying to track him down. It's been only a couple of hours since…" He glanced at Susan.

She stared rigidly ahead, willing herself not to break down.

She forced the stark image of Brian's dead face out of her mind. "Do the police have a motive for the eyewitness?"

Major Savage didn't answer right away. When he did, his words were halting. "Nothing was stolen. So maybe this terrible tragedy is tied into that murder last year of the major I replaced as squadron commander."

In the back seat, the chaplain cleared his throat. "I don't think this is a good time to talk about that."

Susan jerked bolt upright on the seat. "What was his name? That air force captain who was convicted of the murder?"

"Don Albright," Major Savage supplied.

Mulling over the case in her mind, she reached into her memory for bits of information. "Wasn't there some doubt about his suicide?"

"There's been speculation that he faked the leap from the Tacoma Narrows Bridge so he could jump bail and escape." The major's voice was cold and exact.

Susan clenched her hands together so tightly the knuckles cracked. "If Don Albright's alive, he must be the one who killed Brian." Anger released some of her grief, and she didn't try to fight it. "I'll see he pays if it's the last thing I do."

San Francisco

SEATED AT THE TABLE in his cramped room, Archer stared in disbelief at the picture on the front page of the Spokane *Daily Chronicle.* Though the focus was a little hazy, he easily recognized the man facing the camera.

It was himself, in the disguise he'd worn in Spokane. Stiff with shock, he read the news item under the picture.

Have you seen this man? the caption read. *Eyewitness wanted for questioning in the Wade killing.* The article went on to say that the picture was taken by a tourist visiting the cathedral. He'd sent the photo to the paper anonymously because he didn't want to get involved.

Though only the back of the other man in the photograph was visible, the newspaper identified him as Air Force Captain Brian Wade, the officer who'd been murdered two weeks ago.

Archer crumpled the newspaper in his sweaty fists. Were the police trying to find the eyewitness because they thought he was the murderer? Lord knows, he'd dreamed of strangling Wade with his bare hands.

But the police couldn't possibly suspect the man in the picture. With the sophisticated techniques available today, they had to know the bullet was fired from the street, not a foot away. But maybe they thought he'd moved from his photographed position and then committed the murder.

He turned his attention back to the picture. Where had it come from? Not from "a tourist who wanted to remain anonymous." Archer was certain of that. Somebody wanted Glenn Dillon to be charged—either that, or to tell what he'd seen.

What *had* he seen? he asked himself. In the traumatic moment of Wade's death, he hadn't focused on anything but the body toppling toward him. Fuzzy images of a white, late-model sedan with a blond woman at the wheel appeared as indistinct figures in his memory.

He eyed his burgeoning file on Susan Wade. She was a blonde. Could she have been the woman he saw? She certainly had a motive. According to the information he'd collected, Wade's death had made her rich. From her service decorations, Archer knew Susan was an expert marksman on the rifle range, and she could have fired the gun that killed her husband.

By the time a month had passed, Archer knew he'd have to risk another trip to Spokane to meet her and fill in the blanks about her character and objectives. In the automobile garage where he worked, he plotted his every move as he changed oil and replaced worn-out fan belts.

By night, hunched over a flimsy table in his cramped basement room, he examined the newspapers he bought every day and added more information to his growing files. On days off, he compiled the forms he'd need, had them printed and finalized the background information for his cover as an insurance agent.

Two weeks later he was ready.

Spokane

SUSAN YANKED UP the kitchen blind and peered across her deck through the predawn grayness. After the luscious green foliage of Hawaii's Big Island where she'd

spent the past month, the bare trees and yellowed grass
behind her condo looked as bleak as a graveyard. Disturbed by the sight, she released the cord and let the
blind drop with a noisy rattle.

On Major Savage's orders, she'd taken leave in Hawaii shortly after Brian's funeral. Now she'd been
home almost a week, and her spacious condo still
seemed filled with his presence. Glancing from the
kitchen into the contemporary living room, she could
almost see him sitting on his leather recliner.

Why hadn't she told him the truth about her assignment to Fairchild? Maybe if she'd trusted him more,
their marriage would have been better. She'd wanted
to tell him she was here on a covert mission so secret
no one knew about it except key officers at the Pentagon Intelligence Agency. But her sense of duty always held her back.

Now Susan was left with the piercing guilt that she
was somehow responsible for Brian's death. Brushing
her hair off her forehead, she told herself Don Albright
was the killer. But she couldn't help wondering if
Brian's death was somehow tied in to her covert mission—if he might still be alive if he hadn't married
her.

Brian had also left her a lot of money. The authorities had been delicate in their questioning, but there
was no doubt they thought she had a motive for killing
him.

Worse, she had no alibi for that awful afternoon.
Absently, she placed the breakfast dishes in the dish-
washer as she remembered what had happened. A telephone call—allegedly from the wife of one of her air-

men—had led her on a wild-goose chase. The guard at Fairchild's main gate remembered both her and Brian leaving the base within minutes of each other.

She'd told the police about the telephone call and her fruitless search for the airman's wife, hoping they'd realize she'd been set up. They'd asked a few questions and talked to the couple, who denied making the call. Afterward, the police had acted even more suspicious.

Sighing, Susan put on her uniform overcoat. The phone rang as she started out the door. Returning to the kitchen, she picked up the receiver.

"Good morning," she said, hoping it was somebody from the squadron with an urgent assignment for her, something important that would occupy her thoughts.

"Is Captain Wade there?" a man's voice asked.

Susan's heart sank at the friendly tone in his voice. He sounded vaguely familiar. Probably one of Brian's friends, who didn't know about the murder. She dreaded telling him. "No. Are you a friend of his?"

"Not exactly," he said. "I'm an agent with Industrial Indemnity Insurance Company. Is this Mrs. Wade?"

"Yes." Suddenly warm, she shrugged off her overcoat and laid it over the back of a chair.

"This is Derek Archer," he said. "I'm sorry to call you so early, Mrs. Wade, but I'd hoped to catch your husband before he left for work. Could you give me his number at the office?"

"No," she said abruptly. "He doesn't need any more insurance."

"I'm not trying to sell him a policy, Mrs. Wade. I'm trying to service the one he's got." He sounded tired, like a middle-aged man who was fed up with talking to difficult clients. Susan had a good ear for voices. Where had she heard his before?

Trying to be patient, she took a deep breath. "I didn't know we had a policy with your company."

He cleared his throat. "Well, you won't have it long if you don't get caught up on your premiums. Your husband's missed the last two."

Susan's throat tightened. The last thing she wanted right now was more talk about insurance.

"Mrs. Wade?"

"Yes, I'm still here."

"I'll be in Spokane for the next few days at the Riverfront Hotel. That's where I'm calling from. Tell your husband to call me so we can get this settled— Derek Archer from Industrial Indemnity." He repeated his name and then gave her the hotel's telephone number.

Susan didn't bother to write it down. "My husband's been dead two months, Mr. Archer. That's why your premiums weren't paid."

There was a long pause. When he spoke, his tone was grave. "My condolences, Mrs. Wade. That puts a different light on things. Maybe we should get together to discuss your husband's policy while I'm in town. How about lunch in the hotel dining room at noon today?"

Hesitating, she nearly said no. She was trained to be suspicious, and something didn't seem quite right about this agent with a policy she had no record of.

Why was he servicing the policy personally? Didn't the company notify tardy payers by mail?

Then her natural curiosity took over. What was this man up to? Besides, if an insurance company owed her money, she'd be a fool not to collect it. "Fine," she told him.

She started to hang up when he spoke again. "How will I recognize you?"

"I'm blond and I'll be wearing an air force lieutenant's uniform. How about you?"

"I'll have a red handkerchief in my coat pocket."

After she'd hung up, Susan kicked herself for saying yes. After the funeral, she'd examined every document in Brian's file cabinet and safe-deposit box and had contacted the two insurance companies that carried his policies. Industrial Indemnity wasn't one of them.

Better not go, she warned herself.

Quickly she dialed the number of the Riverfront Hotel and asked for Derek Archer.

Nobody with that name was registered.

For an instant she stood there motionless, the receiver clutched in her hand.

What kind of game was Derek Archer—if that was his real name—trying to play? Whatever it was, Susan wanted no part of it. She replaced the receiver on its cradle, even more certain he was up to something—maybe a con game to swindle her out of her inheritance. Still, the agent might be for real. If Brian wanted her to have this policy, she felt obligated to check into it.

By ten o'clock, after she'd finished her third cup of coffee, her curiosity had gotten the best of her. Perhaps the young man she'd talked to at the hotel had made a mistake when he examined the register early this morning. Sighing, Susan dialed the hotel again and asked for Mr. Archer.

"I'll have the operator connect you," said the clerk. His voice sounded like that of the young man she'd talked to earlier.

"Just a minute," Susan said. "When I tried to reach Mr. Archer at seven o'clock this morning, you told me he hadn't checked in. Did you make a mistake?"

There was a short pause. Then a congenial chuckle. "I make a mistake now and then, but this wasn't one of those times."

"Can you tell me when he signed in?"

The clerk hesitated. "I can't say exactly, but I think it was sometime around eight-thirty," he replied finally. "I'll ring his room."

Susan hung up before Derek Archer answered. She spent the time until lunch wondering why he'd tried to give her the impression, early this morning, that he was calling from the hotel when he obviously wasn't.

She'd test him, she decided. If he lied again, she'd know he was up to something.

Chapter Two

Hesitating, Susan glanced around the hotel lobby, searching for a middle-aged man with a red handkerchief in his pocket. The faint smell of woodsmoke from the stone fireplace, along with the subtle fragrance of fresh flowers, enveloped her. A vaseful of yellow roses stood on a rough-hewn table near the door, another sat on the registration counter.

She couldn't help staring when she spotted the red handkerchief. The man wearing it looked years younger than she'd expected after talking to Archer on the phone. Though deep frown lines between his dark brows gave him the disturbing, faintly ominous air of someone on a life-or-death mission, he couldn't be much older than Brian. But in spite of her odd first impression, Susan had to admit he was attractive, in a rugged sort of way.

For an instant she felt an unwelcome tug of interest. *He's been an officer in the service,* she thought, eyeing the sharp creases in his pants, the shine on his black loafers. In his gray business suit, he carried himself with the self-confidence that came with military command.

Though he looked tough and lean, she could see his shoulders straining against the confining fabric of his suit, as if he'd gained muscle recently. A couple of unruly strands of curly black hair drooped over his forehead. His eyes, such a dark blue they were almost indigo, clung to hers with an intensity that made her catch her breath. They were the eyes of a dangerous man, so penetrating they seemed almost as though they'd glow in the dark.

Watch it, Lieutenant, she told herself, surprised at her sudden breathlessness. She was a new widow. She couldn't let herself react to the first interesting man she'd met since Brian's death. And he *did* look appealing, she had to admit, in the frightening way a free-roaming black panther looked alluring. What had happened to give him that tough, predatory look? she wondered.

Starting toward him, she forced herself to remember her plan to trap him into telling another lie. Derek Archer was probably a con artist out to swindle her out of her inheritance. No matter how attractive he was, the sooner she found out what he was up to, the better.

He came up to her with a half smile.

"Mrs. Wade?" He extended his hand.

Susan recognized the smooth baritone voice she'd heard on the telephone. "Yes, I'm Susan Wade." She took his hand. It was surprisingly rough for an insurance agent. His square jaw was thrust forward, as if he expected a confrontation.

Almost without realizing it, she checked for a wedding band. He wore none. She was irritated with herself for feeling relieved.

"Thanks for coming, Mrs. Wade." His voice, deep and sensual, seemed years younger than when she'd heard it on the phone.

He stared frankly into her eyes. When her gaze didn't waver, he cleared his throat and glanced away.

"Excuse me for staring," he said. "When I was in the army, I never ran into any lieutenants as attractive as you."

Susan didn't let herself get distracted by his compliment, despite an unexpected sense of warmth coursing through her. Salesmen were good at buttering people up. If he was working some kind of con on her, this was how he'd start.

"When were you in the army, Mr. Archer?" Her words were quick and sharp. She hoped to catch him off guard.

He took her arm, urging her toward the dining room. "After I graduated from college, I put in my six years to pay off my ROTC commitment."

His reply was so glib, Susan suspected he'd prepared an answer to fit into whatever swindle he was planning. Not until they arrived at the table did she realize that he'd never answered her question.

ARCHER EYED SUSAN WADE, seated opposite him in the Riverfront Hotel's Crown Room. After his months on the run, he was good at sizing people up without their knowledge.

Studying Susan, he decided a picture of her he'd clipped from the local paper didn't do her justice. Instead of looking merely healthy and sturdy, the way she did in the newspaper, she glowed with a kind of inner vitality. Maybe it was the combination of tanned skin, golden hair and brown eyes that gave her such an earthy, vibrant quality. And, close up, she wasn't what he'd call *sturdy,* not in the usual sense. Rather, his experienced eye detected a firm, well-rounded figure beneath the confines of her uniform.

Watching her, an unexpected surge of pure desire washed over him. He wanted to do more than have a meal with this woman, he realized to his chagrin. He wanted to unloosen the hair at the back of her neck so it streamed down her bare back. And he wanted to hold her tight against his naked chest while he was doing it.

Archer recognized his feelings for what they were: simple, unadulterated lust. As he studied his menu, he told himself to back off. For his plan to work, he had to keep his distance from this woman. But he couldn't help stealing another glance, only to find her brown eyes staring back at him. She glanced down, but not before Archer caught what he thought was a gleam of interest. To his dismay, this time his body responded. Heat surged through him, tightening his muscles.

Damn. He'd have to watch his step. The last thing he wanted right now was an unwelcome attraction to Brian Wade's widow, something that would only interfere with his need to get even with the men who'd betrayed him.

"Tell me about this policy you say my husband took out," she said. "How much is it for?"

Her voice was low and musical, more appealing

than it sounded on the phone. But her question made her appear mercenary, like he'd expect a husband-killer to sound. Yes, she might have done it, he decided, eyeing her tempting mouth with its full lower lip. Incredibly, his suspicion made her seem even more attractive, perhaps because it gave them something in common. They were quite a pair: the convicted killer and the grieving widow who might have murdered her husband. For a moment he let himself picture the two of them locked in a lusty embrace, his hands warm on her full breasts.

"It's an accidental death or dismemberment policy for fifty thousand dollars," he said, reluctantly letting the fantasy go. He hadn't had a woman in months and knew the feelings were normal. But why at such an inappropriate time?

He handed her the packet of insurance papers he'd had printed, and she leafed through them.

"Industrial Indemnity doesn't sound like the name of an insurance company that handles this type of policy," she commented, without looking up from the page in front of her. Her lashes, several shades darker than her gold-blond hair, shadowed her high cheekbones.

He shrugged. "Our company's been in business for more than sixty years. We started out with heavy industries where accidents were a big problem. Then, twenty years ago, we began accepting individuals. Your husband said he wanted a sound accident policy that would cover him in war or other violence connected with the military service. Industrial Indemnity is one of the few companies to offer that type of coverage."

She skimmed through the policy. "Yes, I see the limits here in paragraph 4B."

The waiter appeared. Susan ordered a cup of tea instead of a cocktail. Too bad. Archer had hoped to loosen her up with a few drinks.

"My husband was murdered, you know," she said after their beverages had been served and they'd given the waiter their lunch orders. As she spoke, lines appeared on her smooth forehead, giving her a vulnerable look that made him doubt his suspicion. Suddenly he wasn't so sure she'd killed her husband.

"Yes, I know," he returned. "I checked to find out how he died right after I talked to you."

She eyed him quizzically. "Then you must have gone to the newspaper office right after you called from the hotel this morning. The libary's not open that early."

Archer almost said yes, he'd gotten the details of Wade's death from the *Chronicle* files. But something in the expectant way she was sitting, leaning toward him with her back straight and her beautiful brown eyes slightly narrowed, alerted him. Did she have a friend on the *Chronicle* staff ready to deny he'd been there?

He shook his head. "No, I had our research people in San Francisco look into your husband's death."

"And you called them from the hotel this morning?" Her musical voice held a rasp of excitement.

He adopted a tone of irascible patience. "Yes, of course. Where else would I call from?"

When Archer saw the look of triumph on her face, he knew he'd made a mistake. But what was it?

HE'D BETTER HAVE a darn good explanation, Susan thought, watching the play of emotions on his rugged, square-cut face. Why did he have to look so darn sexy? From the swath of dark curly hair falling on his forehead, to his thick brows and firm chin, he struck a vibrant chord within her. And his intense, purple-blue eyes—set wide apart above an aquiline nose—seemed omniscient, almost as if he could see into her mind.

Planning her attack, she took a bite of her fish. He couldn't have called San Francisco from the hotel. He wasn't even here yet at seven o'clock this morning.

"Mr. Archer," she began quietly.

His tight expression relaxed into a smile, but the wary look in his eyes remained.

"You can forget about the formalities," he said with a smile that set her pulses racing. "My friends call me Archer."

She took a deep breath and shook her head. "We're not friends, Mr. Archer. Not while you're playing games with me."

His smile vanished. He seemed speechless in his surprise. As their eyes met, a shock ran through her. Brows lowered and nostrils flared, he gave her a threatening glare that burned into her brain. For a frightening moment, she thought he might slap her.

"What are you talking about, Mrs. Wade?" His usually smooth voice grated harshly.

"About your lies this morning on the phone." She

stared at him. Even as she watched, his expression veered from anger to confusion. He seemed honestly bewildered by her accusation.

"What lies?" Menace remained in his eyes, but a ghost of a smile touched his lips.

"You said you called me from the hotel this morning," she said, her face burning. "When I checked, the desk clerk told me you weren't here. You obviously called from somewhere else. I want to know where—and why you lied about it."

She waited while he took a bite of steak. When he met her eyes, the menace was gone, but there was a deadly coldness hidden behind his direct gaze. What had he expected her to accuse him of?

"When someone in your family dies violently, it's a terrible shock." His sympathetic tone was not matched in his iridescent blue eyes. "No wonder you see suspicious characters lurking behind every bush."

Again, he hadn't answered her question. Her doubts about him refused to go away. What clever line was he giving her now?

"What are you getting at?"

He leaned toward her, a determined look on his face. "As soon as we finish eating, we'll go to the lobby. The clerk will tell you I signed in at eight-thirty this morning, about an hour after I talked to you on the lobby phone."

"Why did you call me before you registered?"

His brows drew forward in a frown. "Because at least fifteen people were in line to check out. If I'd waited, I might not have caught you at home, so I used the pay phone. After I talked to you, I called our research people and had some coffee. Then I registered.''

Susan could hardly believe there could be such a simple explanation. But, surprisingly, she found herself relieved that he had one. Drawn to him, she wanted to see him again. If he was a legitimate insurance agent, she knew she would.

"I'm sorry, Archer." She eliminated the formalities to let him know she meant what she was saying. "You're right. I've become paranoid since Brian was killed. He wasn't robbed, so police know that wasn't the motive. And the one man who might have seen the killer has vanished into thin air.''

Archer settled back in his chair. "If this possible witness disappeared, how did the police find out about him?''

Susan opened her black leather service bag, pulled out a newspaper clipping and handed it to him. "Here's a picture of the eyewitness and a story about what happened.''

While Archer read the accompanying article, Susan studied his face. The frown lines were back between his eyes. He scowled as he read. But no matter how formidable he looked, he was still the most fascinating man she'd met in a long time.

What would have happened if she and Archer had met last year, before she married Brian? she wondered, and then gave herself a quick mental kick. Archer was the last thing she needed right now. Behind his sexy eyes was a menacing coldness that frightened her. To clear her mind, she forced herself to concentrate on a window across the room. Outside in the sun, bare branches starting to bud were silhouetted against an azure sky.

He folded the clipping and returned it to her. "Are you sure this man with his back to the camera is your husband?"

"Positive. Nobody but Brian had hair that curled that way around his ears."

Archer leaned toward her, resting his arms on the edge of the table. "Tell me honestly, Susan. Who do you think killed your husband?"

"Don Albright, the man who murdered Brian's squadron commander last year," she replied quickly.

Susan felt her temper rising just saying Albright's name. The certainty of his guilt relieved her own anguished feelings. Since he did it, she couldn't possibly bear any responsibility for not telling Brian about her covert assignment. "While the verdict was being appealed, Albright jumped bail, faked his own suicide and escaped. The police are still hunting for him."

Archer's scowl lines deepened. "Did Albright have a motive for killing your husband?"

"The best in the world." Susan felt her face flushing as her anger increased. "Revenge. Brian was the one who put the finger on Albright at the trial. If it hadn't been for Brian's testimony, Albright might never have been convicted."

"I remember reading about that trial." Archer's voice was thoughtful. "I never understood how your husband could be so sure Albright murdered the commander. Any one of the six other men at the table might have done it."

"Brian felt Albright move his arm," Susan said,

remembering what Brian had told her. Her fingers tightened around her napkin. "Don Albright had the gun, for God's sake. He killed his squadron commander because of a bad effectiveness report that kept him from getting promoted."

She stared at Archer, daring him to dispute her. Don Albright was guilty as sin, and she wanted the whole world to know it.

Archer met her gaze head-on. "Did they ever find the accomplice?"

"You mean the person who turned out the lights?"

He nodded. "Whoever it was must have known he'd be an accomplice to murder. If that person was a friend, why couldn't the police find him or her?"

"Maybe it wasn't a friend. Maybe Albright paid somebody to help him." Alarm and anger rippled along her spine. "You seem awfully sympathetic to that murderer all of a sudden. For a minute there, I thought I was talking to Albright's defense attorney."

He shrugged dismissively. "Just playing devil's advocate. That's a good way to find out what somebody thinks."

"Well, now you know exactly what *I* think." Susan settled back in her chair.

"I understand several thousand dollars were offered to anyone with information about the commander's murder." There was a subtle undercurrent in his voice. "You're suggesting Albright paid his accomplice. If he'd take Albright's money, why not the reward?"

It was a question she couldn't answer. Disturbed, Susan shifted uneasily on her chair. Why did Archer make her so darned nervous?

"Dozens of people turned up to claim the reward," she said. "But none of their stories checked out. The missing accomplice was one of the weak links in the case."

Across from her, Archer shot her a cynical smile. Then his gaze shifted to something or someone behind her.

"Sorry to interrupt your lunch, Lieutenant Wade."

Susan glanced up to see Major Savage, her squadron commander, staring down at her with his hawklike eyes.

"SORRY TO INTERRUPT," Major Savage said again, after Susan had introduced him to Archer. "But there's been a new development in your husband's murder. The Spokane police want to see you at their headquarters across the river."

Apprehension coursed through Susan as she rose to her feet. What was so important that the police had to see her immediately? She'd already told her story over and over again. Her heart pounding, she glanced at Archer. "Can it wait half an hour or so? Mr. Archer and I haven't finished our business."

Major Savage shook his head. "I'm afraid not, Lieutenant. When the police tried to reach you on the base, I checked your sign-out board and saw you were here. I told them I'd make sure you got there ASAP."

Nodding, Archer helped her slip into her coat. "I'll be at the hotel for a couple of days, Mrs. Wade. We can get together tomorrow and go over these forms."

"Fine," she said, more anxious by the minute.

With a sinking feeling in the pit of her stomach,

Susan allowed Major Savage to escort her across the stone-floored lobby and through the etched glass doors of the Riverfront Hotel.

An air force staff car was parked in front of the lobby entrance. Susan could barely hide her startled gasp when she saw who was inside. Seated beside the driver on the passenger seat was a lanky lieutenant colonel she recognized as John Tinnerman, the commander of the security police squadron at the base. In back was a lieutenant she'd met at the officers' club. With rising concern she identified him as Phil Davidson, a lawyer recently assigned to Fairchild.

A lawyer and a military policeman. "What's going on?" she cried as the car moved away from the hotel.

"Pull into the Azteca parking lot," Major Savage told the driver. "We need some time to talk, and it'll take only ten minutes to get to police headquarters from here." He turned to face Susan. "Detective MacElroy said he had new information about your husband's death. I have no idea what that news is, but thought it best to bring one of our base attorneys along."

Colonel Tinnerman grinned at her from the front seat. "And I'm here for moral support. If you've got questions about the police and how they operate, I'm your man."

"Thank you, sir," she said gratefully. With his round face and button nose, the colonel was one of the homeliest men she'd ever seen, but his down-home manner reassured her.

During the next half hour—interrupted occasionally by Major Savage—she briefed the attorney about her husband's case. When he was satisfied, they resumed their drive across the river.

Arriving in front of the City County Public Safety Building, Susan and the lawyer climbed out of the back seat. Neither Major Savage nor Colonel Tinnerman moved.

Dismayed, Susan peered in the back window at Major Savage. "Aren't you coming with me?"

The major shook his head. "When the police interview you, they won't allow anyone but your attorney in the room. The car will take the colonel and me to the base. It'll be back for you in about an hour."

With a lump in her throat, Susan turned away. Major Savage wasn't the friendliest commander she'd worked for, but she'd counted on his support. Instead, she had a fuzzy-faced lieutenant just out of law school.

"I don't think they're going to charge you," Lieutenant Davidson said, holding the door to the building open for her. "But Major Savage thought it would be a good idea for me to come along, regardless. If they do arrest you at some future time, you'd be better off with a civilian attorney since your husband's murder occurred in a civilian jurisdiction."

The young lieutenant sounded more capable than his youthful appearance indicated. But that didn't keep Susan's legs from shaking as she walked to Detective MacElroy's office.

MacElroy stood and extended his hand when Susan and Lieutenant Davidson entered. She recognized him immediately. A big, barrel-chested man with a florid complexion and bushy mustache, MacElroy was in charge of the on-going investigation into Brian's death. Since the murder had occurred off base, the local civilian authorities had jurisdiction.

After introducing Davidson, Susan shook Mac-Elroy's hand and lowered herself onto one of the two chairs in front of his inspection-clean desk.

"Thanks for coming, Lieutenant Wade, Lieutenant Davidson," MacElroy said. After settling himself, he placed a tape recorder on his desk. "If you don't mind, I'd like to tape our interview."

Susan caught Davidson's nod. "That's customary," he said.

Swallowing hard, she gave a shaky "Yes."

MacElroy started the recorder. When he focused on Susan, his eyes narrowed. "Since you're not under arrest, you're free to leave at any time. Is that clear?"

"Yes." She forced the word out through clenched teeth.

"You have the right to remain silent, you have the right…"

As MacElroy droned on, Susan froze in her chair. *He's reading me my rights, just like I'm a criminal.* When the detective was finished, she turned to Davidson. "If I'm not under arrest, why is he reading me my rights?" Her voice quavered so much she was shocked.

"Don't worry about it," Davidson said. "It's just added protection for you." He focused on MacElroy. "Let's hear what you've got."

The detective folded thick arms against the diamond-patterned sweater he was wearing. He looked first at Susan and then at Lieutenant Davidson. "We've found the murder weapon. It was buried in the atrium at Cavanaugh's Inn at the Park.'' Cavanaugh's was a four-star hotel in Riverfront Park, across the Spokane River from Archer's hotel.

Susan listened with bewilderment. ''That's very interesting, but I don't see what it has to do with me.''

His eyes narrowed. ''Were you in Cavanaugh's lobby the afternoon your husband was murdered?''

Her insides turned to jelly. ''No, of course not. You know where I was that afternoon. In my car on Argonne Road, trying to help an airman's wife.'' She stared at him accusingly. ''I never went near Cavanaugh's.''

''You already know all this,'' Lieutenant Davidson interrupted. ''Lieutenant Wade told me she gave you this information in a signed statement.''

MacElroy kept his eyes pinned on Susan. ''Witnesses at Cavanaugh's claim to have seen a woman who matches your description in the lobby shortly after your husband was murdered.''

Susan could hardly believe her ears. The stuffy little room tilted, and she heard a muffled roaring in her ears. When she opened her mouth to speak, nothing happened.

The witnesses are wrong, she wanted to scream. *I've never been there.*

Beside her, Lieutenant Davidson spoke. ''Captain Wade was killed more than two months ago. How can these people remember a specific day?''

''It was a holiday—Martin Luther King's birthday. Remember?'' A smug smile crossed the detective's face.

''That's right,'' Davidson returned. ''Two months

ago. Why have these employees taken so long to come forward?''

"Because a gardener just found the gun today." MacElroy's expression sobered. "When we asked for a description of people in the lobby that afternoon, several remembered a woman with long blond hair and brown eyes, about Mrs. Wade's height."

"That's impossible," Susan blurted.

"The witnesses especially remembered your long blond hair and the short white dress you were wearing." MacElroy shot her a contemptuous sneer, as though positive he'd find the dress if he searched her closet.

"Not *my* hair," she corrected him. "And I don't have a short white dress." She flashed him a look of disdain. "I never wear white."

His lips twisted into a cynical smile. "If you say so, Lieutenant Wade." A probing query came into his eyes. "Since you're so positive, I'm sure you won't mind letting us take your picture and fingerprints."

Lieutenant Davidson jumped to his feet. "You can't tell me you'd arrest Lieutenant Wade on the strength of a photo ID! Any fool knows how unreliable pictures are."

Unperturbed, MacElroy leaned back in his chair. "Settle down, Lieutenant. A photomontage is just another step in the process."

Davidson leaned over MacElroy's desk. "What's this about fingerprints?"

"If you'll sit down, I'll explain."

Reluctantly, Davidson returned to his chair.

MacElroy's eyes bored into Susan. "We need your

prints to compare with some partials we found on the weapon.'' He lifted a bushy eyebrow. "Incidentally, the weapon was a 357 Magnum revolver registered to your husband. Ever remember seeing it around your house, Lieutenant?''

Clenching her hands so tightly they hurt, Susan forced herself to look directly into MacElroy's accusing eyes. "No, Brian kept his gun at the squadron. It was stolen last November, around Thanksgiving.''

"Was the theft reported?''

"I honestly don't know. Brian didn't say.''

MacElroy's eyes narrowed, and she could tell he thought she was lying through her teeth.

She hadn't believed Derek Archer, she remembered, increasingly anxious. She'd thought he was a con man, trying to work a swindle on her, and now she was in the same position. The image of his expressive face appeared in her mind. What she wouldn't give to be back with him in the Riverfront Hotel right now, worrying about something as unimportant as an insurance policy.

Chapter Three

When the staff vehicle finally reached the Riverfront Hotel where Susan's car was parked, she clambered out so quickly her purse slid to the ground. Bending to pick it up, she saw Derek Archer stride through the lobby doors.

After what she'd been through, she didn't want to talk to him, and turned away, hoping he wouldn't follow her to her car. She didn't want him to see her like this, flustered and scared, afraid the police might actually indict her for Brian's murder.

He didn't take the hint, easily catching up with her as she hurried away from him. "I hope you don't have to go back to work, so we can finish our business."

She looked up at his face. Taller and broader than she remembered, he let his cold blue eyes, now strangely seductive, drift from her face down to her uniform-clad breasts and back to her face again, in a sweeping, deliberate movement.

Her face flushing with unexpected heat, she almost increased her pace and told him to leave. But that would be a cop-out. His insolent glance was a conscious challenge, and Susan couldn't ignore it, no matter how decrepit she felt. So instead she turned and faced him. "It'll have to wait until tomorrow, Archer."

"I don't want to pry into your business, Susan, but I'm a good listener," he said, buttoning his overcoat in the gathering darkness.

So he was curious about what had happened at the police station, was he? That's what his challenge had been about. Disconcerted, she stepped off the driveway onto the sidewalk, trying to decide whether or not to tell him.

Behind those sexy eyes of his lurked a bitter cynicism that made her distrust him. After being photographed and fingerprinted at the police station, her earlier suspicions about him seemed silly. But he was still a stranger, not somebody she could discuss her personal feelings with.

"No, I've got to get home." Susan started toward her car again. "I'm bone-tired. Our business will have to wait."

He fell into step beside her. "So what're you going to do? Go home and have a good cry?"

His abrupt, taunting words took her breath away. "Wha-what do you mean?" At the base of her throat, she felt a pulse beat as though her heart had risen from its usual place.

"Isn't that what you were about to do? Huddle down in a corner somewhere and cry?" His iridescent blue eyes focused on her so accusingly that she shivered.

"I'm not upset," she lied, unable to meet his gaze.

"Of course you are. The police have you scared

witless. Now you're going home and giving up, just like a world-class quitter.''

Susan could feel her eyes filling and swallowed hard, trying to force the tears away. He was right, damn him. She *had* planned to go home and spend the night feeling sorry for herself.

They'd reached the end of the sidewalk. He stopped and faced her. ''What'd they do? Accuse you of killing your husband?''

She blinked her tears away. ''How did you guess?''

''I took one look at your face when you got out of that staff car.'' His eyes were no longer menacing. ''I can help. Let's go somewhere we can talk.''

NEXT TO SUSAN in her Firebird, Archer silently congratulated himself for forcing the truth out of her. He felt an unexpected pang of remorse that he'd made her cry, but told himself not to feel sorry for her: she'd probably killed her husband. Whatever she'd done, the knowing did nothing to lessen his lust for her. When she was around, he halfway forgot his desire for revenge.

Don't screw up by playing around with Brian Wade's widow, he warned himself. *She's only a resource for information to use against those dirt bags who witnessed against me.* But he couldn't rid himself of his awareness, no matter how much he concentrated on the downtown area as they drove through it.

Archer knew where she was headed. High Drive Parkway paralleled the edge of a steep drop-off to the canyon floor over one hundred feet below. The executive homes across the road sat well back from the rim, their windows looking out over miles of breath-taking scenery. On the canyon floor, a freeway snaked its way south.

Susan pulled into a turnoff. Nearby, a bench faced the hill across the canyon, now lined with scarlet in the rapidly fading light.

Archer undid his seat belt and leaned back against the passenger door, giving her plenty of room.

"Did they come right out and accuse you?" He made sure his tone was only mildly interested. She mustn't guess he had an urgent need to know if the police had connected Brian Wade's death to the murder of the squadron commander last year—and if they considered the middle-aged man in the newspaper picture a suspect.

"They didn't arrest me, if that's what you mean." Lifting her chin, she looked him straight in the eye. "The police found the gun they say shot Brian at Cavanaugh's Inn. It's got a skylight and an atrium in the lobby."

She swallowed hard, and Archer waited patiently while she got control of herself. "The weapon was buried in the dirt of a planter in the atrium. When the police questioned hotel personnel, several described a woman who looked like me. They say she was in the lobby that afternoon."

"Several employees described this person? After two months?" Archer whistled softly. "Looks like somebody went to a lot of trouble to make sure those people remembered her, whoever she was."

"Somebody went to even more trouble," she said grimly.

Archer could see her mood veer sharply from despair to anger. "What?" Leaning across the car seat toward her, he caught a faint whiff of female skin and spicy lemon, and had to force himself to inch backward, away from her

Unconsciously, Susan moved toward him, maintaining the same distance between them. "That afternoon Brian was killed, somebody called me at the office, claiming to be the wife of one of my airmen. She said she was calling from a pay station along Argonne Road because she'd run out of gas. She'd left the house to get away from her husband and didn't dare let him find her until he'd cooled off."

Susan gave a forced smile, seeming irritated at herself for being taken in. "I should have known better than to traipse out there—her voice didn't sound right to me. But he's one of my best airmen, and I hated to see him end up in jail for wife beating. You can't imagine how upset I was to telephone their house when I got home and find out she hadn't made the call."

He nodded slowly. "From my army days I remember how close our—" in the nick of time he remembered that a squadron was called a company in the army "—company was as a unit. Like a family."

Her expression brightened. "Then you understand how it was."

To his surprise, Archer found he almost believed her.

"Why wasn't the woman's husband—your airman—in the office with you?" he asked, caught up in her story.

"Because of the holiday," she returned. "The squadron had Hercs—C-130s—in the air, so somebody had to be on duty in all the sections. I let my airmen off, and took the duty myself."

She gave a hysterical little laugh. "And if all that's not bad enough, the police say the gun they found in the atrium was registered to Brian."

"Then you had access to it." Archer whistled softly under his breath. Glancing at her chest he saw her expert marksman's ribbon. He forced himself to concentrate on the decoration and not on the feminine curves underneath her uniform. The sight brought back his fantasy of the two of them entwined in an intimate embrace. He wasn't able to let it go as easily this time.

"When I told them he kept the gun at the squadron, I'm sure they didn't believe me," she added.

A twinge of foreboding rippled down Archer's spine. The mysterious telephone call, the reliable witnesses at the hotel, the late discovery of the murder weapon, its registration to her husband—her story had the touch of a well-thought-out conspiracy.

"Whoever planned this knew a lot about you and your schedule," he remarked, reviewing her words in his mind. "I'm betting somebody's trying to frame you."

He heard her quick gasp. Panic glittered in her eyes.

"My God, what am I going to do?"

"You can get me to look into your husband's death," Archer returned quickly.

HAD SHE HEARD HIM RIGHT? Susan wondered. "What? Are you a private investigator on the side?"

When he shook his head, another lock of black hair dropped casually across his forehead. "No, but I've done some investigative work for my company. Since I've got to spend a few days here, anyway, calling on prospects, I could ask some questions, see what I can find out about your husband's murder."

Be careful, she warned herself, unwilling to trust him too far. *He's a good salesman, and he wants something from me. But what?* In spite of her doubts, she felt herself reacting to his compelling indigo eyes, his square-cut features, the confident set of his shoulders as he sat next to her in the car.

"What makes you think you can locate Don Albright when the police don't have a clue?" she asked, eyeing him suspiciously.

"I'm not talking about Albright." He studied her with curious intensity. "You're not dealing with one man here, Susan. Too much coordination went into your husband's murder to blame it on one individual with revenge on his mind. If one man was responsible for both murders, he had a lot of help."

When Archer paused, Susan could see the wheels turning in his head. "There's no other way to explain why the lights were turned off an instant before the commander was murdered last year," he went on. "Or the fact that somebody was awfully familiar with your schedule—and your husband's, too. They had to be to lure you away from the office at exactly the right time on a holiday when you normally wouldn't be there."

Susan felt herself frowning. "You might be right about accomplices being involved. But Don Albright's behind this. I'd bet a year's pay on it."

The car was getting stuffy. Climbing out, she walked across the yellowed grass to the edge of the precipice. To the south, stands of fir trees circled the emerald green of a golf course beside the divided freeway. Directly below, the steep slope dropped one hundred feet to the valley.

Instantly, the blood rose to her face and the scene swam dizzily before her eyes. Looking straight down had been a mistake. Susan stumbled backward, her stomach a lump of ice. Archer appeared beside her, a large, solid presence. Acutely conscious of his tall, athletic physique, she took another step backward. Did she feel comforted or threatened by his nearness? To her dismay, she wasn't sure.

"Vertigo?" His smooth baritone voice was both soothing and disconcerting.

She gave a shaky laugh. "It's not a phobia. High places don't bother me as long as I look into the distance, not straight down." Deliberately, she forced her gaze to follow the gray ribbon of freeway south until the canyon disappeared on the horizon. Almost immediately, her stomach relaxed.

Turning, he headed toward the bench. "Let's sit down."

Her legs still shaky, Susan stumbled after him. When she slid onto the bench, she left plenty of space between them.

"If heights bother you, I'm surprised you brought me here." His gaze traveled over her face and sought her eyes. Now that the sun had gone behind the opposite hill, his square-cut features were bathed in the sunset's rosy glow. His rugged good looks made her forget her dizziness.

"That's the first time I've gone to the edge," she admitted weakly. "After what I've been through today, this place seemed appropriate."

"I know what you mean about going to the edge. I've been there a few times myself." Moving toward her, he thrust his arm behind her on the bench. Susan wanted to inch away, but couldn't force herself to stir.

"Let me ask a few questions about your husband's murder," he suggested again. This time there was a forced urgency behind his offer, as though something valuable would be lost if she refused. "I know I can help."

To keep herself from being influenced by his nearness, she took a deep breath. The cold, dry air tasted so fresh and clean she wished she could bring some home to her empty condo.

"I don't know," she said honestly. "Your offer's awfully generous. What's in it for you?" As she felt the pressure of his arm against her back, an involuntary quiver coursed through her.

"I don't like what's happening to you," he said. "A long time ago some people I thought were friends sold me down the river. I swore I'd get even if it was the last thing I did."

He sounded so vengeful, she turned, searching his compelling face. With his lips pressed tightly together and deep scowl lines etched on his forehead, he looked so brutal she shivered, sensing the force of his hatred. If people he considered his friends had betrayed him, no wonder he seemed dangerous and vindictive. But the thought of a vengeful man like Archer working for her scared her. It would be like trying to control a black panther with a ribbon for a leash.

Turning back toward the opposite hill, she saw lights blink on, dotting the surrounding landscape. At her side, she felt the heat of Archer's body, warming her through her uniform coat. She resisted the urge to move closer.

"Isn't it funny how things turn out?" she asked, to defuse his anger. "This morning I was sure you were a con man or a swindler. Now I'm thinking about hiring you as a private investigator." To her dismay, there was a note of unsteady laughter in her voice.

"Why did you think I was a swindler?" The thread of tension in his voice hadn't been there before.

When Susan put her gloved hand on his arm, wanting to soften her words, a surprisingly intimate awareness surged through her. Slowly removing her hand, she forged ahead. "First, because you weren't registered at the hotel when I checked this morning. But mainly because I had no record of your company's insurance policy. I can't imagine Brian having a policy with me as beneficiary and not putting it where I'd be sure to find it."

"That does seem strange." But Archer's tone was matter-of-fact, as though this happened all the time. "Have you looked everywhere?"

She nodded. "Before I went to Hawaii."

"How about safe-deposit boxes?" Dropping his arm from the back of the bench to her shoulders, he gave her a little hug. Her heart lurched into her throat. What was there about this man that made her tremble at his slightest touch? Though keenly aware of his body against hers, she didn't move away.

"Two policies were in the safe-deposit box," she said. "Your company's wasn't."

"You only had one box?" he asked in the same cool tone.

Knowing she had to get closer or escape, Susan slid away from him, toward the end of the bench. He removed his arm from her back, leaving an empty space where he'd been.

"Why would we need more than one safe-deposit box?" In spite of herself, her voice trembled.

Turning slightly, he shrugged. "Sometimes people keep separate boxes for different types of items."

Now she saw what he was getting at. "You mean illegal items or anything a person doesn't want his spouse to know about?" She stared at Archer's rugged profile. While she watched, a muscle clenched along his jaw.

"Something like that." Frowning, he paused. "I'm not implying that your husband was hiding anything from you. I'm just saying it's a possibility."

Much as Susan didn't like to admit it, she'd always felt Brian was keeping something from her. A safe-deposit box was infinitely better than the woman friend she'd secretly suspected.

"Yes, it's a possibility," she agreed softly, rising from the bench. Archer followed her to the car.

On the way back to the hotel, he suggested dinner, but Susan declined. She intended to tear the condo apart when she got home. If Brian had a box key hidden there, she intended to find it.

"We still have the insurance policy to go over," Archer reminded her. "And you haven't given me the green light on my offer to help."

"I know," Susan murmured. "Let me sleep on it."

When he didn't press her, she was grateful.

Mixed feelings surged through her when he took her hand before he got out of her car at the hotel. She still didn't trust him, but his touch felt oddly reassuring.

"Tomorrow for lunch?" His gaze held hers.

She nodded, jerking her eyes away to slow her pounding heart. "I'll see you then."

As she drove home, the touch of his hand and sound of his smooth baritone voice replayed in her mind. She'd known him less than eight hours and already he acted almost as interested in her as Brian had before their marriage. *Why?* her suspicious mind kept asking.

It must be the insurance policy, she thought. *There's something about it Archer's not telling me.*

And why hadn't Brian told her about it? If he had had a second, secret safe-deposit box, where would he hide the key?

As soon as she got home, she searched the downstairs, then the two upstairs bedrooms and bathrooms, but found nothing.

From inside the house, she entered the garage through the front hall on the other side of the living room. Brian's workbench was opposite the big double car door. A feeling of sadness came over Susan as she remembered Brian working there. Even before he died she'd realized he wasn't the right man for her, but that didn't ease her guilt and sorrow at his death.

Glancing around the area, she saw the screws and

nails he kept in marked cans on a shelf above his bench. One by one she dumped the cans over, carefully replacing the contents of each before turning over another.

She found the safe-deposit key in the next-to-last can.

WHEN ARCHER RETURNED to his room after a quiet meal downstairs, the blinker on his phone was flashing. Even before he talked to the hotel operator, he knew the message was from Susan. Nobody else had any idea he was here.

He dialed her number, a little surprised at himself for remembering it. He was even more shocked when she recognized his voice.

"Thanks for calling back so soon." She spoke eagerly, full of enthusiasm. "You were right about the second safe-deposit box. I found the key about half an hour ago."

Archer felt himself stiffen with surprise. He hadn't expected her to find a key—had only suggested she look as an explanation for the missing insurance policy. Since she didn't need a copy of the policy to collect the insurance, he hadn't dreamed she'd be so concerned about finding it.

"Good for you!" He strove to eliminate his surprise and put matter-of-fact sincerity into his voice. "I was pretty sure your husband had another box. That's got to be where he put my company's policy. Do you have any idea where the box is?"

"Not a clue." Her voice dropped in volume. "All

that's on the key is a number. I suppose I'll have to call every bank in town to find out where the box is.''

"Don't call,'' Archer said, eager to spend an afternoon with her. "We'll go to the banks tomorrow. When we find out which one has the box, we'll get the contents released to you since you're his widow.''

"Will a bank release the contents? Just like that?'' She sounded doubtful.

"I don't know,'' Archer lied, "but it won't hurt to try.'' He knew damned well no bank would release the contents of a safe-deposit box to anybody but a cosigner—not even a widow—without a court order. But as soon as she agreed to let him help her, she was well on her way to accepting his offer to act as her private investigator. And, if Archer played his cards right, that meant more opportunities to pump her for information and play her off against the other witnesses.

On the other end of the line, Susan warned herself to go slow. Impressed as she was with Archer—especially now that he'd been proved right about the safe-deposit box—she didn't want to do anything impulsive.

But she dismissed the thought as being paranoid again.

"All right,'' she said. "I'll talk to Major Savage and arrange for tomorrow afternoon off. We can go to the banks then.''

"Bring along some ID, your marriage license and a copy of the death certificate.'' Though his voice was solemn, Susan heard a trace of elation. Her heart gave a momentary leap, and she hugged her satin robe more tightly around herself—as if a snug robe were a coat of armor to shut out her confused feelings.

After she'd hung up, Susan shook her head, annoyed with herself. Archer wasn't interested in her. He simply wanted to locate the missing insurance policy to prove Brian had it so she wouldn't think he was a fraud.

His proposal to act as her private investigator was harder to figure out, she thought, drumming her fingers on the table by the phone. He didn't impress her as a man who offered his time without a good reason. Somehow, his explanation that he wanted to help her because he'd been betrayed himself didn't ring true. Was there something else behind his offer? For that matter, was he really an insurance agent? With her special training, she should have checked straight off.

She picked up the phone again and dialed the telephone number written on the insurance forms he'd given her. Though it was after nine at night, maybe someone was in the office to handle claims. If not, voice mail might give her some information about the company, and she could call back tomorrow.

A woman answered. "Industrial Indemnity."

Mildly surprised at getting a person instead of an answering machine, Susan asked for Mr. Derek Archer.

"Mr. Archer will be out of town until next week. If you'll leave your number, I'll have him call you tomorrow."

"You mean next week? When he gets back?" Susan felt her resistance slipping. The more she probed, the more it appeared that Archer was exactly who he said he was.

"No, ma'am. I mean tomorrow." The woman's voice turned patronizing. "He phones in for his messages every day. If you'll leave your number, I guarantee he'll return your call."

"That won't be necessary," Susan said. She'd found out what she wanted to know. Derek Archer really was an agent working for the Industrial Indemnity Insurance Company.

THE CHAIR IN FRONT of Major Savage's desk squeaked when Susan leaned forward. Crossing her ankles primly beneath her, she resisted her urge to squirm in the chair like some ten-year-old called into the principal's office. A drop of sweat ran down her back, cold against her skin.

The major's hooded, hawklike eyes surveyed her from across his desk. "Of course you can take this afternoon off if you need it, Susan."

Her heart plummeted. Something must be wrong. Major Savage called people by their first names only when he felt sorry for them.

"Thank you, sir." She started to get up.

"Before you go, there's something we need to talk about." He motioned her back to her chair.

Sinking down, she leaned toward him.

"I'm sorry to have to do this, Susan," he began slowly, "but now that you're under investigation by the police, I'm going to have to transfer you out of the intelligence office."

Mortified, she lowered her head. "Because of my top secret clearance?"

He nodded. "I'm sure you understand why we can't leave you there."

"Of course." Was that squeaky little voice hers? "I'll help out with some of your unclassified work in the orderly room."

His hooded eyes studied her thoughtfully for a moment. "Sergeant Philips doesn't need any help in the orderly room."

Heat rose in Susan's cheeks. "Then, what?" she stammered.

He leaned back. The movement made him seem even shorter. Susan straightened to see him better.

"Colonel Tinnerman took a shine to you when he met you yesterday. He can use some help in the security police shop—he's got some unclassified research he needs done." His expression softened. "Quite frankly, Susan, you'll probably be better off there than in the orderly room. If you stayed around the squadron, there'd be questions...."

"I understand," she said, not understanding at all. There would be just as many questions if she left and wasn't around to defend herself. Worst of all, she'd no longer have an excuse to snoop around the C-130s and talk to the air and ground crews right after the planes landed. Without that access, her covert mission was wiped out. She'd failed at Operation Macula, her first big assignment.

"Colonel Tinnerman's on your side, Susan," the major went on. "Maybe he can give you some helpful advice and counsel."

"I appreciate that, sir." All she wanted now was to escape the major's forced sympathy and get to a phone. Her Pentagon controller had said not to call unless the matter was urgent. Getting fired from her job certainly qualified, since it meant her investigation was finished.

Opposite her, Major Savage cleared his throat. "If there's anything I can do to help, please ask."

She hesitated, then plunged. "There is one thing. If I could have a couple of days off before I report into Colonel…"

The major began shaking his head before she finished speaking. "I'm sorry, Susan, but Colonel Tinnerman wants you to start on his research project tomorrow morning."

Before she could get up, the major came around his desk, his hand extended. "Thanks for your good work in the squadron, Lieutenant."

Susan took his hand. It felt hot, dry, bony—like a claw. "When I get this mess straightened out, maybe I'll be back."

"Of course you will." His smile seemed phony.

Lifting her arm in a quick salute, Susan didn't smile back.

"WE'LL HAVE YOU reassigned immediately." The well-modulated voice on the telephone was carefully neutral, revealing no emotion.

"You can't do that." Susan kept her irritation under control, her voice as neutral as the man's she was talking to. "I just told you the police consider me a suspect in my husband's murder. They don't want me to leave the local area.''

In the silence that followed, the growl of an eighteen-wheeler shifting into low gear filled the air. She slid the door to the phone booth closed to block out the street noise.

"Did you do it?" the voice asked.

Heat flamed her face. How could her Pentagon controller ask a question like that? "No, of course not." She didn't let her humiliation show in her voice.

"Your husband might have been one of the men we're looking for," her controller reminded her. "Your job for us makes you appear even more guilty." There was a subtle warning in his words. "It's more important than ever that you keep quiet about the operation."

"Don't worry, I know my orders." She'd been cautioned a dozen times that if something went wrong with her operation, she couldn't count on the agency to come to her rescue. As far as the outside world knew, Pentagon Intelligence didn't get involved in cases like this. After she volunteered for the program, Susan received special training so she'd know what to look for.

"We'll leave you assigned at the base where you are for the time being," he said. She noticed he was careful not to reveal her location over the open phone line. "Let me know if anybody's charged in your husband's death. Meanwhile, take yourself off the operation. Though you've found nothing to substantiate the rumors, there may be a connection between your search and your husband's murder."

"Yes, sir," she returned automatically. But in her mind she was already planning to let Archer go ahead with his investigation. If he found out something she could report to her controller under Operation Macula, so much the better.

Chapter Four

She'd forgotten how penetrating his eyes were, how they seemed to know just what she was thinking. Or rather, she hadn't forgotten, she'd simply failed to reconcile their deep-down animosity with the lazy allure of his gaze.

He was looking at her seductively now across the luncheon table, his eyes such a dark blue they seemed almost purple. Or was she imagining—or wishing for—such a look? Staring across at him, Susan knew she'd get no sympathy when she told him about her transfer. She tried to put a humorous touch to her words so he'd see what stern stuff she was made of.

"Now that I'm a suspect, Major Savage doesn't think I should be trusted with classified material, so he's transferring me out of the squadron." But as she spoke, the humiliation of being fired hit her anew, and her attempt at humor failed. She swallowed hard to dislodge the lump in her throat.

Archer studied her intently from across the table. "Don't start feeling sorry for yourself again," he said, lifting one dark brow. "If I remember my army days correctly, people assigned on a temporary basis could pretty much come and go as they pleased. That'll be a plus. In the next few days we're going to need all the time together we can manage.''

She was caught off guard by the sudden vibrancy in his voice, and didn't want him to stop talking, didn't want to lose the warm feeling that coursed through her at hearing his rich baritone.

''You sound like you're looking forward to our time together,'' she said without thinking. As soon as the words were out of her mouth, she could have bitten her tongue.

He held her gaze in a penetrating stare. ''Aren't you?''

She wanted to look down at the table, but she couldn't. His eyes were too hypnotic. ''I'm a widow whose husband has been dead only two months.'' She was proud of the firmness in her voice. ''What I'm looking forward to is seeing Don Albright back in jail where he belongs.''

A half smile crossed his lips. It wasn't reflected in his cold blue eyes. In that instant Susan knew for sure her first impression was right. This man was dangerous.

''And what I'm looking forward to is helping the new widow clear her name.'' The taunting tone was back in his voice.

What was she letting herself in for, she wondered, hiring an almost-stranger as a private investigator? She sucked in her breath, on the verge of telling him to forget their arrangement. But what alternative did she have with the police as good as accusing her of murder and someone out to frame her? Much as she hated the idea, she needed Archer's help.

His familiar mask descended once again, and she felt his hand under her arm, helping her out of her chair. Unlike his taunting words, his hand seemed strong, firm, protective. When they crossed the lobby, she felt him beside her, his powerful, well-muscled body moving with easy, athletic grace.

A dangerous man is what I need, she convinced herself as she fastened her seat belt in his rental car. *If anybody can find a convicted killer, it's a man who's just as deadly.*

Susan felt him watching her, and turned her head toward him as he started the engine. Frowning, he searched her face in that enigmatic way of his, with his lids slightly lowered.

"Where to?"

Susan probed around in her bag until she found the list she'd made last night. "We might as well start with the banks downtown." Eyeing him dubiously, she gave him brief directions to the first one. "When we find the right bank, do you really think they'll let me look inside the box?"

He shrugged. "Since you're not a cosigner, they're not supposed to, but who knows? Maybe we'll get lucky. You can snow them with your ID and marriage license, and your husband's death certificate. Act like they're violating your rights if they don't let you examine the box. Threaten to sue. That always gets people's attention."

At first she wasn't sure he was serious, but one look at his sober expression convinced her. "I don't want

anybody to get into trouble or do anything illegal,"
she protested, her doubts about Archer coming back
full force.

Without saying a word, he swung into a bus zone
near the curb and stopped, the engine idling. "Excuse
me, Susan, but I thought you wanted to find whoever's
trying to frame you." His eyes held hers relentlessly.

She backed away from him, a shiver shooting up
her spine. "What's that got to do with this safe-deposit
box?"

"A hell of a lot." He frowned at her like she didn't
know which end was up. "What's inside that box may
tell us who killed your husband."

SUSAN HIT PAY DIRT at the fourth bank on her list.
While Archer waited for her outside, she took the elevator down one floor to the vault area. Windowless,
with fluorescent lights glaring down on plush carpeting, the place was overheated and smelled faintly of a
flowery air freshener.

Unbuttoning her suit coat, Susan faced the clerk sitting at a desk outside the vault's massive steel door.
"I'm Mrs. Brian Wade, and I'd like to get into our
safe-deposit box, please."

The clerk, an attractive woman about Susan's age,
appeared to recognize the name. "Just a moment. I'll
get your card." Smiling warmly, she swung her chair
around and scooted to a cabinet behind her.

When she faced Susan an instant later, her smile
had been replaced by a worried frown. "I'm terribly
sorry, Mrs. Wade. Your husband is the only signer for

the box. We can't let you have access unless he makes you a cosigner.''

"My husband passed away two months ago," Susan said, allowing her voice to tremble. She placed the death certificate on the desk, along with her laminated driver's license. "Here's the necessary information." Tears filled her eyes and she didn't hold them back. "I'm sure you understand why I need to get into our safe-deposit box."

The woman nodded, her gaze sympathetic. "Why don't you sit down here beside my desk while I call the manager? He has to approve this sort of thing." She picked up her telephone receiver and punched in a number.

A few minutes later a man came out of the elevator and walked toward them. "Now, Mrs. Wade," he began after the clerk had introduced him as the manager. "What can Inland Empire Bank do for you?"

Summoning all her pent-up emotion—as befitted a grieving widow—she told him what she wanted.

"I'm sorry, Mrs. Wade," he said when she'd finished. "I know what a difficult time this must be for you, but I can't let you open the box without a court order." He placed a pudgy hand on her arm. "I'm sure you understand."

"I'm not certain I do," Susan said tearfully. "Since my husband's dead, he can't possibly object to my seeing what's inside the box."

The manager sighed. "I know, I know. Some of these regulations don't make much sense." His expression brightened. "But you should have no trouble getting a court order."

"How long will that take?"

He shrugged. "If your lawyer pushes the right buttons—a day or two."

As quick as that? A thrill of anxious anticipation touched her spine. Some time in the next couple of days she'd learn Brian's most guarded secrets. But now that the moment of revelation seemed near, she wasn't sure she wanted to know them.

The chunky bank manager was watching her closely, one hand thrust inside the pocket of his ample trousers. His sigh of relief was audible when she turned toward the elevator.

Archer was waiting for her outside, leaning against the building's red brick facade. Like her, he was dressed in a business suit. But unlike her, in his crimson tie and Gucci loafers, he looked more cosmopolitan. Susan couldn't help noticing that every woman glanced their way.

"Brian's box is in this bank," she said, starting up the street toward Parkade, the tiered parking garage where they'd left his car.

He swung into step beside her, and she found herself highly conscious of the springy, athletic movement of his stride.

"That's what I figured when you took so long," he said. "Did they let you look inside?" He appeared as eager to find out what was in the box as she was.

"No. I need a court order. The bank manager said my lawyer should be able to get one quickly." When they passed under a covered second-story sidewalk, part of a system permitting inside access to eleven blocks of downtown stores, his hip brushed hers. Susan could hardly believe the way her pulses leaped with excitement at his brief touch.

Take it easy, Lieutenant, she warned herself, fighting the warmth coursing through her. Wouldn't he delight in knowing she heated up like a bonfire when he touched her?

"Where's your lawyer's office?" he asked, not seeming to notice her flushed face.

"On Broadway," she replied without glancing toward him. "Across the river near the courthouse. You can drop me off there, and I'll take a cab home."

The irritated look he gave her made her sorry she'd suggested the taxi. "I'll wait in the car," he said. "When you're finished, we can decide where to go from there."

SUSAN STILL COULDN'T figure out what Archer wanted from her. But she was even more positive that he wanted *something*—more than helping her settle an insurance claim. The suspicion gave her an antsy, anxious feeling, like waiting for the other shoe to drop.

During the few minutes she sat in the plush waiting room while her lawyer finished a telephone call, she ran the possibilities over again in her mind. And, as always, she discarded every angle almost as soon as it occurred to her.

The most logical one—that he was a con artist out to swindle her—didn't add up, now that she knew he was a legitimate insurance agent. And the notion that he might be helping her because he liked her seemed absurd. Men like Archer didn't do favors for people because he liked them. Settling back in the comfortable chair provided by the attorney, she shrugged off the disquieting notion that she'd only seen a small part of him, that he kept most of himself carefully hidden.

When her lawyer escorted her into a small conference area, the first thing Susan did was peer out the picture window overlooking the parking lot. There sat Archer's blue rental sedan. He stood beside it, leaning casually against the closed door. His unselfconscious grace made her think of a resting panther—dangerous even when relaxed.

While she watched, two women sauntered up to him from the nearby sidewalk. During the conversation that followed, he shook his head a few times, then pointed toward a bridge leading across the river. Susan sighed with relief when they walked away. How could one man evoke so many different feelings? she wondered. From tenderness, to suspicion, to plain old jealousy.

"Susan?" She became aware of her lawyer, speaking her name. "Our receptionist said you needed a court order."

In a few words Susan told the attorney about the safe-deposit box and her encounter with the bank manager. But while she talked, all her busy mind could think about was Archer and why he'd offered to help her.

Why not ask him? If he had something to hide, he probably wouldn't tell her. Still, wasn't it worth a try? By the time the lawyer had assured Susan she'd have the court order in the next few days—maybe as early as tomorrow afternoon—she had made up her mind to ask him.

When she returned to the parking lot, Archer was waiting inside the car. He got out when he saw her coming.

"That didn't take long," he said. "Was the bank manager right about the forty-eight hours?" Opening the passenger door, he helped her inside.

"Yes. We'll have the court order in the next couple of days. Now all I need is a few hours off from my new job."

He started the engine. She didn't miss the satisfied smile on his face.

"Before we do anything more, there's something we need to get straightened out," she said, keeping her voice deceptively calm. Might as well get this over with right now, she thought.

Switching the engine off, he turned toward her and leaned back against the door. "So let's have it. What do we need to get straightened out?"

There was a wary watchfulness in his expression that made Susan wish she'd never brought this up. He focused his cold blue eyes on her, and she backed away from him on the car seat, even as she reminded herself she was the boss here, not him.

"Before we go any further with our investigation," she said slowly, "I want to know the real reason you offered to help me." Hardly breathing, she tried to detect any change in his expression that might clue her in as to his thoughts. But nothing changed. His brow remained furrowed, his mouth drawn down.

Then he drew in his breath and drawled an answer in his rich baritone voice. "So you spotted the lie I told you yesterday. For your information, I don't give a tinker's damn about what happens to you, lady.''

Too shocked to speak, Susan stared wordlessly at him.

"There's only one reason I'd take on a two-bit job like this," he continued abruptly. "For the money, of course. I expect to be paid for my services."

He gazed at her with a bland half smile. "You look surprised. Why else would I offer to work for you?"

"Why I...I don't know." The words came out a broken whisper.

It was obvious to Archer that, finally, she believed him. What irony. She wouldn't believe the noble half truth he'd told her yesterday: that he'd been shafted and didn't want to see the same thing happen to her. But she was perfectly willing to accept a crass financial motive for his good deed.

What would she say, he wondered, if she knew the whole truth? That since being convicted of last year's murder, he'd been obsessed with getting even with the men who betrayed him? That she was a mere tool, a means to that end?

"Since you've brought up the money, maybe we should talk about your wages." Sitting up straighter, Susan lifted her chin, forcibly getting a grip on herself.

Looking into her earnest brown eyes, Archer almost named a ridiculously low amount. Why did this woman have to have the widest, most beautiful eyes he'd ever seen? And the softest-looking skin?

But she'd get suspicious again if the amount was too low. He did some quick mental calculation and named the highest figure he thought she'd buy.

"You'd pay three times that for a full-time investigator who's any good."

She gasped. "I can't afford anything like that."

"Of course you can," he said evenly. "You've already said you were the beneficiary of two insurance policies in addition to my company's. Plus, when your husband talked to me about his policy, he bragged about making a killing in the market. His death left you a wealthy woman."

From her startled look, Archer knew he'd guessed right. Just thinking about Wade and how his *friend* had betrayed him made his stomach clench. As Susan's private investigator, he'd have a good excuse to confront the remaining witnesses. If he played his cards right, he could scare the hell out of them. And eventually he'd ruin them, the way he'd planned to ruin Brian and the two who'd died in accidents. He struggled to keep his face calm. He'd been cheated of his revenge for those three. He refused to be cheated for the others.

Susan's brow creased with worry. "How long is your investigation going to take?" Leaning toward him on the car seat, with her golden curls on her shoulders, she reminded him of a picture he'd seen a lifetime ago when he was a boy. The image was of a very pretty young girl with exactly the same shade of hair as Susan's, leaning over a table set with three bowls of oatmeal.

He shook off the thought. Susan might have goldblond hair and brown eyes to die for, but she wasn't Goldilocks in a fairy tale. Then, unexpectedly, his fantasy returned and he was stroking her bare skin, her long hair, and feeling her breasts against his chest. Damn. The fantasy was getting harder to let go of. With her hair down now that she wasn't in uniform, she fit into his lurid dream even better.

But no matter how much good old-fashioned, healthy lust he felt for her, this woman wasn't for him. So why the hell did the air smell cleaner and sweeter when she was around? Why did this crappy world seem more vibrant to him when she sat beside him in the car?

For so long now, he'd thought about nothing but settling the score with the men who betrayed him. But when she was near, he lost his singleness of purpose. Even now, in spite of the plain brown suit she was wearing, he found himself intensely aware of her sculpted figure beneath. Healthy lust. That's all it was.

"So how long will your investigation take?" she repeated, her eyebrows raised inquiringly.

He restarted the engine to get his thoughts back on track. "I'll be here in Spokane a week," he said, turning out of the parking lot. "But I'm guessing I can figure out what's going on in a couple of days—if you give me the green light."

"*A couple of days?* Get real, Archer." She turned in the seat to face him. "The police have been hunting for Don Albright for almost a year with no success. They've spent more than two months trying to find Brian's killer and the only suspect they've come up with is me."

Tears glistened in her eyes. She turned away so he wouldn't see, but he didn't miss much and spotted them right away. *You're a real nice guy, killer,* he told himself, knowing she might expect him to taunt her if he caught her on the verge of tears.

But far from wanting to taunt her, Archer found himself eager to take her in his arms and kiss her tears away. Then he'd kiss those wonderful full lips of hers the way they were meant to be kissed—long, hard, full of passion. After which she'd probably slap him in the face, he thought dryly. Turning back to the road, he told himself to concentrate on his driving.

"I won't guarantee I'll have all the answers for you in three or four days," he said. "But I'll have enough information to make your investment in me worthwhile." Pausing, he tried to figure out what it would take to make her grab the bait.

"Tell you what," he began cautiously. "I'll work for you for the next three days. We'll get together every evening, and I'll tell you what I've found out. If you don't like the way the investigation's going at the end of the three days, you don't owe me a cent."

"And if I do?" He could tell she was intrigued by his offer.

"Then you pay what you owe and let me finish the job—or as much as I can manage during the time I'm here."

For a long moment she didn't move, and he saw the hesitation in her eyes. Then she stuck out her hand.

"Done," she said.

Taking her hand, Archer felt its warmth surge through him. For a moment he held fast to her fingers, reluctant to release them. Then reality set in, and he quickly freed her hand.

TANGLED FEELINGS SURGED through Susan as Archer headed west toward her condo. One part of her gloated that she'd been right all along. He was nothing but a crass materialist, out for financial gain. But another part of her wasn't satisfied with such a simple explanation. She didn't want him to be that kind of person. She didn't know exactly what she *did* want him to be. Anything but what he was, she supposed.

Idiot, she told herself, turning her head to study his aquiline nose, generous mouth. His forehead was creased from his perpetual frown. She wondered what his skin would feel like beneath her fingertips. Since it was late afternoon, his beard had begun to emerge, a dark shadow against his skin. How would the roughness feel against her face? Heat rising to her cheeks, Susan flung her thoughts aside when she realized where they were taking her.

"Is that how you can afford Brooks Brothers suits and Gucci loafers?" she asked pointedly. "By picking up odd jobs here and there on company time?"

"Exactly." He shot her a crooked smile. "Don't get the idea I'm putting something over on my company. They know I moonlight occasionally."

If she'd hoped to embarrass him, she hadn't succeeded. Whisking an imaginary speck off his pant leg, he seemed pleased that she'd noticed his expensive clothing.

"Now that you've come into some money," he advised, "you should try shopping at one of the better stores. Stylish clothes'll do wonders for both your figure and your morale."

Irritated by his frankness, Susan stared straight at

the road ahead. "Thanks for the advice, but I hired you to find the man who's trying to frame me, not to criticize what I wear."

Archer pulled up outside her condo and parked in the driveway. "Thank you, ma'am," he said. "I'll remember that."

He unbuckled his seat belt and turned to face her. Before he could mask his feelings, she saw the unbridled desire in his eyes. Suddenly Susan's heart leaped into her throat. He was going to take her into his arms. She knew it as surely as she knew her own name. Worse, she wanted him to. Her body yearned, ached, for his touch.

She sat frozen, waiting for him to move.

For an instant he sat there motionless. Then the familiar frowning mask descended over his features as though another part of him had taken control. "I'll call you tomorrow, and we'll get together for dinner."

Susan wasn't sure whether to laugh or cry. She'd expected him to reach for her. But her logical mind told her it was for the best. Nodding, she opened the door and got out with as much dignity as she could muster.

"We'll meet for dinner at the Blue Boar," she said, mentioning the most expensive restaurant in town.

His eyes raked coolly over her. "You might as well let me pick you up. The car comes under the heading of *expenses,* so you're paying for it."

"Only if I like your information."

He gave her his cynical half smile. "Don't worry. You'll like it."

She marched up the walk to her condo, her back

straight, listening for the engine noise that indicated he was backing down the driveway. But there was no sound. He didn't leave until she'd unlocked her door and shut it safely behind her.

WHEN SUSAN HAD SEEN Lieutenant Colonel Tinnerman up close in the car yesterday, he'd reminded her more of a rural southern preacher than a man who devoted his life to law enforcement. Susan's new boss, the commander of the security police squadron at Fairchild, had a button nose, thinning hair and cornflower blue eyes. One of the plainest men she'd ever met, he had an angular, scarecrowish body that seemed oddly uncoordinated.

When Susan appeared in his office to report in, he smiled so warmly that she promptly forgot how plain he was.

She saluted. "Lieutenant Wade reporting as ordered, sir."

After standing and returning her salute, he extended his hand. "Welcome aboard, Susan." He had a soft Texas accent and the pleasing manner of a congenial talk show host.

"Sit down." He motioned toward a straight-backed chair beside his desk. "Since we both know why you've been reassigned to my squadron, I see no reason to discuss your visit to the police station yesterday unless you want to."

She sighed with relief. "If I never talk about it again, it'll be too soon."

He laughed out loud. "Good. You're honest. I like that in my people."

Susan stiffened. Why was her new boss being so charming? From the warmth in his voice, he might be welcoming a colonel from the inspector general's office instead of a lieutenant who'd just been kicked off her job. Could he know about her covert mission?

Not possible. The Pentagon said no one at Fairchild would know. And no one in the civilian intelligence community, either.

Her head high, she lowered herself onto the chair.

The colonel eyed her with evident approval. "Did Major Savage tell you anything about my research project?"

She shook her head. "Only that you wanted me to get started first thing this morning."

"That's right, Susan."

He'd used her first name again. After Major Savage's austere manner, Lieutenant Colonel Tinnerman talked like one of the family. Susan wondered if he was as friendly as he sounded or if this was an interrogation method used by security police people to soften up their suspects.

Yes, suspects. She repeated the word grimly in her mind. Whether she liked it or not, she was a suspect in her husband's death. At least that's what Detective MacElroy thought.

"Ever since I got here I've been wanting to do a study comparing the incidence of military and civilian criminal acts in the Spokane area," the colonel said. "But I could never spare an officer to do it."

Susan smiled sympathetically. "I hope I can help."

He rubbed his hands together in obvious satisfaction. "I'm sure you can." He stood and so did Susan. "Come along and I'll show you your office."

The concrete building housing the security police squadron was constructed like an adobe fort, with no windows and a sloping grassy mound covering three-quarters of its outside walls. A tiled hallway led from the front entrance through the center of the building. It was off this hallway that the colonel had set up an office for her.

Peering through the door, Susan liked what she saw. A computer and printer sat on a table beside a gray metal desk. Behind the desk was a metal executive chair. A four-drawer file cabinet stood beside the desk. But best of all, she wouldn't have to go through anybody else's office to get to hers.

"Do you like it?" The colonel watched her with what she interpreted as friendly anxiety.

"Like it?" She flashed him a smile of thanks. "I love it, Colonel Tinnerman. This is nicer than any intelligence office I've ever had." Touched by his kindness, she swallowed hard.

His round, weathered face beamed at her words. "I'm happy to hear that, Susan," he said in his slow Texas drawl. "You're having a hard time just now, and I'd like to make things as easy for you as I can."

She took a deep breath. Was this the right time to ask for an afternoon off?

"I don't want to sound like I'm taking advantage, sir," she began cautiously, "but there *is* one thing I'm going to need in the next couple of days."

The indulgent glint in his eyes matched his approving smile. "I thought there might be."

Susan hesitated no longer. "An afternoon off."

He nodded. "Any particular afternoon?"

"It may be tomorrow, it may be a day or two after that."

He lifted an eyebrow questioningly. Susan knew he was curious, but decided not to tell her nice new boss about the safe-deposit box. Once he knew about it, she'd almost have to tell him what was inside. And *that* was something she might never want anyone to find out—no matter how understanding he was.

Instead, she explained that she expected to receive a large insurance check in the next few days and would need time off during the day to deposit it and talk to her financial adviser.

He seemed to buy her explanation. "As a matter of fact, there's no reason for you to be on a rigid time schedule. As long as the project's done by the end of next month, I'll be satisfied."

His generosity made tears well up in her eyes again. "That's good of you, sir. I appreciate all your consider—"

"You don't have to thank me," he interrupted, patting her gently on the shoulder. "If my daughter had lived, she'd be about your age. I hope someone would have helped her out if she ever got in a fix like yours."

Susan's heart went out to him with new understanding. "What happened, sir?" If he hadn't wanted her to ask, he wouldn't have mentioned his child.

"We lost the baby after my wife was mugged in a department store parking lot." His voice turned harsh. "She never got over the death of the unborn child. A couple years later she took her own life."

Susan gasped. Hearing a horrid story told in such a matter-of-fact tone squeezed the breath out of her. The room spun dizzily around her, and she leaned against the desk for support. "That's tragic, sir," she whispered.

"You're right, Susan. It *is* horrible." His plain features hardened, and a sudden thin chill hung on the edge of his words. "That's why I went into police work. So I could do something about things like that."

He smiled apologetically. "I don't tell many people about that part of my life—it all happened so long ago. Please don't say anything to the people in the squadron."

"Of course." Still horrified by his grim tale, she had to force herself to follow him to the file cabinet. Inside was most of the data she'd need for the study he wanted done.

He spent the next fifteen minutes explaining the system and giving her general instructions about the research. Susan only half heard him. Her imaginative mind kept visualizing his grim story.

If he could live through his terrible experience, so could she, Susan told herself. That must be why he'd told her—to give her the courage to forge ahead. Maybe knowing what was in Brian's safe-deposit box would help her clear her name.

As soon as Colonel Tinnerman left her office, she dialed her attorney. The court order would be ready tomorrow afternoon. Susan received the news with a bewildering mixture of dread and anticipation. What had Brian kept hidden from her?

Chapter Five

Archer knew instinctively when Sergeant Naylor arrived at the clock tower, could feel Naylor's eyes staring at the back of his head. Above, the old clock clanged 8:00 a.m., the time arranged for their meeting. Slowly Archer turned around, away from the tower. Bob Naylor, one of his accusers, stood behind him in his uniform, a strained expression on his weathered face.

"Mr. Archer?" he said, showing no sign of recognition.

Since Archer had last seen him at the trial, Naylor's hair had turned from dark brown to white. He didn't let his surprise show on his face. "Yes, I'm Mrs. Wade's private investigator."

"On the phone you said you had important new information." Naylor's voice grated like a much older man's. He was in his mid-thirties, but he sounded and looked fifty.

Leading Naylor to a bench in the shadow of the tower, Archer told him about the two accidents. "Mrs. Wade and I think they may be tied in to last year's murder trial," he added grimly, though he was sure there was no connection.

When Naylor heard about the accidents, his lined face blanched to the sickly gray color of moldy cottage cheese. "Albright's picking us off one by one," he said, his voice shaky.

"That's what Mrs. Wade thinks," Archer agreed, mentally rubbing his hands with satisfaction. The more terror this man felt, the better.

Naylor got up off the bench and started to pace on the tiled surface below the clock tower. Nearby, a blacktopped path led through the park lawn to a wooden footbridge across the river.

Archer fell into step beside Naylor. "You really think Albright's still alive?"

"Damn right." Naylor spit out the words. "No ghost shot Captain Wade or pushed Jack Evans off that ladder in San Antonio."

Like Susan, Naylor seemed determined Albright was behind the deaths. Everybody figured a man who killed once wouldn't mind doing it again, Archer thought sourly. At least Naylor wasn't blaming Susan for her husband's murder. Reluctantly, Archer had to admit that pleased him.

"The authorities insist those two accidents weren't crimes," Archer commented. "But I'm inclined to agree with you. They're connected to the squadron commander's murder last year and Wade's death in January. The thing that bothers me is Albright's role in all this. From what Mrs. Wade tells me, there's something else going on here, more than just a man out for revenge. Maybe it's a conspiracy of some sort.''

It was the same theory he'd voiced to Susan when she told him about her mysterious phone call and the wild-goose chase she'd gone on the afternoon her husband was shot. Archer tossed out the idea to see how Naylor would react.

Beside him, the sergeant came to an abrupt stop and stared up at Archer. ''What do you mean?'' His mouth took on an unpleasant twist. ''Mrs. Wade's way off in left field if she thinks there's a conspiracy behind the deaths. Albright killed those men because he wants revenge. Period. Nothing else is going on. Nothing.'' Clenching his fists, he looked away from Archer as if sensing his tirade was out of line.

I was right, Archer thought, watching the man's pale, frightened face. *There's something illegal in the works here, and this man knows what it is. Maybe he sincerely believes Albright's behind the accidents, and Wade's murder. But he knows damned well Albright has no connection with the criminal activity, whatever it is.*

Archer spent the next half hour trying to pry more information out of Naylor. But try as he would, he couldn't get the sergeant to reveal anything else significant.

His meetings with the three remaining witnesses were even less productive—probably because each had talked to Naylor before meeting Archer. But by the time he finished with them, he was convinced they were all involved in some kind of crime. Once he found out what it was, he'd drag their names through the mud and ruin their lives the way his had been destroyed.

In high spirits, he drove back to the hotel after his last session. It had been a very profitable day, and the night promised to be even more enjoyable. He imagined the interest in Susan's expressive brown eyes when he told her what he'd learned.

She's just a tool, he reminded himself.

THAT NIGHT WHEN SUSAN opened her condo door for Archer, she watched his gaze drift downward from her face to her red wool dress to her fashionable high-heeled pumps.

"New outfit?" he asked, his expression approving.

She nodded. "I decided you were right. I could use more color and style in my wardrobe."

He stared at her with amazement. "But you seemed so…upset when I mentioned it. What changed your mind?"

Giving a self-conscious little laugh, she glanced down at the soft wool skirt of the dress. "When somebody's right, I try to admit it, even if I don't like what they're saying."

His nod brimmed with reluctant approval. "Good for you. Maybe we'll get along better than I thought."

"*If* you come up with some good information." She turned toward the closet so he wouldn't see his back-handed compliment had embarrassed her. Slipping into her coat, she followed him to his car, parked in her driveway.

"You were right about my transfer being a blessing

in disguise,'' she said after they'd started toward downtown.

"How so?" In the light from the oncoming traffic, Susan saw his familiar cynical smile had returned, along with his wary distrust. She sighed. Why couldn't his expression match the easy grace of the blue blazer he was wearing?

"My new boss acts like a long-lost father," she explained. "He says to take as much time off as I need."

Archer turned toward her with an expression that was frankly skeptical. "You said you were transferred to the security police squadron?"

"Yes. The commander is Lieutenant Colonel Tinnerman."

"Does he treat everybody in the squadron with the same fatherly attitude?" Archer sounded as suspicious as he looked.

She nodded. "I hear what you're saying. I was a little worried that he might have an ulterior motive for giving me preferential treatment, so I checked around the unit. Everybody loves him. He seems to be fair and considerate with them, but hard as nails with anybody who breaks the law."

"He should be fair and considerate with everybody," Archer growled, "including his prisoners. That's what democracy is all about."

"He's got good reason to hate people who break the law." Susan found herself defending the colonel. Quickly she related his grim story. Though he'd asked her not to repeat it, Archer was an out-of-state insurance agent who would never meet Colonel Tinnerman.

When she was finished, she sat in silence, watching him. From his austere profile, she couldn't tell if he'd been moved by the story or not. It was as if he'd shut himself off from her.

"We're almost there," he announced, nodding toward a sign featuring an ugly tusked animal's head. Across the street from Riverfront Park, the Blue Boar restaurant occupied a prime piece of downtown real estate within sight of the Carousel and Opera House.

"So, do you understand where the colonel's coming from?" Susan asked as he parked on a side street a couple of blocks from the restaurant. Downtown was crowded for a Wednesday night, and there weren't as many curbside parking spots as usual.

Archer shrugged at her question. "What's to understand? Something bad happened to him a long time ago, and he's never gotten over it." Pausing, he glanced her way. "At least you know he's not trying to hit on you. Maybe you should count your blessings."

Something about the cold, matter-of-fact way Archer analyzed the colonel's kindness made Susan recoil. What kind of man reacted with so little emotion to a story like the one she'd just told? Remembering the angry rebellion that lurked in Archer's eyes, Susan held her tongue. Maybe something just as awful had happened to him.

IN THE CROWDED RESTAURANT, they sat at a table with a linen cloth and finished a bottle of cabernet sauvignon. The most expensive wine in the house, Archer thought, as he downed his third glass. Susan hadn't flinched when he ordered it, though he was sure she knew exactly what it cost.

"Thanks for the wine," he said, swallowing the last drops in his glass. "It's really quite good."

"Don't thank me yet." Her eyes seemed even larger than usual tonight, like luminescent black opals. When she looked at him with those eyes, it was only too easy to forget the trial and the men he'd sworn to get even with.

"According to our agreement, I don't owe you a cent yet," she went on. "Not until you give me a lot more information than you have tonight."

He favored her with a patient smile. "On the way back to the car we'll have more privacy. I'll tell you then." With satisfaction, he noted her disappointed frown. She'd appreciate his news more if she had to wait for it.

Still, in that red dress with her gold hair brushed away from her face, he was sorely tempted to give her whatever she asked for, no matter how unreasonable. Since he was helping himself by aiding her, he would have worked for free. But such an offer would have made her suspicious. Shifting uncomfortably, he stifled a momentary stab of guilt at using her to get at the men who betrayed him.

Damn, he was doing it again—reacting to her in ways he didn't like. A convicted killer, he couldn't let himself feel anything more for this woman than strong, healthy lust. *She was a tool,* nothing more, and he mustn't let himself forget it.

When he paid the bill, he stuffed a copy in his wallet, making sure she saw him.

"I'll clip all the receipts together when I present my expenses day after tomorrow," he told her in a conversational tone as they started for the door.

"Thanks. I hope your news will be worth it." Her voice had all the warmth of leftover meat loaf. Clearly she thought he was exaggerating his investigative ability.

Outside, the temperature had dropped to near freezing. After buttoning his overcoat against the cold, Archer took Susan's hand and drew it over his arm. Though he knew it was impossible, he would have sworn he could feel her warmth through their heavy clothes. He took a deep breath of the frigid dry air, clearing his lungs—and his mind. But his deep breaths only let him smell her faint woodsy scent all the more.

As he turned off the brightly lit boulevard onto the cross street, he could hear her high heels tap-tapping along beside him and feel the pressure of her arm leaning against him. An unwanted protective feeling swept over him. Something about this woman awakened all sorts of masculine instincts better left in the subconscious where they belonged. He tried to shrug them aside, but the effort only made him more keenly aware of her.

Though it was just a little after ten, the street where Archer had parked the car was almost deserted. Slowing his pace, he scanned the block ahead. Attractive green awnings shadowed the arched windows of modish little shops. But the street's pleasing appearance didn't allay Archer's vague impression that something was wrong. Studying the interiors of the cars parked alongside, he saw nothing. Was this apprehensive feeling another manifestation of his newly awakened protective instinct?

When he glanced down at Susan, she stared up at him with an expectant expression. "So what mysterious new information did you uncover today, Sherlock?"

The faces of the four men he'd talked to appeared in Archer's mind. "I talked to the four remaining witnesses to last year's murder. They agree with you that Don Albright arranged the accidents and shot your husband."

Her disappointed sigh was clearly audible. "I told you that the first time we met. Don't tell me that's all you found out."

They reached the end of the block and started across the street. There was no traffic. Ahead of them a young couple bundled in overcoats climbed into a car parked at the curb. No one else was on the sidewalk.

Beside him, Susan still clung tightly to his arm, making no secret of her need for support in her new high heels. She had a direct, no-nonsense way about her that fascinated him. Would she be the same in bed? he wondered, and was instantly irritated with himself for feeling warmth in his loins.

When they reached the opposite curb, Archer started down the block, careful to pace himself so she could keep up without stumbling. "Now that I've talked to all four men, I'm convinced they were involved in criminal activity of some sort. I'm also sure the three men who were killed participated, too—or, at least, knew what was going on."

She stopped dead in her tracks and jerked her hand

away from his arm. "If that's true, then Brian was involved."

When he turned to face her, Archer caught a slight movement in the alley ahead. A pedestrian passage between two buildings, the brick-tiled alley was used by the adjoining restaurant as a sidewalk café in the summer. Now its trees were bare and its benches empty.

Roughly Archer took Susan's hand and pulled it over his arm. "Start back the way we've come," he ordered, twisting her around.

"What's wrong?" Her voice sounded alert but steady. She must have nerves of steel, he thought, feeling his own rush of adrenaline. Someone lurked in the alley behind them. The skin rose at the back of his neck, and he edged Susan closer to the side of the building where she'd be less of a target.

"Probably nothing." He allowed no sign of alarm in his voice. Though he wanted to pick her up and run, he satisfied himself with increasing his pace back the way they'd come. At any moment he expected to hear footsteps behind them. Or worse, the crack of a handgun. "Someone's waiting in that alley in the middle of the block. No sense getting mugged unnecessarily."

He heard her quick intake of breath. "Thank goodness you saw him." Still holding his arm, she turned and looked over her shoulder as they walked. "You're right, Derek. He's stepped out of the alley." Other than using his first name—which she'd never done before—she showed no panic, only controlled excitement.

Archer stopped walking and swung around. Half a block away a man darted back into the alley when he saw them turn. Wearing jeans and a bright red jacket, he was too far away for Archer to get a good look at his face.

Archer headed back toward the restaurant.

"Do you think he'll come after us?" Susan spoke in the same alert tone, spirited but without a trace of panic. Her brown eyes glistened with excitement, not fear.

He glanced over his shoulder. "Doesn't look like it, but no sense waiting around to find out." For a tense few minutes, he continued toward the restaurant and safety at the same hurried pace. Not until they were inside did he let himself relax. "You wait here. I'll get the car."

Gripping his arm, her fingers showed surprising strength. "It's not safe. Let's call the police."

He took one look at her wide, frightened eyes, and something inside him melted. At last she was showing signs of fear. It was for him, he realized. For the past long year, no one had given a damn whether he lived or died. But now Susan did.

Annoyed, he warned himself not to go soft. If she knew who he *really* was, she wouldn't give a damn, either. Or maybe she would. She'd want him dead.

"I was probably wrong about him being a mugger," he said, knowing he couldn't afford an encounter with the police. After they took his name and address, they might check up on him. A few telephone calls and they'd realize Derek Archer hadn't existed before last year.

Before she could stop him, he hurried outside. As he strode past the alley, he glanced along the tiled passageway. Empty. Too bad. He was spoiling for a fight. The SOB was probably afraid they had called the police. By the time Archer picked up Susan in front of the Blue Boar, his adrenaline had stopped flowing.

"You were awfully calm back there on the street," he said grudgingly as they drove away from the restaurant. "Is the air force giving its intelligence officers special training these days?"

"What do you mean *special training?*" Her musical voice had a sharp edge he hadn't heard before.

Archer glanced at her face. In the shadowy glow from the oncoming traffic, he caught her wide-eyed expression of alarm—considerably more concern than she'd shown at the sight of the mugger. For some reason, she seemed unduly upset by his reference to special training.

A disturbing thought struck him. If she'd had such training, could she be an intelligence agent, assigned to Fairchild on a covert mission? Archer decided to go over her file when he got back to the hotel. Even if the training was disguised as something else, there might be some evidence of it in the information he'd collected about her.

Had he stumbled onto something important?

SETTLE DOWN, Susan told herself. Derek couldn't know about the special training she'd received. She'd over-reacted and she knew it.

"I thought maybe you'd taken one of those self-defense courses advertised on TV," he explained.

But that wasn't what he'd implied an instant earlier with his reference to special air force training for intelligence officers.

"You were right the first time." She settled back on the car seat. "The air force offered a course in self-defense at my last base. Anybody could take it."

Derek nodded, paying more attention to her than to the road. They'd left the downtown area and were headed toward her condo.

"You were smart to take the course," he said. "From what I hear, you can discourage a mugger just by appearing confident."

He believed her. She went limp with relief. "That's what our instructor said."

"What base were you assigned to?" When she didn't answer right away, he glanced in her direction. "Before you came here, I mean."

Susan felt her face flush. Lying might be part of an intelligence operative's job description, but there was no way she'd ever get used to it. "Did I say base? I meant the Pentagon. That was my last assignment." The blood began to pound in her temples.

In the headlights from an oncoming car, she saw his derisive grin. Though he asked no more questions about the training, she sensed he knew she was lying about it.

So what? she asked herself. At least he didn't know why. In a way it was too bad she couldn't tell him. If Derek knew about her covert mission, he wouldn't lose respect for her because she lied.

Her covert mission. She hadn't given it more than a passing thought since her controller had taken her off the job yesterday. In the eight months she'd been here, she'd uncovered absolutely no evidence that anything illegal was going on at Fairchild. Yet Derek, after only one day snooping around as her private investigator, had come up with a notion similar to the Pentagon's.

For the first time Susan realized she'd been calling him by his first name. And he hadn't corrected her. How she wished she could tell him the whole story.

"The mugger interrupted your report," she said as he turned into her driveway. "Come inside and let's talk about what you found out."

THAT MUGGER DID ME a favor. He got me inside the house. Seated next to Susan on the oversize leather sofa in her living room, Archer tried to keep his creative imagination from picturing her without a scrap of clothing, her long golden hair falling luxuriantly around her bare shoulders.

Susan studied him with an expectant look. "You were saying you thought my husband's crew was involved in something illegal." Instead of the negative attitude she'd shown earlier, she leaned toward him as though eager to hear his theory. Watching her full breasts strain against the dress's light wool fabric, Archer's fantasy came back more vividly than ever. He could feel her skin beneath his hands, her softness curved against his chest. Breathing deeply, he had to force himself to concentrate on their conversation.

"I think the crew was using the C-130 for smuggling," he said abruptly. "I think that's why your husband was killed. Maybe he was about to squeal and the organization found out."

"You mean Don Albright found out," she corrected him. "If something illegal was going on, he had to be behind it."

What would she say, he wondered, if he told her he was Don Albright, the convicted killer she so despised? His gut tightened at the thought.

"Maybe so," he agreed, "but he sure had a lot of help. Like I said before, this smells like a conspiracy." Smiling, he remembered the scared look on Sergeant Naylor's face when he'd used that word.

"Drugs?" She whispered the word breathlessly, as though it were the worst profanity imaginable.

He shook his head. "I don't think so. This conspiracy has too much finesse for drugs. That telephone call to you was obviously part of a carefully orchestrated plan to frame you. From what I hear, drug lords don't think that way."

"And you're saying Brian knew about this conspiracy, whatever it is?" Her face had fallen.

How much did Susan love her husband? Archer wondered, surprised at himself for even thinking the question.

"Your husband had to be involved, Susan. As pilot, he was the aircraft commander." Seeing the glint of tears in her eyes, Archer felt the unexpected urge to comfort her and gave himself a swift mental kick. What he wanted to do with Susan Wade had nothing to do with comfort and everything to do with throwing her down on this couch and holding her bare body against his.

"Maybe Albright killed Brian because he was going to tell the authorities what was going on." Her voice was weak, without conviction.

"That doesn't make sense," he returned. "It assumes Albright was still working with your husband." Archer slid closer to her on the leather couch. "After your husband did his best to put Albright in prison for the next forty years or so, I doubt they'd still be working together."

She nodded in agreement. "I was wrong when I said that. Brian might have had his secrets from me, but one thing I did know. He had no qualms about revealing how he felt about Don Albright."

"And how was that?" Archer probed while watching the light play across her face and wishing it were in his hands.

"Brian was sure Albright would try to get back at him for causing his murder conviction—if he was still alive, that is. He worried about it all the time." Her forehead creased in thought. "So, of course, he hated Albright."

She looked so downcast, his foolish urge to comfort her returned. He wanted to hold her in his arms and stroke her golden hair, and tell her everything would be all right. But if the convicted killer did that, she'd end up hating him. To his surprise, he realized how she felt meant something to him. He'd been strangely humbled when she began calling him by his first name. Liking the sound, he'd come to expect it.

"Shall I meet you at the bank tomorrow afternoon or pick you up here at your place?"

With this new subject, the worry lines on her forehead disappeared.

"Here, I guess," she said. "I want to get out of my uniform before we go to the bank."

When he rose to go, she stood up with him and touched his hand. She was so close he could feel her warmth, could smell the mint liqueur she'd drunk after dinner. He felt her touch from his heart down to the soles of his feet.

"One thing we need to get clear, Derek," she said, her businesslike tone bringing him back to reality. "I want to be alone when I see what's inside that box. Once I've looked, I'll decide who else needs to know."

"Of course," he said, hiding his disappointment. "I'll wait outside the bank while you're in the vault."

IN HIS ROOM at the Riverfront Hotel, Derek took the bulging manila folder labeled Susan Campbell Wade out of his locked suitcase. By studying her file, he hoped to confirm his newly aroused suspicion that she was a trained intelligence agent.

First he examined her service record, obtained from the National Personnel Records Center in St. Louis through the Freedom of Information Act. Among other information, the record listed her promotions, awards and duty assignments. He found no reference to what he was looking for: attendance at a secret intelligence training school.

Next, from the service record and the snippets of

information he'd collected about her, he constructed a day-by-day record of her military service on his laptop computer. By including her leave time and temporary duty, away from her permanent station, he could account for almost every day of her three-and-a-half years' service in the air force. There were no blank periods during which she might have attended a secret school.

He must have missed something.

Doggedly he went through the material again. Only this time he examined her monthly utility bills. He'd gotten her telephone, electric and gas bills by calling the various companies and claiming to be Lieutenant Campbell, since she was unmarried then. If she'd been gone for any length of time, her heating and electric bills should reflect her absence.

He found the discrepancy almost immediately. Her gas, electric and phone bills were considerably less during the two winter months before she was reassigned from the Pentagon to Fairchild.

Then he looked at the dates and places she'd charged gas on a government credit card—information also available through the Freedom of Information Act. Bingo! During the same two winter months, she'd charged gas three times at stations in Denver. Her service record showed no indication of a temporary duty to that part of the country.

From the data in his computer, Derek was almost certain the air force had sent Susan to a covert intelligence collection school before she was assigned to Fairchild. If he was right about her special training, she might have been assigned here to find out about the smuggling activity Derek could smell every time he turned around.

But why had she married Brian Wade, who he now suspected was probably involved in the smuggling? Was that, too, part of her covert mission? His fists clenched at the thought. If she'd married Wade to help her penetrate the smuggling ring…

He didn't like the idea, he realized. *Dammit all, Archer,* he warned himself. *Why can't you see her simply as a means to an end? Then she'll never disappoint you.*

Chapter Six

Susan backed her Firebird out of the garage and waited behind the wheel until Derek showed up at exactly 2:00 p.m. After he'd parked his rental car at the curb and started toward her, he held her gaze, not letting her look away, even if she'd wanted.

She didn't want to.

With this afternoon's warmer weather, Derek carried his leather jacket over one arm. His jeans had seen better days, but their much-worn appearance in no way detracted from the eye-catching way they clung to his muscular body and accentuated his long legs. Today he looked sexier than ever, and she'd be kidding herself not to admit it.

His cotton chambray shirt, open at the throat, stretched tautly across his broad chest. In his pointed cowboy boots, he seemed much more blue-collar and infinitely more accessible than before. An unwelcome surge of excitement swelled through her.

"Right on time as usual," she said without smiling, so he wouldn't guess what she'd been thinking. "Get in. I thought I'd drive today."

Without a word, he opened the passenger's door and

got in, tossing his jacket on the back seat next to her briefcase.

As she turned out of her driveway and started for town, she could feel him looking her over. Out of the corner of her eye she saw his gaze drop from her face to her breasts, to her long pleated skirt. A delicious warm feeling spread through her loins.

"Good choice of uniform," Derek commented casually.

Susan had spent over an hour choosing her clothes and dressing for the afternoon. She found herself inordinately pleased by his approval. But when she turned to look him full in the face, she saw not approval, but his usual cynical smile.

"I don't want to be too conspicuous in the bank," she murmured.

"In that dark skirt and sweater, you won't be," he said. "With your hair pulled back and no makeup or jewelry, you look exactly like what you're supposed to be: a grieving widow. You couldn't have picked a better outfit if you'd been *specially trained* for the part." From his slight emphasis on the words, she suspected he'd used them on purpose. Thanks to her idiotic overreaction last night, he'd guessed she had special training.

Well, let him speculate all he wanted. He'd never be sure of anything if she could manage to keep her wits about her. Admittedly, that was a big *if*. When he was around, all she could think about was his muscular body and what his skin would feel like under her fingertips. She wanted to touch him, she realized, shocked at herself, wanted to know how his muscles rippled under those tight jeans, wanted to run her fingers through the chest hair curling through the vee in his shirt. She breathed a long sigh. With thoughts like these, no wonder she'd put her foot in her mouth about the special training.

Beside her, Derek sat silent, the usual distrustful smile on his face. He didn't speak until they reached the downtown area.

"While you're inside the bank, I'll wait by the door where I was the day before yesterday." He paused just long enough for her to sense something was bothering him.

"I'm sure I'm not telling you anything you don't know," he began. "But don't spend a lot of time in the vault. The quicker we move, the more difficult for somebody to get whatever's in that box away from us. Just stick everything in the briefcase and come right on out."

She maneuvered the Firebird into a parking space.

"How melodramatic," she taunted as they started to walk toward the bank. On the street, the sun seemed brighter than in the car. She handed her empty briefcase to him while she put on her sunglasses. The tinted lenses offered protection from more than the sun. "Why don't you come right out and say you want to see what's inside the box?"

If she'd hoped to fluster him, she didn't succeed. He turned toward her with an expression of pained tolerance. "I'd be a liar if I said I wasn't curious. Finding out what's in your husband's safe-deposit box is almost as interesting as watching Geraldo open Al Capone's vault." His face darkened. "But even more important than seeing the contents is keeping them safe.''

"Who's going to take them?'' Susan wanted to laugh but couldn't. A tendril of foreboding curled up her spine. "Nobody knows about the box but you and me and my lawyer. What's to be afraid of?''

He took her arm as they crossed an intersection. "According to what you told me, nobody except your husband knew you were working in your office on the Martin Luther King holiday last January. So who called pretending to be an airman's wife? And how did your mysterious caller find out you were there?''

A cold knot formed in Susan's stomach. "Do you think someone might be following us?''

"It's possible.'' Derek paused for a moment, and she shivered, seeing the coldness in his eyes. "It's also possible that someone you don't suspect is interested in what you're up to.''

"Like who?'' The knot in her stomach grew bigger.

"Like someone in your lawyer's office?''

Stubbornly, Susan shook her head. "Not likely.'' She tried to ignore the tightness in her stomach.

"How about the personnel at your squadron? Even though your colonel lets you take off whenever you want, don't you have to sign out or let someone know where you are?''

Defiantly, she shook her head. "Nobody at the squadron knows anything about the box or the court order—or even whether or not I'm in the office.''

"If you say so.'' Clearly Derek thought she was underestimating the curiosity of her fellow airmen.

They'd reached the bank. Her heart thumping

madly, Susan mounted the shallow stairs and pushed the door open to the black marble interior. What would she find in Brian's secret hiding place?

THROUGH NARROWED EYES, Derek watched Susan go inside. With her head high and her back ramrod straight, she reminded him of a picture he'd seen once of Joan of Arc marching into battle. Her dark outfit reinforced that image. He expelled his breath in an exasperated sigh. She wasn't a saint. She was Susan Wade, possible government agent and killer, just like him, about to discover the innermost secrets of her philandering husband.

But no matter what she was, he wished he could be there with her when she opened that box. If her husband had put something inside that would destroy her emotionally... He gave himself a quick mental shake. Why should he care how she felt when she saw the box's contents? He couldn't let himself go soft, not now when he was in sight of his goals. Instead of worrying about her feelings, he had to figure how to get the damn stuff away from her—or at least how to get a good look at it. Whatever was in that box might give him the ammunition he needed to even the score at last. He had to get his hands on it.

Usually thoughts of vengeance toughened his resolve. But not today. He kept picturing Susan lifting her chin in that spunky, defiant way, her brown eyes flashing fire. What would she do if he told her the truth about himself?

Hell, he knew the answer to that one! She'd call the

police and turn him in, and he'd go to jail for the rest of his life.

What a hopeless situation! With a start, Derek realized he was thinking about a relationship between the two of them.

Don't screw up by falling for Wade's widow, he warned himself for at least the tenth time since meeting her. He didn't realize he'd spoken aloud until a pretty young woman in a business suit glanced at him and smiled.

"I beg your pardon? Did you say something?" she asked.

He noticed her hopeful expression and favored her with a smile. "Sorry. My wife's taking longer than expected and I was muttering under my breath."

Now, where had *that* excuse come from? Never before in his life had he used a nonexistent wife to get rid of unwanted female attention. Never before had he given a rip about being nice to someone he wasn't attracted to, even in the days before he became Derek Archer. Where were these noble intentions coming from?

"Well, have a nice day," she said, obviously disappointed.

He leaned against the stone building, enjoying the warmth of the sun on his face. A moment later, he deliberately moved into a shaded area. He'd been enjoying life too much these past few days. Instead of lounging around in the sun, he needed to figure out how he was going to get a good look at whatever was inside Brian Wade's safe-deposit box.

He mulled the question over in his mind, not satisfied with the alternatives. After reminding himself she was nothing more than a means to an end, he came up with the only viable answer. If Susan wouldn't show him the contents voluntarily, he'd take them away from her. There was no way she could stop him.

THE STOCKY BANK MANAGER hurried over to Susan shortly after she stepped inside the marble lobby. He thrust out his hand. "Good to see you again, Mrs. Wade. Your lawyer phoned and said you'd be in this afternoon."

Her heart sinking, she shook his hand and said hello. Derek was right again. How many other *invisible* people knew exactly where she was and what she was doing this afternoon? The tendril of foreboding she'd felt before crept farther up her spine. Pasting on a smile, she pulled the court order out of her bag and gave it to him.

He glanced at the paperwork and nodded. "You know where the vault is, but we have a new cle₁... I'll introduce you."

Susan followed him across the lobby to an inconspicuous elevator, marbled to blend in with the marble walls. He pushed the down button, and the doors slid open.

A moment later they got out on the floor below. The area, dominated by the massive round vault door, still smelled faintly of air freshener, the way it had two days ago. Susan's stomach churned with anticipation and dread. She'd soon know what scandalous secrets lay in Brian's box.

A middle-aged woman sat at a desk facing the elevator. She greeted Susan and the manager with the same charm-school smile of the rest of the bank staff.

"This is Mrs. Brian Wade, Martha," the manager said, showing her the court order. "She needs to get into her husband's safe-deposit box." He turned to Susan. "Martha will be pleased to help you."

"Of course," the woman murmured, her polished smile still in place. "I'll get the signature card." Rising, she went to one of three four-drawer file cabinets lined up against the wall behind her, and returned with a card. Susan could see it had a list of dates and Brian's signatures.

"I'd like to jot down the dates my husband looked inside the box," she said. Without waiting for approval, she took a small notebook from her bag and began listing the dates. To her relief, she noted he'd rented the box several months before he met her. That meant he hadn't taken it just to hide something from her. Maybe its contents wouldn't be as disturbing as she feared. She didn't look up until she finished her list and signed her name below Brian's on the card.

"Can you handle things from here, Martha?" the manager asked. At the clerk's nod, he turned toward Susan. "If you need any help, call me, Mrs. Wade."

"Thanks," she returned, touched by the sympathy in his expression. Like her, he realized that husbands who kept safe-deposit boxes hidden from their wives were apt to have embarrassing secrets.

The woman returned the card to the file and pushed the drawer closed. Then she took the few steps to the massive vault door. "If you'll give me your key, Mrs. Wade."

Susan followed her inside the vault. About fourteen-by-eight, the room was lined from floor to ceiling with rectangular metal boxes. Brian's box was located on the top row, and the clerk had to climb a small ladder to reach it. After twisting the keys in the two locks, she drew the box out and handed it down to Susan. About four times longer than it was wide, it felt heavy and awkward in her hands.

She followed the clerk to one of the small adjoining rooms and closed the door behind herself. Along one wall was a kitchen-height counter. A bar-type chair sat in front of it.

Gingerly, as though the box might be filled with explosives, Susan set it on the counter and placed her briefcase and handbag beside it. Holding her breath, she flipped the latch back and opened the long lid.

Neatly arranged, in Brian's meticulous way, were a key, two credit cards and some papers.

Where was the insurance policy from Industrial Indemnity? It had to be here. Hastily, she leafed through the papers. There was no sign of it. She'd been so sure the policy would be in the box, she could hardly believe it wasn't here.

More carefully, she shuffled through the contents again.

On top was a key attached to a red plastic tag with the name and address of a local mail distribution center printed on it. Beneath the key were two credit cards belonging to someone named Stephen Ellis and a three-by-five index card with a name and telephone number in Seattle written in Brian's neat script.

Next was a small notebook filled with dates and

figures that made no sense to Susan. Finally, on the bottom, was the folded deed to some property in South America.

The insurance policy from Derek's company definitely wasn't here. How odd. And she noticed something else peculiar: the name on the file card was different from the one on the credit cards. But, thank God, nothing seemed connected to her or their marriage. If Brian had illegitimate children or fond mistresses, Susan could see no evidence here. At the realization, a heavy weight shifted off her shoulders.

Mindful of Derek's warning to hurry, she thrust the items into her briefcase and twisted the combination lock. Then she poked her head outside the door.

The clerk looked up. "Are you finished, Mrs. Wade?"

"Yes." In another minute, the box had been returned to its place and Susan was in the elevator, the locked briefcase in her hand.

She stepped off the elevator into the bank lobby with the odd sensation that everybody was staring at her. Quickly she scanned the few patrons in the bank. Though no one so much as glanced in her direction, Susan felt like every eye in the place was focused on the briefcase in her hand. She had to get outside to Derek, where she'd have some protection. Conscious of every step, she hurried though the marble lobby to the polished brass door and down the few outside stairs to the street.

He wasn't there.

Susan felt momentary panic as she glanced around the street corner, searching for him. An instant later he emerged from the shadows beside the bank's wall. A swell of relief surged over her at the sight of his solemn, square-cut face.

He reached for the briefcase. "Here, I'll take that."

She jerked it back, out of his reach. "It's not heavy. I can manage." Surprised at his grim, tight-lipped expression, she gave him a welcoming smile. "Your company's policy wasn't there."

"Then your husband must have put it somewhere else." He didn't seem as surprised as she thought he'd be. "Care to tell me what *was* inside?"

Hesitating, Susan ran over the contents in her mind. Was there anything she couldn't share with her private investigator?

Nothing she'd found seemed remotely connected to Derek or to his insurance company. He was probably right about the policy. Brian had filed it elsewhere. Or maybe she'd inadvertently thrown it out. Goodness knows she'd been disturbed enough after the funeral to do something like that.

And she *had* hired Derek to investigate Brian's death. Now that she knew there was nothing scandalous in the box, she needed him to help her make sense of the mysterious items she'd found. The thought of the two of them hunched over a table together, examining the box's contents, made her feel warm all over.

Her mind made up, Susan described the five items in the briefcase. "We can look them over carefully in the car." She stepped up her pace toward her Firebird.

"Good thinking." She heard approval in his voice. As they headed for the crosswalk, Susan heard quick breathing behind her and felt the air stir. Automatically she tightened her grip on her shoulder bag and turned her head to look.

A man stood behind her, so close she could smell his body odor. Her own startled face was reflected in his silvered sunglasses. She jerked to one side, away from him. He grabbed for her briefcase, and she yanked it away. He grabbed again, catching her wrist in a steel grip and pulling, hard. Her arm felt yanked from her shoulder, but she held on to the case.

Half a second later he released her and she flinched, sensing he was going to hit her. The next instant something solid whacked the back of her left leg. Pain shot through her calf, and she crumpled to the sidewalk. An instant later his shadow blocked the sun. She tried to shove the briefcase away from him, but he scrambled on top of her, wrenching it from her hand.

Then, above her, she heard a fierce growl of rage. There was a sudden movement, and the shadow shifted. A pair of sunglasses clattered to the pavement. The mugger squealed with pain and dropped the case. It clunked to the sidewalk beside Susan. As she struggled to her feet, she grabbed the handle, holding it with a deathlike grip.

Standing, her attacker twisted on the sidewalk like a boneless rag doll, his arm bent at an odd angle. Derek had him, she realized with a shudder. He had pulled him off her.

With a sudden twist of his body, Derek kicked the mugger's legs out from under him. He landed on the pavement with a sickening thud. Staring down at him,

Susan saw him gasping for breath and writhing in pain.

Derek caught her eye, an oddly gentle expression on his face. "Are you all right?" His familiar caustic smile was gone.

The agony in her leg was so bad she could hardly stand. She forced herself to stay upright, to put equal weight on both feet, not to show how bad it hurt.

Swallowing hard, she said, "I'm fine."

His eyes narrowed and he frowned, as though he sensed her pain. Then he looked down at the mugger, still lying on the sidewalk.

His loud gasps had quieted. Susan noticed he was older than she'd thought. His red jacket and long, unkempt hair had fooled her. With his lean, muscular body, he looked more like a trained fighter than an adolescent thug.

A small circle of interested spectators gathered around them at a respectful distance. In a moment the police would notice the disturbance.

The police. A jab of panic twisted through her as she thought of the questions they'd ask, the insinuating way they'd try to connect this incident with Brian's murder. Could they confiscate her briefcase as evidence?

"We've got to get out of here," she said in a panicky whisper.

Derek stared down at the man on the pavement. "First, I think our friend here needs a little lesson."

The mugger stared back with rocklike black eyes.

"Where I come from, a man doesn't kick a lady." Derek's words were so soft only Susan and the mugger could hear them. The man's eyes widened, and he put up his hands to shield his head.

What's he going to do? Susan thought, swallowing the scream that trembled in her throat. Then, horrified, she watched Derek's pointed cowboy boot connect with the mugger's ankle.

The man's screech ripped through the afternoon air. Derek tensed. Susan was sure he was going to kick again.

"No," she screamed. "He isn't worth it." Grabbing Derek's arm with her free hand, she tugged as hard as she could. The muscles underneath her fingers were taut, like coiled springs.

When Derek glanced down at her, his face was filled with rage. But as he stared, she saw his anger lift. Shifting his position, he took the briefcase from her with one hand. He put the other under her arm. "Can you walk okay?"

Still in shock, she could only nod.

The little group gathered around them stood in absolute silence, absorbing the violence with placid acceptance, as though watching it on the five o'clock news. Then someone stepped forward and patted Derek on the shoulder. "Good show, man," he said. There was a murmur of agreement.

Their approval sickened Susan. Couldn't they see that something awful had just happened? And not just to the mugger. She'd seen the hate on Derek's face and it frightened her.

As they passed through the fringe of onlookers, a woman asked, "Aren't you going to wait for the police and press charges?"

Derek smiled pleasantly at her. "Nothing was taken, and that pile of garbage on the sidewalk got the worst of the deal. Why should we press charges?" He kept walking, not waiting for the woman to reply.

Behind them, Susan heard the squeal of tires at the curb. Was it the police? She forced herself to limp faster. But she'd taken only a few steps when Derek stopped and glanced back at the mugger. She turned, too. Her attacker was now sitting up and rubbing his ankle.

While she watched, two men jumped out of a van that had pulled up at the curb near him. In an instant they had lifted him bodily off the pavement and into the van. In another instant the vehicle turned the corner and disappeared.

Stunned by the attack, Susan caught Derek's vengeful scowl. "What were you going to do to him?"

If he noticed her shocked reaction, he didn't say so. "Break the bastard's leg." His eyes narrowed, and she caught a hint of the rage she'd seen on his face when he kicked the mugger. It was still there, festering under the surface.

Shaken, she stared at him. Vengeful wrath boiled off his tall muscular body in waves so intense she could almost see them. "You probably did break it."

"No. He's just got a bad bone bruise. Like yours." She felt his hand under her arm again. "Are you positive you're okay?"

"I'm fine." As they started toward the car, she tried not to limp. No sense making him angrier than he already was. "Do you think he was waiting to steal the briefcase?"

"I'm sure of it. Muggers don't usually have backup cars waiting to pick them up when a victim resists." He paused, as though wondering how much to tell her.

For Susan the sunny downtown street took on a sudden chill. "Is there something you're not saying?" Fear tightened her muscles and made her forget the throbbing pain in her leg and hip.

"I'd bet money that mugger was the same man we saw last night. He had the same body build and was wearing a similar red jacket."

"But I didn't have the briefcase last night."

His face displayed a knowing awareness. "Somebody knew you were picking up the court order today, that you'd find out what was inside Brian's box." Susan heard an urgency in his smooth baritone voice.

"I think that mugger meant to take you hostage last night," he continued, "and force you to give the box's contents to whoever hired him."

Susan couldn't stifle her gasp of disbelief. "But you were with me. He'd never dare something like that unless I was alone."

At her implied compliment, Derek gave her an appealing smile that sent her pulses racing. "Thanks for the vote of confidence." There was a hint of amusement in his glance. "But fists are no match for guns. That man probably had his friends waiting around the corner in their van. If we'd kept walking last night, I suspect I'd be dead by now and my body buried in some out-of-the-way spot."

They reached her Firebird. Susan's hands shook when she fumbled in her purse for her keys. "But there was nothing incriminating in Brian's box."

"Whoever hired the mugger doesn't know that, and neither do we," he said soberly. "Either of the men whose names were on those cards could be behind your husband's murder."

Her keys slid out of her trembling fingers and dropped into the gutter. Stooping, Derek picked them up. "Want me to drive?"

She shook her head, grateful for his offer but wanting to prove—as much to herself as to him—that she was in control. "I can manage."

He opened her door and helped her inside, then went around the car to the passenger side. Putting the briefcase on the floor behind his seat, he studied her face with an anxious expression. "You're sure you're all right to drive?"

"Positive." She glanced at the briefcase, fighting her apprehension. "Maybe we should take this stuff to that bank down the street. I could rent a safe-deposit box there after we've looked at it."

Decisively he shook his head. "After our scene with the mugger, too many people downtown this afternoon will recognize us. We don't want to get stopped by a conscientious police officer trying to find out what happened—or by one of the mugger's friends hoping to finish the job."

What a frightening thought: somebody was after them and they couldn't go to the police. Trembling, Susan started the engine. "Where to, then?" No matter how dangerous Derek seemed, she had to trust his judgment. She had nowhere else to turn.

For a long moment he sat in silence. "Let's go to

my hotel room to look things over. We should be safe there.''

She'd be alone with him in his hotel room. The thought brought unwanted warmth to her face. *Don't be an idiot,* she told herself fiercely. *This man is interested in the money you're paying him. You're flattering yourself if you think he's got designs on you.* But she couldn't help wishing he did.

Chapter Seven

Derek eyed Susan as she lowered herself to the chair, and he wondered how she'd react if he pulled her to her feet and kissed the breath out of her. He'd seen the flush on her face when he suggested coming to his hotel room, and suspected she was as ready as he was.

He stifled his unwelcome impulse. Right now he had more important things to do than make love to a woman who would despise him if she knew who he really was.

Without being obvious, he glanced at the briefcase on the table next to her chair. He had to see what was inside.

She glanced at her watch. "It's nearly four. The banks will be closing soon. If we're going to put this stuff in a vault, we'd better decide which one."

"Of course." *Be patient,* he told himself. *Don't be eager—no matter how much you need to see what Wade hid in his safe-deposit box.* She said she'd show him. And if she didn't, he'd take the contents away from her. It was as simple as that.

She got up, went to the nightstand beside the bed and reached for the telephone directory. "I'll call a bank near my condo—see if it's got a vault and how late they're open."

For the first time since the mugging, she wasn't by his side. As she walked away from him, Derek saw her limp. She tried to hide it, but he knew she was in more pain than he'd realized. Cursing under his breath, he moved toward her. As he drew near, she stood facing him with her back to the bed, her eyes full of questions.

Lord, but he wanted to feel her mouth on his, her shapely body curved against him. For one petrifying instant he stood in front of her, so close he could smell the clean woodsy scent of her. Her eyes widened and she stepped backward against the bed. At the pressure, an involuntary grimace crossed her face.

"Turn around," he ordered.

"Wh-why?" Her voice trembled as she spoke. He couldn't tell if she was eager or frightened. Perhaps both.

At that moment he wanted nothing more than to throw her on the bed and have her. His body told him to go ahead, that what he saw in her eyes was obliging anticipation. His mind said this wasn't the right time or place. He couldn't take advantage of her willingness, of the trust that willingness implied.

Don't be an ass, he warned himself, upset at his unexpected concern for her feelings when the important thing was examining the papers inside the briefcase.

"I want to see what that bastard did to your leg." He was surprised at how husky his voice sounded.

"Oh." Was that disappointment he heard? But dutifully she turned around. "I'm sure it's not serious or I couldn't walk." Her tone was apologetic.

He took one look and swore out loud. "I should have broken his damned leg." Her stocking was torn across the calf. Underneath, the flesh had already begun to swell. Lightly he ran his fingers over the swelling. She flinched at his touch.

"The skin's not broken, but you'll have a bad bruise." He tried to control his anger. "You can start by sitting on the bed with your legs up while you call the bank."

"Why don't *you* call the bank?" she said, smiling. "While you're on the phone, I'll make a list of everything that was in Brian's box."

"Fine," he growled, pretending a reluctance he didn't feel. This was exactly what he wanted. If he sat on the side of the bed while he talked on the phone, he could examine the papers when she took them from the case.

She settled herself with her feet up, two king-size pillows behind her back. She looked so *right* on his bed that he had to force himself to turn away before he said or did something he'd be sorry for.

The briefcase was on the floor by the closet. Crossing the room, he leaned to pick it up.

"Derek." Her voice was a soft whisper.

Startled, he turned toward her.

"Thanks for not waiting around for the police." She laughed, but without humor. "The last thing I needed right then was more attention from Detective MacElroy. If he'd gotten involved, he would have had all kinds of questions about what was in the briefcase."

"I figured you wouldn't want them brought in." *And I sure as hell didn't want them nosing around,* he added to himself, acknowledging the real reason he'd insisted on leaving. Derek put the briefcase on the bed beside her and watched while she twisted the combination on its small lock.

"Maybe we should report what happened now, even though this much time has passed." She opened the briefcase but didn't take anything out. "The police might be able to connect the van with whoever hired those men."

Derek's gut tightened. Why was she being so slow? He resisted his urge to grab the briefcase from her. "I doubt the police could identify the van's owner without the license." He made sure his voice didn't betray his anxiety.

Closing the briefcase, she slid it off her lap to her other side. Had she changed her mind about showing him the contents?

"I got the license number." Her brown eyes sparkled with pride.

Momentarily diverted, he stared at her in disbelief. "How'd you manage that?"

"I've got a photographic memory when it comes to numbers."

"If we've got the license, we don't have to go to the police to find out who owns the van," he said. "I can get the name in less than an hour."

Her expression turned frankly skeptical. "I thought the licensing people protected that information."

Derek shook his head, a lock of curly black hair falling across his forehead. "Just the opposite. It's available from the state to anyone who doesn't mind waiting."

"Really." She still sounded skeptical.

"To save time I can access a commercial data net and get the name from an information broker in an hour or so."

Still doubtful, she glanced around the room. "You brought a computer?"

He eyed her without smiling. Was she ever going to show him what was in the damned briefcase? "Yes, but I don't have a modem. I'll have to use the hotel fax machine to access the broker."

"I think you should do it. We need to find out who owns that van." Her fingers drummed nervously on the side of the closed briefcase, and he sensed she was stalling.

Frustrated, Derek eyed the briefcase, tempted to grab it and dump the papers out on the bed. Had she changed her mind about showing them to him? His mind shifted into overdrive. He'd have to leave her in the room alone while he was at the fax machine. Would she seize this chance to search his room?

You bet, he told himself grimly. She was an intelligence officer. She wouldn't be worth her salt if she didn't. Had he left any files unsecured? He was sure he hadn't, but just to be safe, he went to the closet and—squatting so she couldn't see him from the bed—double-checked the lock on the suitcase where he stored them. No problem, he thought with satisfaction. Even a trained locksmith would be hard put to open the sophisticated lock without smashing it.

When he left the room with the printed license plate

number on a sheet of yellow paper, Susan was leaning back on the bed with her eyes closed. Outside his closed door a few seconds later, he smiled knowingly to himself when he heard the faint *click* of the night latch sliding into place.

Let her snoop all she wants, he told himself. Maybe then she'd be convinced he was Derek Archer, insurance agent, with nothing to hide.

As soon as Derek left the room, Susan got off the bed and slid the night latch into place. She didn't want him walking in on her in the next ten or fifteen minutes. Though she'd told him generally what Brian had kept in his safe-deposit box, a twinge of doubt remained about actually showing him the contents.

She wasn't sure why she still doubted him when she felt so secure when he was with her. Maybe *turned-on* was a better description of how she felt, she admitted grudgingly—and that was exactly what the problem was. But if she looked through his things and found nothing to contradict what he'd told her, she'd be more comfortable sharing Brian's secrets with him.

It didn't take long to glance through the few clothes he'd hung in the closet and laid neatly in the dresser drawers. Though obviously expensive, his suits looked several years old. Interestingly, one had the label of a local store sewn inside. He must have visited Spokane off and on over a period of years. No wonder he knew the town as well as he did.

A compassionate feeling swept over her when she saw handkerchiefs with his initials frayed at the edges and T-shirts coming apart at the seams. He wasn't kidding when he said he needed to supplement his income.

Ignoring her throbbing leg, Susan dropped to her knees outside the closet and carefully opened his two unlocked suitcases. Nothing was inside. He'd obviously put everything he considered confidential in the one with the lock. When she lifted the locked suitcase, she was surprised at how heavy it was, probably filled with books or papers.

Taking his laptop computer from the closet, she set it on the table and turned it on. After a few experimental jabs, she discovered which program he used. A client list including Brian's name appeared on the screen. But when she punched *Wade, Brian*, the screen came up blank. She tried two other names on the list. Nothing. The only thing on the disk was the list of client names and a blank insurance form.

How odd, she thought. Why haul a laptop computer around the country if you're not going to use it? Maybe there was another disk in the case. A quick search of the machine's carrying case revealed another disk, but when she put it in the machine, it was blank. If he had a work disk, it was locked up in the suitcase.

Maybe he doesn't know how to use his computer.

A light knock on the door startled her. If Derek saw the computer on the table, he'd know she'd been snooping.

The rap came again. Louder. She peered out through the peephole. There he stood with his usual distrustful smile. He held something in his hand. Through the peephole, she couldn't tell what it was. Wrapping her composure around her like a suit of armor, she slid the bolt back and opened the door.

He stepped into the room, taking in the computer with eyes that were all too knowing. "Find anything interesting?"

Susan managed a tremulous smile. "You know I didn't."

"What were you looking for?" he asked pleasantly. "Anytime you want answers, all you have to do is ask."

"I wasn't looking for anything special," she lied. "I've never used a laptop and was curious." That, at least, was the truth.

"So what's the verdict?"

"I like it," she replied sincerely. "If you want, I can explain the program to you."

He stared at her, baffled. "Why would I want you to do that?"

When she glanced at the screen, the blank insurance form stared back at her. "Well, when I realized you weren't using your computer, I thought..."

"You thought I didn't understand the program." His expression softened so much he looked like a different man. "My clients' files are confidential, so I keep them locked up." His rich baritone voice sounded raspier than usual. "If you really want to be useful, get back on that bed and put this ice on your leg."

Susan focused on the plastic bag in his hand. That's what he was carrying. How could she not trust a man so concerned for her comfort? In that moment, she made her decision: she'd show him Brian's secrets.

Without a word she went to the king-size bed and settled herself squarely in the middle.

He handed her a towel and the bag of ice. As the soothing coolness calmed the angry heat in her swollen leg, she opened the briefcase and patted the edge of the bed. "Sit down, and let's see what Brian thought was important enough to lock up."

AT LAST. Sinking to the mattress, Derek masked his exuberance. His unexpected concern for Susan's injury had momentarily taken his mind off Wade's papers. Now, with the moment of truth finally at hand, his eagerness returned.

The first thing she handed him was the key to a post office box. Mentally he noted the box number and station location in Dishman, north of the city. Next she passed him two credit cards and an index card. He made a mental note of the two men's names on the cards. *Stephen Ellis* on both credit cards. *Ted Lindsey* on the index card, along with a telephone number, in Wade's handwriting.

"What do you make of this?" she asked, handing him a small notebook with spiral binding at the top.

Derek took one look inside and recognized the numbers. "They look like flight dates and times along with coded numbers—probably for smuggled cargo and cash payments."

"Good for you, Derek." The admiration in her voice made him feel like he'd just won the lottery. What was happening to him? With a few brief words she'd made him feel like a winner. There were other figures, too, but he didn't bother to analyze them. That would come later, after he'd copied everything.

"Now, here's something I don't understand." Her head bent, she untied the ribbon around a small sheaf of papers. "It seems to be the deed to some property in Paraguay, but it's in Spanish." She glanced hopefully at Derek. "You don't read Spanish by any chance?"

"A little," he said, itching to get his hands on the papers.

She shoved them at him. "Here. Maybe you can make sense of them."

Sucking in his breath, he skimmed through them. "The property's in the name of Stephen Ellis, the name on the two credit cards."

"Is that significant?" Her beautiful brown eyes gazed into his, distracting him.

"Yes, I'm sure it is." His mind struggled with the problem, trying to add two and two and come up with four. Then, suddenly, he knew the reason for the property deed and the credit cards. Wade was an even worse SOB than he had imagined. Seeing the hopeful look in Susan's eyes, he had to look away.

"Brian must have been keeping this safe-deposit box for Mr. Ellis, whoever he is," she said. "The post office box key is probably in Ellis's name, too."

"Maybe." Why couldn't he come right out and tell her what he suspected?

She seemed to sense he was hiding something. "I've told you my explanation. It's only fair you tell me yours."

"You may well be right," he began, uncharacteristically cautious. "My idea's pretty farfetched."

"So, give," she prompted, irked by his reticence.

For half a second he considered lying. But this was something she needed to hear and accept. "I think your husband planned to assume another identity and leave the country." He reached for her hand, but she jerked it away.

Her jaw dropped and she shuddered, as though he'd struck her. "I can't believe he'd do such a thing. If he were going to leave, he'd need a passport. Why wasn't it in the box?"

Watching the confused play of emotions on Susan's expressive face, he wished Wade were still alive so he could smash his fist in the man's lying mouth. To Derek, there was no doubt Wade meant to abandon her. He meant to leave her hanging, perhaps for years, not knowing if he was dead or alive.

Derek knew a man could disappear completely, as though he had never existed. Not without careful planning, of course, but it could certainly be done. He himself was living proof.

"As I said," he went on, wondering why he was trying so hard to make things easier for her, "the idea's probably too farfetched."

She'd been staring down at the folded paper in his hand. When she looked up, he saw a swift shadow of anger sweep across her face.

"It's not farfetched." Her tone was oddly detached and didn't match her frown, as though she was struggling to disavow her anger. "Even during our honeymoon, Brian put me at the bottom of his priority list. If some stranger wanted to play tennis, that took priority over a swim in the pool with me. We went to Las Vegas and he stayed out gambling most of every night we were there. I rarely saw him.''

''Gambling on your honeymoon?'' Derek felt vindicated. Susan had just confirmed what he'd known in his gut all along. Brian Wade was a cold, insensitive man, one who would have no moral problem betraying his wife—or his best friend.

Carefully he took her hands, and this time she didn't jerk them away. Instead, she leaned toward him, her eyes glistening. ''I don't want to mislead you, Derek. For Brian, gambling wasn't a problem. He was a winner, not a loser. Every morning he'd tell me how much he'd won. Then he'd sleep most of the day and leave me to my own devices. I often wondered why he married me.''

Derek studied her arresting face, dominated by sparkling brown eyes. ''The question is, why did *you* marry him?''

At his implied compliment, a flush brightened her cheeks. ''Because I loved him, of course. Or at least I thought I did. To quote an old cliché, he swept me off my feet. You can't believe how nice he was before we were married. But afterward, well, he simply wasn't the same man.''

Derek felt some of the tension leave him.

She paused, thinking. ''You know, Derek, it was almost as though he married me for a reason—like someone ordered him to. He had to be nice until he got that ring on my finger. Then it didn't matter anymore.''

Derek's elation grew. "Why didn't you leave him?"

She looked down again. "I intended to." Her voice broke. "I kept putting off telling him, thinking he might change."

"But of course he didn't."

As he watched, she studied her hands, clasped tightly in her lap since he'd released them. "Every day he seemed more inconsiderate and harder to get along with. If you're right and he meant to walk out on me, I can see why. He probably had some Latin beauty waiting for him in Paraguay."

Derek saw the tears brimming in her eyes and could resist no longer. With one quick motion he gathered her into his arms. She didn't pull away. At the feel of her breasts against his chest, he had to fight his desire to crush her mouth with his. His attraction to her must not get out of hand, not here in this hotel room with so much riding on their investigation.

She buried her face against his chest. "How could I have been so stupid?"

Stroking her silky blond hair, he felt her tremble. "Your husband was intelligent, and being a fellow officer, he spoke your language. I'm sure he could be quite charming when he wanted to be. Most women would have reacted just as you did."

He felt her swallow hard and knew she was fighting tears. "Even my mom and dad liked him. I had no idea a person could turn into somebody else the way he did, overnight."

At her softness in his arms, heat flowed through him and he forced himself to resist his body's rebellious desire. "Do you have any idea why he'd want to change his identity and disappear?" Disturbed by his physical reaction, Derek tried to back away, but she clung to him.

"It must have something to do with that smuggling you were talking about." Her voice, buried in his throat, was muffled. "Somehow, in some way, Brian must have been involved. Maybe he got in too deep and wanted out."

Or maybe he decided to take his profits and run. Derek wanted to embrace her more tightly, but he knew that would be dangerous. Instead, he kept stroking her hair.

"It's after five," he said. "If we're going to take this stuff to a bank vault, we've got to get going."

She didn't move in his arms. "The hotel must have a secure place for its customers' valuables. We can leave everything there overnight."

His stomach tightened. "You're not registered here." Did she intend for him to take custody of Wade's secrets?

"But *you* are." Her smile was so trusting he felt like what he was: a convicted killer with dirt for a heart. If he had a shred of honor left, he'd forget this damned obsession of his and walk as far away from Spokane—and Susan—as he could get. While he still could.

IGNORING THE PAIN in her leg, Susan glanced at Derek's face as they headed back to her condo. In the light from an approaching car, she saw that his usual wary smile was back.

"You never did tell me who owned the van that mugger used." She turned toward the road. When he was beside her she found herself concentrating on him more than her driving.

"You'll never guess," he returned, a cold edge of irony to his voice.

"Don't tell me I know the person." Her stomach tightened with apprehension. From the wicked way he was smiling, she suspected she'd be shocked by his reply.

"You bet," he said. "It's registered to your new boss, Colonel Tinnerman."

"You're kidding." She gave him a sidelong glance of utter disbelief. "That's too big a coincidence. That information broker you faxed has got to be wrong."

For a long moment he considered that. "You're right about the coincidence. There's got to be some kind of connection when the same man who's after your briefcase drives off in the colonel's van. I'd guess the van was stolen. Listen to the talk around the squadron tomorrow morning and you'll find out."

"I'll do better than that. I'll ask the colonel." The car behind them flicked its lights to bright. Susan adjusted her rearview mirror to reduce the glare.

"Are you going to tell him you were mugged?"

"Do you think I should?" To her surprise, Susan realized she valued Derek's opinion. For a little while, back in his hotel room, she'd caught a glimpse of an understanding personality lurking beneath his tough exterior. Did he really have sensitive feelings, or were her instincts wrong again, the way they'd been with Brian?

"No," he said flatly. "Don't tell Tinnerman. Somebody's playing games with us, Susan. Until we find out the rules, let's not tell anyone what's going on."

"They're not playing games with *us*." Her breath seemed to have solidified in her throat. "Nobody's after you. It's me they want."

"Correction. As long as you're paying for my help, it's *us* they're after." His voice turned cold, businesslike. "You've got one more day to decide if you want to continue with my services."

Damn him, she thought. Why did he have to remind her he was here only because she was paying him? Just when she'd hoped his tough shell was cracking. A disturbing thought struck her. Could Derek have arranged the mugger's attack to scare her so she'd keep him on and pay him after the three days were up?

For one intense moment she weighed the possibility. Then, remembering the thug's agonized shriek when Derek kicked him, she cast the notion aside, irritated with herself for even considering it.

He'd never let me get hurt if he could stop it. Deep down she knew that. But he still had some explaining to do.

"You found out who owned the van hours ago. Why did you wait so long to tell me?" She found herself annoyed and pleased by his silence. Upset because he hadn't told her. Pleased because the delay meant he'd seen the connection between the van and the mugger and knew it represented an additional threat to her, one that would upset her. No matter how cold he seemed, he *had* been considerate of her feelings.

Would he lie to protect his tough-guy image? Susan firmed her lips. She wasn't going to let him off the hook even though she appreciated the reason.

"I saw no reason to frighten you unnecessarily," he said, after a moment's hesitation. She smiled to herself, glad she'd been right for once.

"And along that line, there's something I've been meaning to talk to you about." He cleared his throat. "Your condo isn't secure, Susan. Living there alone is a bad idea. Until I find out what's going on, you ought to move to a hotel."

"The Riverfront Hotel?" She couldn't believe that squeaky little voice was hers. The last thing she wanted was a room near his.

"Any good hotel would do," he replied, "but mine's the best choice, since I'm staying there. We could meet every night to compare our progress."

To her embarrassment, an image of Derek, his muscular body glistening from a shower, raced through her mind. What was she thinking? She shook her head defiantly. "My condo's as safe as any hotel. I've got a security system."

Glancing at her, he frowned. "Not good enough. If your alarm went off, it might be half an hour, maybe longer, before the police got there. A couple of thugs can do an awful lot of damage in that amount of time."

She refused to let his warning frighten her. "In my neighborhood police respond in minutes."

"Suit yourself." His abrupt words sounded totally unconcerned.

"I can help you just as well from here," she insisted. Ahead she saw Derek's car parked in her driveway where he'd left it that afternoon. Opening the garage door with her remote control, Susan drove past his car into the garage and closed the door.

He got out when she did and stood behind her while she unlocked the door to the kitchen and flicked on the lights. When she pressed the four-digit code to disarm the security system, she could feel the warmth of his body close behind her. She didn't step to one side when she turned around.

Facing her, he stood so near she heard the raspy sound of his breathing. Like her, he seemed to be gasping for breath. His indigo eyes caught and held hers.

Suddenly she knew what was coming. *He's going to take me in his arms.* Not in the comforting way he'd held her in the hotel. But passionately, the way a man holds a woman when he makes love to her. And she wanted him to. Yearned to feel his body close to hers, his arms wrapped tightly around her.

But she couldn't let him. Not yet. Not as long as his only reason for being with her was the money she'd promised him. Moving while she still could, she forced herself to step aside.

His eyes followed her hungrily. He wanted her, all right. But his wanting would be purely physical. She needed more than that from a lover.

Expelling his breath in a huge sigh, he gave a slight

nod, almost as though he knew what she was thinking and agreed with her. Studying his square-cut face, she wished she hadn't moved.

Damn! Why did he have to look so cursedly sexy?

Chapter Eight

Frowning, Derek nodded toward the security control panel, as if the electric moment they'd just shared had never happened. Even with his attention diverted, Susan could feel the force of his high-powered sexuality. Thank goodness his eyes had lost their predatory air. If he stared at her again the way he had a moment ago, she was afraid she wouldn't be able to resist.

"How long since you checked the system?" he asked. Like a bloodhound tracking a familiar scent, he seemed determined to uncover a flaw. Or was he focusing on the security system to mask his feelings?

"A couple of weeks before Brian died, the monitoring company did an annual inspection."

"Then it should be working okay," he said, but his frown remained.

Now that Susan had been standing for a few minutes, the pain in her leg returned. She felt the blood drain from her face and sagged onto a kitchen chair.

"I'm sorry, Derek. I think I'm going to pass out." She hated to admit her weakness, but that was better than fainting.

He could have said *I told you not to drive.* But he

didn't. Instead, he did something totally unexpected. He knelt beside her and stared into her eyes. She caught her breath.

"Put your arms around my neck, Susan. I'm carrying you to the living room."

Obediently she did what he asked. An instant later she felt his strong arms under her legs and back. Tensing, he lifted her out of the chair. She couldn't miss the musky smell of him as he held her close against him.

Feeling the muscles in his chest against her breasts, a hot ache grew in her throat. His closeness was so male, so bracing, that blood coursed through her veins like an awakened river. From feeling faint, her body heated to flushed excitement.

In the living room, he set her on the leather couch with her legs stretched out and a pillow behind her back. After he'd switched on a light, he placed his hands on his lean hips and looked her over intently. His gaze suddenly warmed, the way it had in the kitchen. Then, right before her eyes, he squelched his desire, and his eyes turned cool. The impression was so intense, Susan felt as though she'd been scorched and then dipped in cold water. Craving his touch, she wasn't sure she hid her disappointment well enough to fool him. But if he noticed, he gave no sign.

"You seem better already," he said.

Her cheeks heated even more under the intensity of his gaze. "All I need is a good night's sleep and I'll be fine."

Lord help her, more than anything she wanted him to fall on top of her and explore every inch of her with his bare hands, wanted to feel his muscular body harden against her. But desires like that were off limits with this strange man whose only attraction to her was the money she'd promised to pay him.

"Then I'll be on my way as soon as I take a quick look around so you can get to bed," he said. Not sure whether to be grateful or frustrated, her heart sank as he turned toward the stairs, away from her.

Don't leave, she wanted to cry out. *Stay for a while longer and hold me in your arms. Let me know how your lips feel, how your tongue tastes when it's inside my mouth. We'll build a fire and listen to music.* But she didn't dare speak that way to a man who was almost a stranger, who kept himself carefully hidden from her even though she'd confided in him this afternoon about her marriage as she had to no one else.

He went upstairs, and she could hear him opening and shutting doors. Ten minutes passed before he reappeared.

"Are you sure you're okay to get to bed by yourself?" Sitting down on the couch beside her, he cupped her face in his large hands. It was as if he had to touch her before he left. His rough, calloused fingers were almost unbearable in their tenderness.

For an instant she considered lying. If she needed help, he'd have to stay. But did she want him to see her as a stricken woman, unable to function because of a few bruises? More important, did she want a man who could turn his back on her and walk away when she desperately wanted him to stay?

"I'll be fine," she said firmly.

"Be sure you set your alarm as soon as I walk out that door." He dropped his hands, his eyes hooded.

She managed a mock salute. "Yes, sir."

For a moment he looked at her. Then, as if he couldn't help himself, he lifted a hand to caress her face. His touch sent a warming shiver through her.

"Now I'm going to do something I'll probably regret," he said. The lust was so plain on his face that she flinched.

Susan felt his breath, warm and moist against her skin, and her heart raced. She tensed, willing herself to resist. No matter how much she desired him, she couldn't let herself fall for him.

Then his lips met hers.

She expected his mouth to be cruel and hard, his emerging beard to scrape her sensitive skin. She could have battled that.

But his lips were surprisingly gentle, tantalizing her with a feather touch. They moved from her lips across her cheeks and closed eyes with a soft exploring that left her defenseless. Caressing more than kissing, he trailed a line back to her lips, pressing them apart with a gentle massage.

Catching fire from his searching mouth, she found herself burning with desire, yearning for the wild, dangerous kiss she'd been determined to fight. At that instant he released her. She felt an aching need for more. Shocked by her eager response, Susan stared at his face.

As he rose from the couch, his lips twisted into his familiar cynical smile. With only one lamp burning, dark shadows filled the room, leaving Susan with an odd sense of foreboding. Was it Derek she was afraid of or this condominium, so filled with Brian's essence?

"I'd better go." Lazily Derek's gaze roamed over her body stretched out on the couch. "You seem to be okay, but I'll be glad to stay if you need me."

It seemed to Susan that he put more emphasis than necessary on *need*. His mocking smile was like ice water. She froze. Was that all his kiss meant? That he'd play stud if she required his services? "Thanks, but I'm fine." She could barely force the words out.

"I still think you should check into a hotel tonight." He stared into the room's shadowy corners with an intensity that made her shiver. With her security system she couldn't possibly be in danger staying here, but the warning tone in his voice scared her, anyway.

"I'll be fine." Looking up at him, she emphasized the words as she repeated them. His indigo eyes were shuttered, his emotions carefully hidden. He was standing so close, but in spite of his nearness, he seemed unreachable.

But with a quick movement, he dropped beside her on the couch. Susan's heart skipped a beat. Was he going to kiss her again? Half of her wanted him to, desperately. The other part was angry at him for his nonchalance and afraid of what would happen if he did.

Before she could stop him, he leaned over her and drew her into his arms. Lowering her head to the pillow, he held her close against him as his mouth descended.

She lay beneath him on the couch, trembling as the wild lips she'd been hungering for moved eagerly on hers. They were hard, and wet and demanding—the way she'd imagined they'd be—and she could no longer resist.

When he thrust his tongue inside her mouth, it was mobile, brutal, demanding. She thought she was ready for him, but her hungry eagerness surprised her. The feel of that part of him inside her, thrusting and tantalizing and playing with her tongue, was unbearably erotic. She found herself clutching him around the neck with both arms and pressing her lips against his with such force that they almost hurt.

Without releasing her, he swung his legs up on the couch beside hers and she felt his hardness against her thighs, the muscles of his chest against her tender breasts. She could feel warmth flow through her like molten lava and knew there was only one thing she desired. She wanted him closer. Lord help her, she wanted him to tear off her clothes and make love to her.

Sensing her desire, he thrust one leg over hers. Pain shot from her calf to her thigh, and she jerked backward, away from him. Not even her passion could numb the cramping pain.

Breaking the kiss, he moved his legs away from her. But if she expected sympathy, it was a forlorn hope.

"You said you were okay." In spite of its huskiness, his voice sounded accusing, but his breath on her cheek was warm and sweet.

She wanted to cry at the emptiness inside her. "I thought I was."

"Obviously you're not." He stood and she saw that his eyes had lost their cold, cynical stare. "Sometimes you surprise me, Susan.'' And she knew he wasn't talking about her leg.

She felt her face flushing, and sat up on the couch so her self-consciousness wouldn't be so obvious. ''You caught me at a weak moment. Don't count on it happening again.'' Damned if she'd let him know how he'd affected her.

He studied her with those knowing eyes of his. ''We'll see about that.'' Then he went to the kitchen and retrieved his leather jacket from the back of a chair where he'd hung it.

''Be careful going back to the hotel,'' she said, suddenly worried about him.

''I'm always careful,'' he assured her. ''Call if you need me.'' While there was a mocking note to his voice, the frown lines around his eyes had relaxed. ''Now, come to the door with me so you can set your alarm as soon as I leave.''

With the door ajar, she watched him walk down the driveway to his car. He didn't look back.

WALKING AWAY FROM Susan's front door was the hardest thing Derek had ever done. She wanted him to stay. He could sense her desire in every breath she took. But much as he wanted her, he couldn't have her. Not as Derek Archer, alias insurance agent. And certainly not as Don Albright, convicted murderer.

As he returned to town, he glanced in his rearview mirror to be sure no one was following. Clenching his fists tightly at his side, he almost wished someone were. If something didn't happen soon, he thought he'd explode.

He could feel the tension in his belly, boiling inside him like hot oil. Ever since pulling the mugger off Susan this afternoon, he'd had to restrain himself so she wouldn't notice. Kissing her had made his edginess even worse. Damn. Why couldn't he keep his hands off her?

It was after ten when he got back to the hotel. Still early, he thought, fighting the tension in his gut. Maybe if he concentrated on the figures in Wade's notebook, he could stop lusting after his widow.

Stopping at the lobby desk, he retrieved the small black notebook from the hotel safe and shoved it in his jacket pocket. Then he took the elevator to the fifth floor.

The bed had been turned down for the night, and a foil-wrapped chocolate lay on each of the two king-size pillows. The sight made him think of Susan—lying on this bed with her gold hair spilling over her bare shoulders and onto the fresh, white pillowcase. He could feel her lips so willing as they met his, her body so soft under his. Wanting her so much he hurt, he breathed a heavy sigh.

How concerned she'd been when she thought he didn't know how to use his computer properly. If there was one thing he'd learned to do well, it was operate a computer. During the past year, he'd become something of a whiz, using the machine to collect and file detailed information on his accusers. After hanging his jacket in the closet, he reached for his laptop.

It was gone.

But that couldn't be. He must have missed it. Feeling foolish, he bent down to inspect the closet floor.

His two suitcases were stacked neatly in back. The computer was gone.

A numbing anger swept over him. How could this happen in the best hotel in the city? He gazed around the luxurious room. The housekeeping staff must have let someone in.

The locked suitcase. The one containing the detailed files on Susan and the four airmen. Where was it?

His anger turned to a white-hot rage. The suitcase was gone, too.

Furious, he paced the length of the room. What now? He couldn't complain to the hotel without involving the police—a course of action he couldn't pursue.

As he paced, he cursed out loud, using vengeful obscenities that sounded strange because he hadn't used them the past few days. Since meeting Susan, he'd begun to forget his hatred for the men who witnessed against him. Now, in the face of this disaster, it returned with a vengeance. He mustn't let her distract him again.

Susan. Was she okay? If they'd break into his hotel room, they might do the same to her condo. A feeling of momentous urgency washed over him as he thought of her alone and unprotected. He had to warn her.

He lifted his phone and started to tap out her number. Surprised at himself, he realized he'd memorized it. Before he finished dialing, he lowered the receiver. She'd been hurting and dead tired when he left her. Maybe there was a better way to make sure she wasn't bothered. Why not park outside her place and keep an eye on things?

He fingered the Saturday night special in his jacket pocket, the result of a few minute's haggling early this morning on a Spokane street corner. Last night's near encounter outside the restaurant convinced him a gun might come in handy. He hadn't needed it this afternoon. Perhaps he would tonight.

SOMEBODY WAS INSIDE the condo.

Suddenly wide awake, Susan jerked bolt upright in bed. What had she heard? She held her breath, listening. Her heart pounded so loudly she had to strain to hear.

There it came again. The tiny squeak on the stairs down the hall from her bedroom. Mingled with normal daytime sounds, the step would be unnoticeable, but it screeched a warning in the deathly silence of the night.

Clutching her blanket to her chin, Susan pictured the stairs. She knew exactly which one squeaked. It was near the top, only a few steps from her bedroom. The intruder would be at her door in seconds. Panic like she'd never known before turned her insides to Jell-O.

Her first impulse was to run and hide. But where? He'd surely find her if she stayed in the bedroom. And by the time she unlocked the sliding glass door to the balcony, he'd be inside the room.

The alarm should have gone off. Frantically she eyed the control panel by the door. Its tiny lights were flashing green, not red. Somehow the intruder had managed to disarm the system.

Sheer black fright swept over her in huge waves.

Her heart beat so loudly, its thumping seemed to fill the room.

Quick, she had to do something. She couldn't just lie here, waiting. She leaped out of bed and dashed to the security panel beside the door. With her index and third fingers she punched the two buttons that would set off the panic alarm.

Nothing happened. Every nerve in her body tensed. She punched again. Still nothing.

This is impossible, she thought, gasping for breath. The panic alarm went off whenever those two buttons were pushed, whether the system was armed or not. Why weren't horns blaring and lights flashing?

She heard movement in the hall outside. Then the doorknob turned and the door burst open. Susan let out a shriek. A hulking brute of a man stood framed in the doorway, his face dimly visible in the tiny green lights on the control panel. In the reflected glow, his square bulldog's face looked grotesque, like something out of a monster movie. Dressed all in black, he wore a knitted stocking cap that made his small head seem even tinier. At least six-and-a-half feet tall, he smelled of cigarette smoke, garlic and sweat.

Slowly he moved toward her, his raised hand clutching something. Light from the flickering panel glinted on a knife's steel blade. Rooted to the floor, she pictured the blade arcing toward her. How much pain would she feel when he thrust it deep inside her?

Instinctively, Susan covered her breasts with her arms. Her breath was so tight in her throat that she was afraid she'd faint. "Get out," she screamed.

"Go sit on the bed nice and quiet like a good little

girl.'' He ground the words out between his teeth in a hoarse, low voice. "You've got something you're dying to tell me."

"No. No," she cried, trembling with helpless anger. "What you want isn't here."

He caressed her cheek with the point of the knife. "Then tell me where it is or I'll do some carving on your pretty little face."

Slowly she began to back toward the bed. If only she'd listened to Derek and gone to the hotel. Or if she'd swallowed her silly pride and asked him to stay. But she hadn't, and he wasn't here to help her. She had no one but herself.

Was there anything she could use in defense? Frantically she glanced around the bedroom. A shoe? A metal trash basket? Nothing seemed effective against a razor-sharp knife.

In the dark hall behind the intruder, she saw something move. God help her if there were two of them. Her legs turned to water, and she dropped to the edge of the bed.

Seconds later the overhead light flicked on.

"Drop the knife." It was Derek's voice. He was here. A wave of relief swept over her.

"What you feel in your back is the business end of a .38," he growled at the intruder.

Susan stared at him, hardly believing her good fortune. How had he shown up at exactly the right time?

From the astonished look on the big man's face, he was as surprised as Susan. His knife fell to the carpeted floor with a dull thud.

"Now, turn around and face the wall with your hands up."

The intruder swung around, and Susan finally found her voice.

"How did you get here?" she cried. "How did you know?"

"Later." Derek's one word brought her back to reality. "Are you okay? If he touched you, I'll kill him right now."

Her heart leaped into her throat. "I'm fine."

"Good," he said. "Grab that knife and throw it in the corner." His eyes never left the intruder's massive back.

On trembling legs, Susan slid off the bed and picked up the knife. Gingerly she placed it in the farthest corner.

"Now let's find out what our friend here was up to." Derek stuck the gun in the man's face, making sure he could see it.

Grabbing her robe from the closet, Susan took a good look at her intruder. In the bright overhead light, with Derek's gun pointed at his ear, he didn't look nearly as threatening as he had only moments before. Like a snake that's been defanged, the monster had lost his power to terrorize her. With her robe belted around her, she sat down on the side of the bed.

"What's your name?" Derek prodded his captive with the pistol. When he started to turn, Derek put the pistol against his head. "Keep your face to the wall and your hands up."

"Krakow." His voice was so low Susan could barely hear him.

"All right, Krakow," Derek said. "I've got a couple of questions. If I get the right answers, you'll walk out of here with your skin intact."

Stiffening, Susan couldn't believe she'd heard right. Surely Derek didn't intend to let this criminal get away scot-free after he'd broken into her home and threatened her life.

"I don't know nothing, mister," the man whined.

"Then I guess I'll have to put some memories back in your head." Derek's tone was deceptively quiet. "Take off your shoe and sock, please, Krakow."

The big man twisted his head sideways. "Wh-why?"

"Just do it." The gun prodded Krakow's head.

As the intruder stooped, Derek glanced over his shoulder at Susan. "Get me one of your scarves and a pillow."

Quickly she found a scarf, then handed him a king-size pillow. Derek dropped the pillow on the floor beside him.

"What you doing, mister?" Krakow's voice quavered with fear.

"First I'm going to give Mrs. Wade the gun and let her point it at your gut while I tie this scarf around your mouth." Derek's voice was filled with loathing. "Then you won't scream and wake up the neighbors when I shoot your big toe off."

"No," Susan shrieked. "You can't do that."

"Of course I can," Derek growled. "I'll use the pillow for a silencer. Anybody who breaks into a lady's condominium in the middle of the night deserves to have a toe shot off, don't you think, Mrs.

Wade? And if that doesn't bring back his memory, we'll try a part of his anatomy that's a little higher up.''

Without hesitating, Derek handed the weapon to her—almost as if he knew she'd won a medal for marksmanship. Feeling nauseated, she aimed it at Krakow's stomach.

Right before her eyes, the big man wilted. Sickened though she was, a small part of her enjoyed seeing Krakow's terror.

Before Derek could tie the gag snugly, Krakow spoke through the loose cloth.

''I'll tell you what I know.''

''Good.'' Derek kept his voice deadly calm. ''Who are you working for?'' Out of the corner of his eye, he saw Susan lean forward on the bed. She seemed okay but must have been scared to death. His fingers tightened around the gun handle.

When Krakow didn't answer, Derek prodded his head with the pistol. Then he reached for the pillow on the floor next to his leg. It would make an effective silencer.

''You heard the question, Krakow. You've got five seconds to answer or you'll lose a toe.'' Grimly he began counting. ''One…two…three…four…''

''Stop.'' Anxious desperation filled the big man's voice. ''Nobody hired me. I was working on my own.'' He spoke slowly, pausing between words, as if his brain wasn't equal to his imposing size.

''We both know better than that,'' Derek said with chilling certainty. ''You'll save us both a lot of trouble by answering a couple of simple questions. If you don't…'' He let his finger play with the gun's trigger. "We can do it the easy way or the hard way. Your choice."

The big man sagged against the wall, all his resistance gone. His small head, topped with the black stocking cap, wagged nervously as he spoke. "You'll let me go if I answer?"

"That's right." Derek jabbed him in the ear with the gun. "Tell me what I want to know, and you're outta here with no police and all your body parts intact."

Silence engulfed the room. Derek could hear Krakow's heavy breathing. His body odor and the garlicky smell of his breath hung in the air like a sour cologne. Derek began counting again.

"All right, I'll tell you." The words jerked out of his mouth. "But it won't do you no good. We only talked on the phone, and I didn't get her…er, his name."

Derek heard Susan's quick gasp of astonishment. He glanced at her over his shoulder. Her eyes bored into his with the urgency of someone whose life depended on what she'd heard.

"Were you hired by a woman?" he asked, careful to keep the surprise from his voice.

"It was a woman's voice. That's all I know." Nervously Krakow shuffled his feet. His shoes, like his sweatshirt and pants, were black.

"How did she get your name?"

"I don't know."

Was Krakow lying about the female voice? Probably not. Derek was reasonably sure Krakow's slip of the tongue was genuine. He jabbed the big man's ear again with the gun. "What did this woman tell you to do here tonight?"

Now that Krakow had started to talk, his words flowed more easily. "Find out from Mrs. Wade what was in her husband's safe-deposit box and where she put it."

That, Derek was certain, wasn't a fabrication. "What if Mrs. Wade wouldn't talk?"

Krakow hesitated just long enough to make Derek suspect he was inventing an answer. "I was to tie her up and bring her along."

Sure you were, you no-good jerk. White-hot rage shot through Derek. The bastard had probably been ordered to kill Susan to keep her quiet. But there wasn't time to force the truth out of him. Someone might already have called the police. Derek couldn't afford to put himself in an official spotlight and focus more attention on Susan.

"Where were you going to meet this woman?"

Krakow stirred uneasily. "I—I wasn't," he returned. "We only talked on the phone. She said to leave Mrs. Wade tied up in the car on a road near the Arboretum. I figured she'd pick her up in another car."

More lies. "What a trusting soul you are," Derek said sarcastically. "If you only talked on the phone, how was this woman going to pay you?" He prodded his captive again on the side of his head. "You can do better than that."

Krakow jerked his head back. "By—by messenger."

His immediate response made Derek doubt it was a fabrication. "Explain," he said curtly.

"Half now, the remainder when the job's finished."

"You really think she intended to send a messenger with the second half of the money?"

"Yeah. I don't give her the papers she wants until she pays."

The answer made sense. When Derek glanced over his shoulder at Susan, he caught her nod. She, too, thought Krakow was telling the truth about his employer.

"Next question," Derek said. "How did you get the combination for Mrs. Wade's security system?"

"The woman gave it to me."

"The woman who hired you?" Derek asked, incredulous. "She had the combination to Mrs. Wade's alarm?"

"Yeah."

"What is it?"

When Krakow repeated the four-digit combination, Derek heard Susan's quick intake of breath. She half rose from the bed. Without turning, he waved her back down. Stepping back, he motioned toward the door with his gun hand. "Get the hell out of here, Krakow."

With his hands still in the air, the big man took a cautious step toward the hall as if unable to believe his good fortune. He seemed to fear a shot in the back if he moved too quickly.

"If I ever see your ugly face around Mrs. Wade again, I'll aim a foot or two higher than your feet." Derek's finger on the .38's trigger itched to apply more pressure. How he'd enjoy putting a shot or two through Krakow's tail section. Picking up the pillow beside his leg, he fired through it, the shot striking the floor near the big man's bare foot.

Krakow took off down the hall running, not stopping to collect his shoe and sock. Derek heard him thudding down the stairs three at a time. The crash of the front door as it slammed behind him seemed to shake the building.

Shoving the pistol back in his leather jacket, Derek turned toward Susan. She sat on the bed staring at him, her luminous eyes wide with shock and amazement. She seemed to be angry. That was too bad, he thought, but there was no other way to handle Krakow. He steeled himself for a confrontation.

"Why did you let him go?" she cried, her voice rising. "We should have called the police. Don't you realize this woman who hired him might be the one those people at the hotel thought was me?"

"He was probably lying." Derek hoped to throw her off the track. If Susan insisted on calling the police, he'd have to walk out on her. Damn. Why should that bother him? He simply couldn't risk close scrutiny by the authorities.

"He wouldn't lie about a thing like that," she retorted, jumping to her feet. "He didn't lie about why he came here."

She brushed past him toward the phone on the other side of the bed. Derek reached her side as she picked up the receiver. "We'd better talk before you do anything hasty. Telling the police about this could have some nasty ramifications."

He took her arm, intending to stop her from calling 911. When he felt her body trembling, the familiar murderous rage welled up in his throat. But now it was combined with an odd protective feeling that was new to him.

Putting an arm around her waist, he got her away from the phone and lowered her to the side of the bed. Instead of moving away, Susan leaned her head against his shoulder. Something deep inside him cursed the monstrous barriers between them. If only he could hold her without any pretense. Maybe then the raging demons inside him would go away.

"I'm sorry I got angry, Derek," she murmured. "If it weren't for you, I probably wouldn't even be here now."

Her brow furrowed. "Just how *did* you get here in time to come charging to my rescue like the U.S. cavalry?" Her voice sounded much stronger now.

He hesitated, unwilling to tell her he'd spent the last three hours sitting at the curb beyond her driveway. Such an admission smacked of devotion above and beyond the call of duty. He didn't want her to get any wrong ideas about him.

Chapter Nine

"So give," Susan said, sensing Derek was keeping something from her. "How did you get here in such a hurry?"

For a long moment he didn't answer. Suddenly his nearness made her unheated bedroom feel unbearably hot and crowded. She rose and went to the chair on the other side of her nightstand. "Is there something you're not telling me?"

He didn't dodge her direct glance. "Somebody got in my hotel room while we were here earlier tonight. They took my computer and some work files I'd brought along."

Watching his grim smile, a wave of compassion swept over her. "Oh, Derek, I'm sorry. It's all my fault. They must have been after Brian's papers."

"Don't be ridiculous. It's not your fault." She watched him shrug off the importance of what must be a major loss for him. "Risks like that are what you're paying me for."

Damn him. He would bring the money up again. He was eyeing her with such an intense expression that

Susan looked down at her hands, clenched tightly in her lap.

"It's a good thing I was burglarized," he growled. "I figured if they'd go to all the trouble of getting a hotel passkey so they could search my room, they might know how to penetrate your security system. That's why I came back. God knows what might have happened if I hadn't been here."

Susan stared wordlessly across at him, her heart pounding. "Do you mean you were parked outside watching my condo?"

He just shrugged his shoulders. "If I'd been on my toes, I would have stopped Krakow before he got inside. He came in through the back door, and I didn't realize anybody was here until I saw his flashlight through the window."

Susan wasn't sure whether to hit him or hug him. "What if I'd been the one with the flashlight? I've been known to use one when I creep around the house at night."

"You don't usually leave the back door unlocked, do you?" Derision and sympathy were mingled in his glance. "That's how I got in."

Her stomach clenched tight. "If it was open, then he must have had a key. And he knew the master combination to the alarm system, too, Derek. That's the one I use when I change the code. It'll override the others." Disturbed, she paced the length of the room, then dropped to the bed beside him. "Just thinking of that monster able to walk right into my house…"

"Somebody's gone to a lot of trouble to gain access

to your home.'' His eyes narrowed, and his lips formed a hard, thin line. ''Any idea why?''

''None, unless...'' Susan's mind churned with a crazy mixture of hope and fear. ''Unless this has some connection with Brian, and I've gotten in the way somehow. Maybe whoever hired Krakow got the key and combination when Brian was still alive. Maybe they wanted to spy on him, not me.''

''That's what I think.'' Derek hugged her against him, a gentle pressure that made her all too conscious of her nightgown and robe. ''But now that they're after you, there's one thing for sure—you've got to get out of here and into a hotel.''

''Oh, Derek, we've got to report these break-ins to the police.'' Susan would have gone to the phone, but he was sitting so close she'd have to stand right in front of him to use it. Her comfortable terry robe suddenly felt even more insubstantial. Pulling it close, she tightened the belt as if that would end the erotic feelings welling up inside her.

''I can't stop you if that's what you want to do.'' Derek gazed at her levelly. ''But you'll be wasting your time. MacElroy won't believe you.''

Susan twisted uncomfortably on the bed. Every natural instinct told her this was a serious crime that should be reported. ''Of course he will. The police might even be able to catch Krakow.'' She glanced across the bed at the well-worn shoe in the doorway. ''Most robbers don't leave shoes behind.''

''Exactly.'' He spoke the word with an authority that bewildered her. Why wouldn't the police believe her?

"There's no sign of breaking and entering," Derek went on, "no harm to you physically. Detective MacElroy might even get the notion he was working for you."

"Working for me?" Susan's breath caught in her lungs. "How could anybody think such a thing, especially after you tell them he came after me with a butcher knife." She stared at him, confused by his doubting expression. "You *do* plan to admit you were here?"

Derek shook his head, his eyes guarded. "If you say anything about my role in this, MacElroy's going to think I spent a good part of the night in your bed. That might not be a good idea for a widow under suspicion for killing her husband."

In dazed exasperation, Susan crossed her arms over her breasts and pointedly looked away from his knowing eyes. "Then you think that man and whoever hired him ought to get away?"

"Not at all," Derek returned. "What I have in mind for them is considerably more painful than what they'd get in police hands." Standing, he walked around the bed and picked up Krakow's shoe and sock. "But first we have to find out who's behind these murders and exactly what's going on."

Shivering, Susan watched him as he stood in the doorway to her bedroom, the shoe in his hand and the familiar wary smile on his lips. By now she knew him well enough to realize his smile hid something dark and dangerous.

THOUGH IT WAS NEARLY four o'clock in the morning, the night clerk at the Riverfront Hotel checked Susan in without any problem.

"If you'd like, we can get you an adjoining room with Mr. Archer by the end of the week," he offered.

To her embarrassment, Susan felt her cheeks burn at the suggestion. "No, I—"

"Thanks, we'd appreciate that," Derek interrupted. "Until then, put her in the closest available room and get her a key for my box in the hotel vault."

"Yes, Mr. Archer." The clerk smirked at Susan. "Will you be paying with a credit card, Mrs. Wade? Or is Mr. Archer…?"

Susan quickly handed the clerk her card, her face growing hotter at his insinuation. But the image of only a door between them provoked sensual thoughts that set her on fire. She'd had virtually no resistance in her tonight when he kissed her. She didn't kid herself about what would happen if he did it again, once they were settled into their adjoining rooms.

As Susan turned away from the registration desk, the clerk asked if they needed a bellhop.

"We can manage." With ease, Derek lifted her two suitcases. She took the key from the clerk and picked up her tote bag.

After a quick trip on the elevator, they reached the fifth floor. Her room was almost directly across the hall from his. Inside, they switched lights on, bathing the king-size bed and thick wine carpeting in a warm glow.

Despite the room's inviting appearance, Susan knew there'd be no sleep for her for the rest of this night. She still quivered with semishock, knowing she'd picture Krakow's face every time she closed her eyes.

And the knife. She could still see it glittering in the green light from her security system.

"How about some coffee?" She didn't want to be alone. Derek placed her suitcases on the floor and turned toward her, moving with the easy grace of a trained pugilist.

He nodded. "There's an all-night restaurant just across the river. Over breakfast, we can decide where we go from here."

But Susan had her own idea about what she wanted to accomplish in the next couple of hours. She wanted to find out what made Derek Archer tick. One minute he growled at her like an angry panther. The next, he appeared with a bag of ice for her bruised leg and treated her with surprising warmth. There was something about him that didn't quite ring true—like he was two different people sharing the same body. But one thing was for certain—nobody would lay a hand on her when he was around.

They took his rental car to the coffee shop, leaving her Firebird in the hotel parking lot. The restaurant smelled of coffee and frying bacon. A fortyish waitress with puffy eyelids showed them to a well-lighted booth and took their orders.

"I'm starving," Susan admitted, ordering a huge country-style breakfast. After the waitress brought their coffee and left, she added, "When that man came at me with that knife tonight, I thought I'd never be hungry again."

"If he'd had his way, you never would have." Derek's dark face set in a vindictive expression.

The skin on the back of her arms prickled. "If he meant to kill me, why didn't he have a gun?"

Derek shrugged. "Who knows? Maybe he's a slasher who works with knives, and that's why he was hired to make you talk."

Shuddering, she stared at her coffee to blot out her memory of the leering face and the horror she'd felt when the knife point grazed her cheek. When she looked up, Derek was studying her intently. She saw the heartrending tenderness of his gaze and sensed that he understood her terror.

"All I know is we're damn lucky he didn't have a gun. If I'd had to kill him…" Abruptly, he stopped speaking.

"The police would get involved," she finished, remembering how upset she'd been when Derek let the intruder go. "First this afternoon and now tonight, you don't want the police involved." She paused, considering how firmly he'd resisted her desire to call the authorities. "It's almost as though you've got personal reasons for avoiding them."

The corner of his mouth twisted with exasperation, and he took a long swallow of coffee before he answered. "As long as I'm working for you, you're the *personal reason* for everything I do in connection with this case, including avoiding the police. But you're the boss, Susan. Go ahead and report what happened. See what the cops say." A warning glint appeared in his eyes. "But I'd advise you to call your lawyer first."

"Are you saying the only reason you came to my house tonight was because you're working for me?" Her heart pounded in an erratic rhythm as she considered what her question implied: that he might have done it out of concern for her.

The familiar mask descended over his face. "What other reason would I have?"

She took a deep breath. "You might care what happens to me."

For one of the few times since they'd met, he didn't meet her direct gaze. "You're giving me too much credit, Susan. I'm not one of these caring new-age males. I'm out to get everything I can from you." His voice was uncompromising, yet oddly gentle. "Including, but not limited to, the money you're going to pay me." When he finally looked up, the smoldering flame she saw in his eyes belied his harsh words.

"I don't believe you," she said.

His mask fell away, revealing his bafflement.

The waitress chose that moment to deliver plates loaded with eggs, bacon, home-fried potatoes and pancakes. Susan felt her mouth water and breathed deeply of the enticing aroma.

"Almost getting murdered must stimulate my appetite." She poured syrup on the pancakes. "I can't remember ever being this hungry." She took a bite, then licked the syrup from her lips.

Across the laminated tabletop, Derek stared at her in confusion, not touching his food. "What did you mean when you said you didn't believe me?"

"Just what I said. I don't think you're nearly as selfish as you say you are." Feeling more sure of herself, Susan relished the dismayed expression on his darkly handsome face. Chalk one up for her. She'd gotten to him for once.

"Didn't you learn anything from your bad experience with your husband?" he asked. "The country's full of selfish men like him and me who are out to take advantage of you."

"Maybe so," she agreed. "But you're not the least bit like Brian. In the few short months we were married, he never treated me with anything like the concern you've shown in the past few days. He was never there for me when I needed him." Susan watched him intently. "You've always been there."

"Because you're paying the bills," he muttered, picking up his fork.

"Stick it in your ear," she murmured softly. "On a hunch because someone broke into your room, you must have waited half the night outside my condo to be sure nobody got inside, even after I assured you the security system was top-notch. That doesn't sound like an employee just doing his job."

"I'm warning you, Susan, don't convince yourself I'm something I'm not."

Shaking her head to silence him, she refused to stop. "And how about the ice for my leg this afternoon? And not accusing me of searching your computer files. You must have known what I was doing."

For the first time since they sat down, he took a big bite of food and swallowed it. "Just why *were* you snooping through my things?"

In a flash Susan realized she wanted, even *needed,* to tell Derek about her covert mission. It seemed more and more obvious that Brian's murder was connected to the illegal activity going on at Fairchild, the activity she'd been secretly sent to investigate. If so, her life might depend on Derek. Three times in the past two days he'd saved her. If she couldn't trust him... Casting aside the nagging doubt that still plagued her, she decided to level with him—the way she'd never leveled with Brian.

"There were a couple of reasons I was curious about your files," she admitted slowly. "Since the policy from your company wasn't in Brian's box, I wasn't convinced you were an insurance agent."

"Are you now?" he asked, his eyes slightly narrowed. He seemed to have forgotten his half-eaten breakfast.

She nodded. "I saw nothing to indicate you aren't."

"What's the other reason?"

Putting down her fork, she shifted uneasily on the vinyl seat. "That's a little harder to explain."

"Start at the beginning," he said, leaning toward her. Why did she have the impression he already knew what she was going to say?

Here it comes, Derek thought, watching the conflicting play of emotions on Susan's expressive face. Reluctance and loyalty to her cause battled with her desperate need for his help. Need won, as Derek had hoped it would. She was going to trust him with her real reason for being at Fairchild. Glancing down at his plate, he took another mouthful of food so she wouldn't feel pressured.

"You know that illegal operation you think Brian was involved in?" She eyed him so intently, Derek wondered if she guessed what he suspected, that she was a covert investigator.

For a moment Susan hesitated, and he had to content himself with a quick nod of his head.

"Somebody at the Pentagon agrees with you." She spoke eagerly, no longer hesitant.

"Who?"

"The Pentagon Intelligence Agency." The warmth of her smile echoed in her voice. "They sent me here to check covertly into some rumors about smuggling. Nothing dangerous or chancy. Just keep my eyes open for anything out of the ordinary."

Pretending surprise, he leaned toward her. "Thank God you told me. That may be why these people are after you."

"Not possible." Unconsciously her brow furrowed. "Nobody knows about my assignment except the covert operations people at the Pentagon. None of the civilian agencies were in on it, only a few top brass at the Pentagon Intelligence Agency. Plus, I found out absolutely nothing. The operation's been canceled."

"What did the people at the Pentagon say when you told them about your marriage?" Derek felt like a rat for asking, but he had to know if she'd married Wade as part of her mission.

"They didn't like it," she said, frowning at her empty plate. "But I thought we loved each other, so I went ahead." She gave him a quizzical look. "So where do we go from here?"

Pushing their plates aside, Derek took out his list of the safe-deposit box contents and laid it on the table between them.

"Let's decide right now," he said.

THE PHONE WAS RINGING when Susan walked into her small office later that morning. Eagerly she grabbed the receiver, thinking it might be Derek.

Alarm shot through her when she heard the familiar raspy voice of her former commander, Major Savage. What now? she asked herself, her blood pressure soaring.

"Call Detective MacElroy ASAP," Savage said tersely. "He's been trying to reach you at home since early this morning. Our number here at the squadron was the only other one he had for you."

Susan heard the accusation in the major's voice and knew she should have called MacElroy to give him her new work number. "Did he say what he wanted?" she asked, knowing the major would have found out for her if he could.

"No, but I suggest you call him right away."

She let her breath out in a slow sigh. "Thanks, I will."

Something's wrong, she thought. Had new evidence turned up to incriminate her? Heart pounding, she hung up and tapped Detective MacElroy's number on the telephone. A few moments later she reached him at police headquarters.

"Just a routine check, Mrs. Wade," he said in his booming bass voice.

So relieved she thought her legs would collapse, Susan lowered herself to the chair behind her desk. "Did Major Savage tell you I've been transferred to the Security Police Squadron?"

"Yes. Be sure you notify me of any other changes

in your address or phone. You *are* still living at your home address?''

Susan's stomach sank. He'd probably think she was trying to put one over on him. ''No, I moved to the Riverfront Hotel last night,'' she blurted. ''That's why you didn't catch me at home.''

''I see,'' he said, a warning note in his voice. ''Any special reason for the move?''

''Not really.'' Nervously she opened her bottom desk drawer and dropped her purse inside. Derek was right. It was best if no one knew he'd been there with her—or that they'd let Krakow get away. ''The condo seemed lonely, so I moved to the hotel for a few days.'' The ease with which she lied no longer amazed her.

She heard MacElroy's exasperated sigh. ''Be sure you let me know if you have another sudden impulse to move.''

Feeling like a criminal, she said she would. After she hung up, she called to let Major Savage's first sergeant know where she was staying, and then went to her own orderly room to report the new address. With that small chore finished, she headed for the squadron's coffeepot at the back of the room behind a folding screen.

After pouring herself a cup, Susan lingered, hoping to overhear news about the theft of the colonel's van. She hadn't sipped her coffee for more than two minutes when an airman on the other side of the screen mentioned the robbery to a buddy at the next desk.

''The local police found the paddy wagon last night,'' he said conversationally. Though Susan had been in the squadron only a couple of days, she knew the squadron troops referred to the colonel's van as the *paddy wagon* because he was always using it to haul his people to athletic events. How different Colonel Tinnerman was from Major Savage, who seemed to consider any friendliness toward his troops a mortal sin.

Stepping out from behind the screen, she turned to the airman who had spoken. "What's this about the colonel's van?"

The airman stood. "Good morning, ma'am."

"As you were," she said, giving him permission to return to his chair. "Now, tell me about the colonel's van."

He sat down. But before he could answer, Susan felt a light touch on her arm. It was Colonel Tinnerman.

"Good morning, Susan," he said, smiling warmly. Cup in hand, he headed for the coffeepot. "Join me in my office and I'll give you the whole story while we drink our coffee."

"YOU CAN'T BE SERIOUS." Colonel Tinnerman's homely face contorted with astonishment.

"I'd never have known the mugger used your van except that I've a good memory and got a quick look at the license." Enjoying the amazed look on the colonel's face, Susan sat back in the chair beside his desk and took a long swallow of coffee. "Of course, as soon as I found out you owned it, I realized it must have been stolen."

Puzzlement replaced his surprise. "How'd you trace the license number?"

"My insurance agent did it for me. Remember? I told you about him the day I reported in." Susan examined her commander's face. His cornflower blue eyes glowed with the warm interest she sometimes saw in her father's gaze.

"Well," she continued, "the agent was with me when I came out of the bank after depositing the check from his company."

Susan had already decided to stick with her original story about needing the afternoon off to invest insurance funds. She shrugged off a minor twinge of guilt at lying to a commander so concerned with her welfare. If he knew about Brian's box, he might insist she tell the local authorities about it. She wasn't ready to do that, not until she and Derek had finished their investigation.

"Did your insurance agent see the mugger, too?" the colonel asked.

"Yes. He's done some investigative work and knew how to find out who owned the van from the license number." Remembering how Derek had brought ice for her leg, she permitted herself a small smile.

The colonel's round face grew thoughtful. "Sounds like this man's made quite an impression on you. Sometime in the next couple of weeks, I'd like to take the two of you to dinner."

Susan stared at him, speechless, touched again by his warm generosity. Even though she knew the colonel enjoyed treating his people to fun outings, she hadn't even considered that he might invite her to dinner.

"That's very generous of you, sir," she began, surprised at how emotional her voice sounded. "But Derek—that's the agent—will be here only until Monday. He's based in San Francisco."

"Too bad." The colonel really did look sorry. "I suppose you young people will be too busy to have dinner with your commander between now and then—" He eyed her questioningly.

"It's purely a business relationship," she said quickly, to head off an apparent misunderstanding. "He's just helping me straighten out my financial affairs."

"He must be a talented man," the colonel commented dryly, sounding more like her father by the minute. "He's an insurance agent, an investigator and now—a financial adviser."

Why deny it? "Yes, sir, he's been a big help."

The expression in the colonel's blue eyes showed a depth of concern she'd rarely seen. "The first sergeant tells me you've moved to the Riverfront Hotel for a few days. Is that where your agent is staying?"

Though Susan saw only warm consideration on the colonel's face, she felt her cheeks flush. "It's not like you think, sir," she protested. "My condo was broken into last night, and I was afraid to stay alone. So I moved into the hotel."

"My dear girl." His voice had an infinitely compassionate tone. "Why didn't you call me? I would have arranged for you to stay with one of the women in the squadron."

"Sir, it was three o'clock in the morning. I'd be on somebody's hate list if I got her up at that hour."

A swift shadow swept across his face. "Are you telling me you were alone in the house when someone broke in?"

When Susan saw his worried expression, she wished she'd never mentioned it. She should have known how upset he'd be after what had happened to his wife. "I was upstairs in bed."

"Did the police catch the man?"

How to answer? Thinking fast, Susan stared down at her hands, clenched tightly in her lap.

"I didn't call the police, Colonel Tinnerman." When he started to speak, a dismayed frown on his face, she forged ahead. "Whoever it was must have heard me. He took off before I got a good look at him. Since nothing happened to me and he didn't take anything, I saw no reason to involve the police."

More lies, she thought, ashamed but determined to stick to her story.

"Instead of going downstairs, you should have dialed 911," the colonel said, shaking his head.

"I know," she agreed quickly. "I'd awakened from a sound sleep and wasn't thinking straight." She hoped he wouldn't insist she report the incident. "Now that it's over, I don't want to call attention to myself. So far the police haven't believed a thing I've said. Sometimes I think they'd like nothing better than to take me into custody—for my own good, of course." She gave a humorless little laugh.

A half smile broke through his concerned expression. "Our civilian counterparts don't operate that way—but I see why you didn't report it."

He scribbled something on a card and handed it to her. "Here's my home phone. My number at the squadron is on the front. Don't leave this office until you've memorized both numbers. If anything threatening ever happens again, please call me, no matter what time it is."

He's almost too good to be true, Susan thought, still reeling from his dinner invitation and his generous offer to let her pick her own duty hours. She scolded herself for her cynicism. If she didn't watch out, she'd end up like Derek, wary of everyone.

Slowly sipping her coffee, she glanced at the card. With her photographic memory, she needed only an instant for both numbers to be indelibly imprinted on her brain....

Chapter Ten

Susan's hand tightened around the doorknob when she took her first look at Derek, standing outside her hotel room early that afternoon. With his open yellow sport shirt revealing a mass of curly black hair, he aroused longings she had trouble keeping hidden. After he'd come in, her room felt ten degrees hotter and a whole lot smaller than it had only moments ago.

"Did you call Seattle yet?" he asked. The call, carefully planned last night, was the first item on their schedule for today. The second was a visit to the sub-urban mail-to-go center where Brian had rented a box.

Hearing the rasp of excitement in his voice, Susan met his direct gaze. "No, I was waiting for you. I'll do it now." Taking a small notepad out of her bag, she flipped to the page where she'd copied the name and telephone number listed on the index card from Brian's safe-deposit box. Quickly she dialed.

The woman who answered repeated the telephone number in a businesslike way, but gave no other information.

"Mr. Ted Lindsey, please," Susan said, motioning Derek to sit beside her on the bed so he could hear.

"May I ask who's calling, please?"

Susan didn't hesitate. If they expected Lindsey to level with her, he'd have to know who she was. "Mrs. Brian Wade."

"Mr. Lindsey will be with you in a moment, Mrs. Wade."

Susan held the receiver so Derek could hear. His face was so close to hers she could smell his spicy after-shave. He must have showered just before meeting her. A delicious shudder ran through her as she pictured his bare chest, with its mat of curly black hair lathered with soap. Dismayed, she realized each image of him she came up with was more detailed, and barer, than the one before it.

"This is Ted Lindsey, Mrs. Wade," a pleasant male voice said, interrupting her thoughts. "How can I help you?" His tone was smooth, like a radio announcer's.

"I'm not sure what your connection is to my husband," Susan began slowly. "I found your name on some of his papers. I was hoping you could tell me."

"Connection? I suppose you'd call me a friend, Mrs. Wade."

"Did you know he'd been killed?"

"Yes," he said, after a moment's pause. "I should have sent condolences. But I didn't know you, and I'm not very good at that sort of thing."

Catching Derek's slow nod, Susan forged ahead with the first of the questions they'd outlined over breakfast early this morning.

"Do you mind telling me where you met Brian and how long you've known him?"

Silence. Then he said, "I'm sorry, Mrs. Wade, but

I'm at work, and don't have time for chitchat.'' His tone turned abrupt. "I'm sure your husband's death was a terrible shock, and I'll do anything I can to help. But since he never mentioned me to you, it should seem obvious that we weren't much more than good drinking buddies.''

Again, Susan glanced at Derek. "Go for it,'' he mouthed silently.

"I've been talking to his friends, trying to find his murderer,'' Susan said boldly. "Could you meet me for a few minutes next Saturday morning?''

"It would be a waste of both our times, Mrs. Wade. Now, if you'll excuse me, I've got to get back to work.'' Lindsey seemed about to hang up.

"Wait,'' she cried. "If you want to help, this is how. I've hired Stephen Ellis, the private investigator. He'll be with me when I talk to you. All we ask is a few minutes.''

Using Ellis's name was Derek's idea. Since *Ellis* and *Lindsey* were the two names in Brian's safe deposit box, Derek thought there might be a connection. Maybe he was right. As soon as Susan said Stephen Ellis, Lindsey stopped resisting.

"I still think it's a waste of time, but I'll be glad to get together with you and your investigator if you think I can help,'' he offered. "Where would you like to meet?''

She breathed a silent sigh of relief. "Eleven o'clock Saturday morning at Ye Olde Curiosity Shop on the Seattle waterfront.'' It was the only place she knew in the port city. "How will I recognize you?''

"You don't need to recognize me,'' he returned.

"Your husband showed me your picture." He didn't say goodbye.

After Susan replaced the receiver, she went to the chair beside the table. Having Derek so close on the bed made her edgy, unable to think clearly. Now that she knew for sure they'd be together in Seattle over the weekend, a shiver of excitement raced through her. Somehow, the two hotel rooms in Seattle—three hundred miles from Spokane—seemed more intimate than the two they had now.

From across the room, Derek gave her the okay sign. "Nice work on the phone, Susan."

Heat rose to her cheeks at his compliment. Why did she feel so darn pleased at the slightest hint of praise from this man? Rising, she started toward the door, but he didn't follow.

"Before we leave, there's something you need to know."

She whirled around, vaguely frightened by his change of tone.

Making no move to get up from the bed, he pulled a slip of paper from his pocket. "This morning I was doing more work on the figures in your husband's notebook. On several pages there are lists that look like bank deposits." He inclined his head toward her chair. "Why don't you sit back down while I go over this with you."

Numbly she returned to her chair. What secret dealings were about to be revealed? She sucked in her breath, not sure she wanted to know.

"At first I thought it was part of the illegal shipping record," Derek said, his dark eyebrows slanted thoughtfully. "Then I noticed some numbers and letters at the bottom of the page. After I checked this morning, I found out it's the identification for an account in a bank in Fribourg, Switzerland."

"A Swiss bank account?" Susan's mind spun with bewilderment, refusing to register the significance of his words. "But Brian had no foreign bank accounts."

"Maybe not," Derek agreed. "But if I were you, I'd get my attorney to check on it. From these figures, it's not clear exactly how much is in the account, but it could be in the millions, depending on how he recorded the deposits." He grinned that cynical smile of his that never quite reached his eyes. "If I'm right, you can afford a full-time private investigator."

Susan was too shocked to appreciate his dark sense of humor, and stared blankly at him.

He handed her the paper. "All the info's here. We can stop by your attorney's office on the way to the post office."

Trembling, Susan put the paper in her bag. "You say there's a lot of money in this account. But Brian didn't have that kind of capital. He couldn't have stolen it—could he? If he did, it's not mine."

"Then whose is it?"

She shook her head helplessly. "I don't know, Derek, I just don't know."

THE CONTRACT POST OFFICE where Wade had rented a mailbox was located at a shopping center in Dishman, a suburb north of the city. Derek didn't think he and Susan were followed from her attorney's office, but took the precaution of parking at the Northtown

Mall before they took a taxi to the shopping center. He figured they shouldn't be more than a couple of hours, and if the car thieves who had been plaguing the mall parking lot wanted his rented car—what the hell, it was insured.

From inside the mall, he called a cab for the ride out the freeway to Dishman. Whoever was behind the attacks on Susan knew about the safe-deposit box. By going through the papers in his stolen suitcase, they also knew that Derek had more than a business interest in her. He couldn't allow them to find out about this secret mailbox as well.

He glanced at her sitting quietly beside him. In her black slacks and red turtleneck sweater, with her hair loose on her shoulders, she looked more like a college student than an air force lieutenant. Derek's gut tightened at the sight of her. Why couldn't he keep his hands off her?

She hadn't said much since he dropped that bomb on her at the hotel. Outwardly she looked as poised as always, but when he put his arm around her shoulders, he felt her tremble. He didn't blame her for being a little shell-shocked. It wasn't every day that a woman found out she was probably worth millions.

The cab soon appeared and they headed out on the freeway. When they arrived at the shopping center, Derek paid the cab driver, then he glanced around the spacious parking lot. Most of the cars were lined up in front of the single-story row of businesses, with a dozen or more clustered at the lot's center near the grocery store.

Had they been followed? While he watched, a van

turned into the lot. A woman with a baby got out, disappearing a moment later inside a discount shoe shop.

Nothing to worry about, he thought, heading for the mail-to-go center with Susan close beside him. According to the big red, white and blue sign over its plate-glass window, the business offered copying, wrapping and mailing services as well as rental boxes. He opened the door and they went in.

A row of copy machines stood to their left. At a counter on their right, a thin young man with a gold earring asked if they needed help.

"Just going to our box," Derek said. Susan flashed a reassuring smile at the clerk.

Derek could feel the clerk's eyes on their backs as they went to the rear of the room where the mailboxes were located. He probably knew the regulars who picked up their mail every day. Would he try to stop two strangers he didn't recognize?

After a brief search, they found the box with a number matching that on the key. Susan inserted it. The door swung open.

The box was empty.

She glanced at Derek with a surprised expression. "Do you suppose somebody else—maybe Stephen Ellis—has a key?"

A warning alarm rang in his head. If this was someone else's box, did he or she know Wade had a key?

"Need some help?" a man's bored voice said from behind them. At Derek's nod, the copy clerk opened the door beside the mailboxes and appeared behind the counter half a second later.

Taking the key from Susan, Derek held it up so the clerk could see the number. He scowled, pretending to be annoyed.

The clerk's smile vanished. "Something wrong with your box?"

"It's empty. What's happened to my mail?"

The clerk took another look at the number on the key. A flash of recognition crossed his angular face. "Just a minute, I'll get it for you."

He turned away. A moment later he plopped two bulging shopping bags down on the counter. "The owner said to tell you we'd appreciate it if you'd stop by a little more often."

"Thanks," Derek grumbled, picking up the bags. He waited until they were outside to speak to Susan.

"Let's see who this stuff's addressed to," he said when they were out of the clerk's sight.

"I already know." She sounded discouraged. "Stephen Ellis. When we were walking out, I saw the name on that catalog on top. Since the mail hasn't been picked up for months, Brian must have been getting it, not somebody else."

He nodded, fighting another surge of hatred toward Wade. "Looks like I was right. Your husband intended to assume another identity—Stephen Ellis."

Derek's suspicion was confirmed beyond doubt an hour later. At a quiet table in the downtown public library, they examined every piece of paper in the two shopping bags—all addressed to Stephen Ellis.

As Susan breathed in the book smells and heard the quiet rustlings of people browsing through the shelves around her, she felt the pain and tension draining out of her. Why should she feel hurt because Brian hadn't loved her? She hadn't loved him, either, not at the end. If she'd loved him, she could never respond to Derek with the pulse-pounding intensity she felt every time he was near.

Susan stole a sideways glance at him, sitting beside her at the library table. His back straight, his head bent slightly, he appeared very relaxed, as though he spent hours at a time in a similar position. Maybe he did, she thought, realizing again how little she knew about him.

Like Brian, Derek had a mysterious side, a strange, dangerous personality he kept carefully hidden. She'd been honest with him, confiding her innermost secrets about her relationship with Brian and her covert mission to Fairchild. And what had he told her about himself?

Nothing.

Still, he'd come to her rescue three times, practically pulling her from the jaws of death last night. And she had this deep *knowing* that he was worthy of her trust. Despite his tough-guy assertions that his only interest was what she paid him, she knew more than money was involved. At the thought, that certain warmth he inspired flowed through her, a liquid silkiness heating her insides.

With a sigh, she turned her attention to the pile of mail in front of her. Most was advertising. But no matter how mundane the item appeared, she listed it and put it on the stack for Derek's review. Nothing would be discarded until they'd both examined it carefully.

"Take a look at this," he whispered, handing her an envelope with government markings.

With trembling fingers she pulled out a U.S. passport. The name was Stephen Ellis, but the picture was Brian's—incontrovertible proof that he'd intended to assume another identity and presumably to walk out on her.

Susan thought she'd come to terms with Brian's abandonment, but she was wrong. At the sight of his round, boyish face staring soberly at her from the passport picture, she felt her eyes filling.

"Are you okay?" Derek murmured. She heard the concern in his voice.

She longed to throw herself into his arms. If only she could feel his hands caressing her hair, his firm chest against her breasts, maybe then her hurt would be lessened.

Swallowing hard, she bit back her tears. "I'm fine."

He took her hand and held it softly between his. "That's my girl."

Looking at Derek's face, she imagined he could feel what she was feeling—from the deep-down hurt at Brian's plan-ned abandonment to the breathtaking desire he aroused in her. But the calluses on his hands reminded her again of how little she knew about him. She'd have to find out more.

Soon.

Before it was too late...and she fell in love with him.

AT THE LIBRARY, Susan and Derek spent nearly three hours sifting through the mail in the two shopping bags and listing every item. When they'd finished, there were only a few pieces that appeared to be of special interest: the passport; credit card bills for charges made in Buenos Aires last December; bank statements from two out-of-state banks; and four hand-written letters in Spanish, also from the Argentine capital.

Instinctively, Susan knew the four letters were from a woman. Since she didn't read Spanish, she couldn't tell what they said. After making a copy of each at the library, she handed the four copies to Derek. "Would you mind getting these translated?"

He gave her a slow-sweet smile with none of his usual cynicism. "Do you want to see the translations?"

"Not really," she admitted. "But I suppose I should. The attacks on me seem to be tied to Brian. If I'm going to get out of this mess alive, I need to know what was going on in his life."

"Agreed." Without further comment he stuffed the copies in the pocket of his leather jacket. "Did you know your husband was in Buenos Aires last December?" He nodded toward the credit card invoices lying next to the letters on the library table.

"Yes. His C-130 was part of the rescue mission after that big earthquake in northern Argentina." Susan compared her copy of the figures in Brian's black notebook with the invoices. "The December date's listed in his notebook. He must have made some charges on his Stephen Ellis card when he was in Buenos Aires." Her voice rose, and a middle-aged woman glowered at her.

"Let's get out of here," Derek muttered. "We need to talk."

After putting the junk mail back in the two shopping bags, Susan placed the significant pieces, along with her lists, in her bag. Derek called a taxi from the library pay phone.

Outside, night had come, along with a swift drop in temperature. Shivering in spite of her wool sweater, Susan slipped into her lined car coat, grateful she'd brought it with her.

During the taxi ride to the Northtown Mall, she couldn't help reacting to Derek, sitting close beside her with the shopping bags next to him on the seat. Her senses spinning, she drank in the sight and smell of him.

Particularly his leather coat. It gave off a rich outdoorsy scent faintly tinged with cigar smoke. The odor brought back an elusive memory of something she couldn't put her finger on.

"Do you smoke cigars?" she asked softly, not wanting to pry but determined to find out more about him.

He stiffened at her question, innocent though it was. "No, why? Do you smell smoke on me?"

"Yes," she said, suddenly remembering why the smell seemed familiar. "When Brian and I were going together, he had a leather bomber jacket almost exactly like yours. It smelled the same way." She paused, trying to recall the last time she'd seen it. "He never wore it after we were married. I gave it to charity along with the rest of his clothes."

"Interesting coincidence," Derek commented. But

unperturbed though he appeared, she got the impression that he was bothered by what she'd said. Wondering why, a tiny thread of doubt uncoiled in her mind. A few minutes later they arrived at the Northtown Mall, and Susan thrust her suspicions aside.

As before, Derek made certain the taxi driver didn't connect them with the rental car. Alighting from the cab on the far side of the mall, they walked down a wide corridor and then through a department store to reach their vehicle.

Outside again, they headed for their row at a leisurely pace. A cold wind more reminiscent of winter than early spring chafed Susan's face and tugged at her hair. Wishing she'd brought a scarf or hat, she raised the collar on her coat and shoved her hands into its pockets.

Tall overhead lights shone brightly on the hundreds of cars parked in the mall lot. They turned into their row. Just ahead a car backed out and swung around, blocking their way. Derek guided Susan to one side, then picked up his pace again. Suddenly, with no warning, he stepped in front of her and stopped.

She ran right into him. One minute she was striding along beside him. The next she was pressed against the back of his jacket. Grabbing for his arm, she managed to keep her balance.

"Follow me between these two cars," he ordered in a calm voice. "Be quiet. Two guys are about to steal my vehicle and we need to get out of here before they see us."

Her heart pounding, she did as he asked. From the shelter of the parked car, she peered down the row.

Instantly she felt his hand on her shoulder, pushing her down.

"Don't attract their attention." His steady voice didn't match the steely tension in his hand as he crouched beside her.

Susan heard the slam of a car door, then the soft whir of the starter. The engine caught. An instant later the night exploded into a million blazing fragments.

"Let's get out of here!" Derek grabbed her hand and pulled her toward the mall entrance.

"What happened?" she cried, running to keep up with him.

"Some poor bastards got blown up when they tried to steal our car." They reached the door and he yanked it open. "Five minutes sooner and it would have been us."

Attracted by the blast, a crowd of shoppers burst toward the door, pushing Susan and Derek aside. Feeling suffocated, her breath caught in her throat. "The bomb was meant for us?"

"You bet." He elbowed his way through. "Excuse us, please. Excuse us." He pulled harder on her hand. "Hurry up, Susan. We've got to call a cab and get away from here."

Already she could hear the screeching whine of sirens. The crowd around them swelled, heading outside.

"What happened?" someone asked, rushing past her.

Susan didn't bother answering. All she wanted was to escape the chaos behind them. Summoning her last ounce of strength, she managed to maintain her composure while they dashed to the far side of the mall where Derek called a cab.

Finally safe on the back seat, she fell into his arms. He held her so tightly she could feel the pulse beat of his throat against her face. Thank God they'd escaped.

"It's okay," he murmured, stroking her hair. "We got away. They didn't hurt us."

"But they almost did," she whispered, forcing her breath from her laboring lungs. "Who are they, Derek? Why are they trying to kill us?"

"They're afraid we'll be able to nail them," he said grimly. "As long as we keep snooping, we're a real threat."

He kept stroking her hair until she stopped shivering. "We can't go back to the hotel, Susan."

She stiffened. "You think they're waiting for us there?"

"No. They think we're dead." His blue eyes darkened as he held her gaze.

"Then, why..." In spite of her resolve not to, she started crying. She felt his hand on her back, soothing her.

"As long as they think we're dead, we'll be safe. If they check with the hotel and we haven't come back, they'll be sure their bomb got us. Listen to me, Susan. This is terribly important."

Though his voice was low, it vibrated with tension. Could the cabbie hear them? Probably not, but she noticed that Derek lowered his voice to a whisper meant for her ears only.

"We've got to get out of Spokane right now." His breath warmed her cheek. "Without leaving a trail.

Our weak link is Lindsey. If he's tied into this smuggling ring, they'll know we're alive and in Seattle as soon as we meet him tomorrow morning. But that can't be helped. Every other indication that we might still be around has got to be eliminated.''

"Does that mean I can't notify the squadron?" If she didn't report in by Monday, she'd be considered AWOL. The realization brought a panicky tightness to her chest.

His gentle stroking on her hair continued. "Your squadron's the first place anybody would check, Susan. There and the hotel."

He leaned forward, his voice rising to speak to the cabbie. "You can let us off at that fast-food place up ahead."

Getting out of the taxi, Susan breathed in the smells of French fries and hamburgers, and thought she was going to be sick.

"Some coffee might do us both good," Derek suggested, noticing her drawn expression.

"As long as I don't have to go inside."

He grinned back at her. She had never seen him grin in such a boyish way.

"If you'll ride herd on these two bags of mail for our friend Stephen Ellis," he said, "I'll get the coffee." A few minutes later he was back with two steaming foam cups.

Before removing the lid from hers, Susan let the warmth permeate her chilled hands. After following Derek to a telephone booth near the building, she took a long swallow. The jolt of caffeine took away the last of her shivers. "How long do we have before whoever planted that bomb realizes we weren't blown up in your rental car?''

"A couple of days, maybe a lot longer. I'm no expert, but it seems to me the police will need at least that long to identify the remains.'' Pausing, he examined her face. Apparently deciding she was sufficiently recovered to hear more, he went on. ''From the sound of that blast, there may not be enough left of the bodies to tell much about the gender of the victims.''

Turning back toward the telephone, he dialed a number. Susan heard him ask for flight schedules. Setting her shopping bag down, she clutched her cup in both hands again, not hearing his words or feeling the cold wind.

With the car bomb, the threat had turned even more sinister than with the man with a knife. He, at least, had a face. But this bomb reeked of terrorists who hid behind black stocking masks. Like Derek had said all along, some kind of global smuggling ring must be after her, an organization that sent muggers and assassins, that set bombs to explode in her face when she least expected them. But even Derek couldn't know where every assassin lurked, where every bomb lay hidden. Tough as he was, he wouldn't be able to protect her much longer.

He was right. They had to stay hidden, even if she had to break the law by going AWOL from the squadron. She yearned to feel safe again, secure somewhere with Derek. Would Seattle provide the sanctuary she longed for?

Chapter Eleven

Seattle

An unfamiliar pressure on her chest woke Susan from a deep sleep. What was causing it? And where was she? Still dressed in her red sweater and black slacks, she lay quiet until fully awake.

She opened her eyes. In the soft light from the bedside lamp she saw pale walls reflecting the dancing glow from the TV screen opposite the bed. With the sound turned low, she could barely hear the animated voices and cheerful music of an early morning program.

Where was Derek? There, beside her in the bed, his arm across her chest. Turning her head slowly so she wouldn't waken him, she surveyed his sleeping form. Lying on his back in his undershirt and pants, with his eyes closed and his breathing deep and regular, his powerful body seemed more vulnerable than brawny. *My brave, wounded Derek,* she thought, wondering for the hundredth time what had happened to make him so determined to keep his emotions in check and act so tough and indifferent.

He hadn't been gruff and insensitive last night when he'd comforted her in the taxi, or when he'd held her tenderly until she dropped off to sleep. They'd flown to Seattle under assumed names, as a married couple, because that would make them harder to trace. They'd checked into this downtown hotel under the same names and paid cash, in advance, for the two nights they planned to stay. Understanding Susan's terror and insecurity, Derek had comforted her and avoided any moves that might inspire passion.

Thank God for his consideration, she thought, remembering her sick, empty feeling last night. But now they were in bed together. She reached out and took his hand in hers. So many calluses. He did much more than sell insurance.

He awoke, then, and squeezed her hand. "It's half past seven. Why didn't you wake me sooner?"

"I was enjoying my nice safe feeling. Last night I was afraid I'd never feel this way again."

"I know." She felt him shudder as he drew in a deep breath. "There's nothing like anonymity to make you feel safe."

"That sounds like the voice of experience," she said, sensing an opportunity to probe.

"More the voice of observation," he returned, not taking the bait. "It's the animal that stands out that gets hunted. The anonymous ones that melt into the herd get to live another day."

For a moment they lay there on the bed, holding hands. Then Susan shifted, lifting herself to one elbow. "Where did you get the calluses on your hands, Derek?"

"Working on car engines." She heard no hesitation in his voice. "When I'm in San Francisco, I spend more time at the garage than the office."

"Is that where you work on the engines? At your garage?"

"It's not my garage." He turned his head to look at her. "It belongs to a friend. He lets me keep my clunkers there in exchange for help around the shop."

What an impressive liar I've become, he thought, disgusted. But he couldn't tell her his calluses came from an eight-to-five job in a gas station garage, not if he expected her to keep believing his insurance agent story.

She inched nearer. To his dismay, his rebellious body reacted. He couldn't let himself do what his hardening body demanded. Not without telling her who he really was. If he did, she'd end up hating him. *So what?* he asked himself, despising the sinking feeling in his gut because it meant he cared for her.

"Do you fix them up, then drive them yourself?" she asked.

He scowled at her. "I don't own a car for personal transportation. The company provides the one I use for work. After I fix up my old clunkers, I sell them."

Seeing the tenderness on her face, he felt even worse. When she searched his room she'd seen his frayed handkerchiefs and worn suits. Dammit. He should never have told her he'd been sold down the river by his friends. She probably thought they'd swindled him and now he was struggling to start over. How would she react if she knew the truth: that every penny went into his vengeful campaign to even the score with her dead husband and his fellow conspirators?

Stupid question, Archer, he told himself. He knew exactly how she'd react. Loathing would replace the concern he saw now in her lovely brown eyes.

"As long as you live in San Francisco, you don't need a car," she said sympathetically. "With parking the way it is there, you're smart not to have one."

"Sure I am." His words dripped with sarcasm. What could he say to turn her off? "I'm smart to live in a basement apartment, too. Face it, honey, I've got nothing to offer you but trouble, and the quicker you figure that out, the better for us both."

Susan sat up and folded her arms across her chest. Derek's tight smile was not convincing. And calling her "honey" sounded affected to her.

"You're wrong," she said, "and you know it. If not for you, I might not be alive. What I can't figure out is why you've decided to be nasty this morning when you were so kind and comforting last night."

Sitting up, he moved backward on the bed and propped a pillow behind him. "Basically, I'm not a nice guy, honey. I've never pretended otherwise."

"What's with the *honey* crack?" she asked pointedly. "And what's so different about this morning?" Still determined to trust her own instincts, she was convinced Derek wasn't nearly as bad as he claimed.

"We're registered as a married couple," he murmured softly, looking down so she couldn't see his eyes. "That's sure different."

She studied him shrewdly. When he met her gaze, she saw the raw desire in his eyes, and her heart lurched. Trying not to be obvious, she scanned his body. Though he was still dressed in the dark pants he'd worn yesterday, his arousal was hard to miss. A delightful shiver of wanting coursed through her. If he wanted her, why this sudden attack of meanness?

"Now that I've had a good night's sleep, are you afraid I'll take advantage of you, Derek?" she taunted. Was he protecting her from an intimacy both of them might regret later? Last night, in her exhaustion and near shock, she hadn't been in any condition for more than gentle comforting. This morning she wanted more than comfort, and he knew it.

He raked her boldly with his gaze. "Since you won't believe what I say, I guess I'll have to show you just how nasty I can be."

She sucked in her breath and held it, half afraid of what was coming, but eager, nonetheless. One minute she was sitting there on the bed, daring him with her eyes. The next, she was locked in his arms and his lips were hard against hers, smothering her. His thrusting tongue probed her mouth, short-circuiting her senses. She felt him in every cell of her body, as though she'd been torched with liquid fire.

Susan wanted to resist, to push him away, to tell him yes, she believed him, so he'd return to the self he'd been last night. But she did none of those things. The same eager energy she'd felt when he kissed her before swept over her, and she clung to him, wrapping her arms around his neck and kissing him back in a savage response that amazed her.

The coarseness of his emerging beard against her sensitive skin aroused her to further heights. Sensing her passion, Derek deepened the kiss, holding her even closer and pulling her down beside him.

Finally he backed away.

"Don't stop," she cried, though her lips and chin burned from his fiery touch.

"Are you sure?" Wonderment had replaced his usual knowing expression. "I didn't mean for this to happen. I thought you'd tell me where the hell I could go."

Susan had no words. She shook her head and held out her arms. He pulled her to him, holding her tightly, but in a way that was poignantly different from his bruising caress only moments ago.

From the television came Neil Diamond's baritone voice singing of love gone wrong. It was a passionate song of betrayal and failure, a song meant for late-night hours, not for early morning, when love was fresh and new. She did love Derek, she realized, loved him and wanted to protect him the way he protected her. Across the room, the voice rose with despair, a lament to a romance that could not be.

"My darling Susan," he whispered, his dark blue eyes intense in his rugged, square face. "I've pictured you in my arms like this from the first minute I saw you. Lord forgive me for taking advantage of your gratitude."

"It's not gratitude," she murmured, wanting him to understand. "There's something else, something more—"

"I know," he groaned. "When I'm with you I feel different. Nothing matters except the two of us. But that doesn't change things." He reached over and turned off the bedside lamp, as if he didn't want her to see his face.

Susan knew she should ask what he meant when he said things hadn't changed, but the next minute his mouth descended on hers and she felt herself drowning in desire. Then his hands were at her sides, easing her sweater over her head, and the lacy cup of her bra aside. His lips touched her nipple with tantalizing possessiveness. Before she quite knew what happened, she was suddenly naked, her clothes in a small heap on the floor.

Gently he eased her down on the bed. Somehow he'd managed to shed his clothes while she was intoxicated from the touch of his mouth on her body. Naked, now, he hovered over her, his hand searing a path down her belly and across her thighs. In the flickering light from the television, she saw the hard muscles in his shoulders and arms, a strength that became tangible when he lowered himself to her.

Closing her eyes, she welcomed the sleek caress of his body on hers. Though his kiss was not as punishing as the first, it was more savage than gentle. He crushed her to him, pressing his mouth to hers with passionate intensity.

It was like nothing Susan had ever experienced, like nothing she'd imagined in her wildest fantasies. After his first kisses, Derek slowly explored her body's most sensitive places, instinctively knowing what aroused her, what made her cry out with pleasure. Flicking his tongue around her sensitive nipples, he knew exactly how much pressure turned her insides to fire. And his fingers caressed her most intimate places until her ecstasy was so intense it was almost painful.

Fully aroused, he guided her to the awesome center of his masculinity, letting her know him in a way she'd never known anyone else. Not until she'd caressed him all over with her fingers and tasted his salty sweetness with her tongue did he lower himself to her.

She was so ready for him that his slow entry turned her painful longing to a wanting so intense she could scarcely bear it. Arching her hips, she rose to welcome him, gasping as his fullness slid into her.

Moaning, he lay snug and deep inside her. For a long moment she was still, enjoying the feel of him on top of her, letting her desire build to a fever pitch. When she could bear the ecstasy no longer, she began to move up and down, toward him and away, reveling in her erotic excitement.

"No, not yet," he groaned, and she sensed the full measure of his barely contained passion.

Reaching down, he pulled her legs up around his hips. Instinctively she moved with him, welcoming then releasing, tightening then letting go.

Desperately she wanted him to take her all the way, to a place where she'd never been before. Her desperation was so acute that, as she strained against him, she cried out. But for what? She had no idea of the sensation she was striving for. She only knew that he was the man she wanted to share it with.

As his thrusts quickened and deepened, she trembled all over, sensing that a long-denied pleasure awaited her soon. Above her, Derek held her tightly in his arms.

Then something wonderful happened. She exploded into an Eden of incredibly delightful sensations, and Derek was right there with her, his erotic cry of pure pleasure ringing in her ears.

Afterward she lay exhausted in his arms, enjoying the rough feeling of his chest hair against her breasts, and her sense of warm fulfillment. She heard his heart thudding against her own, felt his strained breathing, and wondered if he knew what he'd given her. For the first time in her life, she felt completely satisfied.

It was a long time before her breathing had finally returned to normal and she could speak without gasping. "Derek, you tried so hard to turn me off this morning. Now that you didn't, are you sorry?"

Lightly he kissed the top of her head. "If you mean am I sorry we made love—no. It was the best thing that ever happened to me."

"Me, too. I've never had a sensation like that before." Embarrassed, she looked down at the sheet covering them.

"You mean you've never climaxed?" He put his hand under her chin and held her head so she couldn't turn away.

"Nothing like that's ever happened to me," she admitted slowly, staring into his eyes, now not cold at all. For a long moment she hesitated, remembering the sensations and wanting him to make love to her again, soon. "If you enjoyed it as much as I did, I can't figure out why you acted so mean this morning."

"I didn't want you—us—to make a mistake." He paused. "There are things you don't know about me,

Susan, things I had to do in my life that I'm not proud of.''

"Whatever happened to you before isn't going to affect how I feel about you now." Shrugging off the tiny frisson of foreboding that raced down her spine, she focused on the TV screen. A chattering talk show had replaced Neil Diamond's melodious tones.

Following her gaze, Derek got up to turn it off. Watching him stride across the room, Susan's eyes drifted downward to his firm buttocks. A jagged, dark purple scar marred the skin on one side. Now that she'd noticed it, she couldn't stop looking. About five inches long, it left a noticeable indentation in the skin.

Like a dog bite, she thought, suddenly remembering a story Brian had told at one of the first parties she'd gone to with him. A crewman on his C-130 had been attacked by a pack of wild dogs on the runway after a flight to Lima. He'd been badly bitten on the buttocks. The wound had gotten infected and hadn't healed properly for a long time.

Telling the tale, Brian had laughed about how close the dogs came to emasculating the victim. His laughter and crude language about a serious injury had irritated Susan so much that she never forgot the details.

"How did you get such a terrible scar?" she asked Derek, after he'd lain down beside her again.

"Got bitten by a dog when I delivered papers as a teenager." The answer flowed off his tongue like warm honey.

"It looks more recent than that," she observed, "like it happened in the past couple of years, maybe."

He shook his head. "Nearly twenty years ago. The

damn thing got infected and the medics had to open it up and do surgery. They said it would look like that the rest of my life.''

How odd that he would have a scar from an infected dog bite, exactly like the one Brian described.

Susan lay back in his arms. "What a shame to mar such a beautiful derriere with an ugly scar like that."

Obviously proud of the scar, he lifted a bushy eyebrow. "*Au contraire,* madam. That scar is a trophy to my manhood, a stark symbol of the victory of man over beast." He spoke the stilted sentence glibly, as though he'd said it many times before, in men's locker rooms, perhaps.

Hadn't Brian used almost the same words when he jokingly repeated the tale about his hapless crewman? Even then she'd realized he was quoting the victim. But how come Derek knew the words, too? He'd never been on Brian's crew, had never even been in the air force. *Or had he?*

An awful sinking sensation began in Susan's stomach. Could Derek have been that crewman who got bitten in Peru?

Not possible, she told herself fiercely. Brian's story had absolutely nothing to do with Derek. But Susan didn't believe in coincidences. And this one was staggering. If Derek was that crewman, why was he pretending to be someone else?

There could be only one reason.

Much as she wanted to, she couldn't deny the possibility that Derek…was Don Albright, convicted murderer, who had been Brian's copilot and the only crewman she'd never met.

No, no! It couldn't be.

Derek touched her and she recoiled. He released her then and yanked the sheet back over them. "Having second thoughts?" An I-told-you-so expression crept over his face.

Susan wanted to sob out her suspicions and let him reassure her, the way he had last night. Heaven help her, she wanted him to make love to her again. But she couldn't, not until she'd had a chance to think. She couldn't accuse him until she was sure.

She managed a reassuring smile. "What I'm having isn't a second thought. It's the urge for a good soak in the tub."

Understanding replaced his wary expression, and he grinned. "Be my guest."

WHEN SUSAN EMERGED from the bathroom forty-five minutes later, Derek sat at the end of the bed with his back to the door, watching the morning news on TV. He seemed so comfortable in his nakedness that she had to resist her impulse to come up behind him and put her arms around his neck. Barely an hour had passed since they had made love, and already she yearned to feel his hard body joined with hers, to melt under the caress of his firm hands.

Shocked at herself, she shook away the unwanted impulses. That mustn't happen again, not until she'd satisfied herself that Don Albright had no connection with Derek Archer.

Don Albright and *Derek Archer.* The two names appeared in her mind in the boldface print of a newspaper headline. Both had the same initials.

People who change their names often keep the same initials to avoid changing monograms and help them make the transition. The sentence came from an intelligence manual. Another unbelievable coincidence.

Wrapped in one of the hotel's fluffy white towels, Susan walked barefoot into the room. "The bathroom's all yours."

Derek looked up at her approach. Slowly and seductively his gaze slid downward. He held out his arms. "Come here, woman."

She longed to leap into his arms. Instead she smiled coyly, hating herself. She couldn't stand flirty women who played hard to get. "I'll be here after you shave and shower." By then she should have some answers.

Wearing nothing but his early-morning beard, he didn't try to hide his aroused condition. Susan's eyes were drawn to the jutting evidence like a magnet. When she finally forced herself to look up at his face, he stood there in the bathroom door, grinning with approval at her interest. "I'll see you in a few minutes."

She waited until the door shut behind him, then rushed to the phone. *Hurry,* she told herself. *You have only a few moments.* Quickly she dialed information in San Francisco and got the number for the Industrial Indemnity Insurance Company. It was different from the one Derek used on his stationery, she noted. With her talent for remembering numbers, she easily recalled the one he'd given her.

What if it is? she asked herself. Didn't most companies have several telephone numbers?

She checked her watch. Only a few minutes past

nine. Even though it was Saturday, somebody ought to be there.

She got a message service. After pressing a couple of numbers, she reached a service representative.

"Can you tell me how to get in touch with Mr. Derek Archer, who works for your company?" Her heart thudded in her chest like a runaway trip-hammer. *Please let him work there,* she prayed.

There was a long pause while the representative checked the company's listings. "Can you tell me Mr. Archer's department?"

Susan's heart sank. Frantically she searched her memory. "I'm not sure, but I think it's something like Military Term Insurance."

"I'm sorry, ma'am, but we have no department with that name." The representative's voice was congenial.

"Spokane is part of his territory," Susan offered.

"That's not possible, ma'am. Industrial Indemnity isn't organized into geographical areas." The representative's voice lowered. "And I have no Derek Archer on my personnel list."

But what about Brian's policy? "Mr. Archer claims my deceased husband was one of his clients. Can you check your files and see if my husband, Brian Wade, had a policy with your company?"

"I'm sorry, Mrs. Wade. Industrial Indemnity doesn't release information about policyholders over the telephone. If you'll send us a letter or visit our office in Seattle, we'll be glad to answer your questions."

"Thanks, I'll do that." When Susan hung up, the icy lump in her stomach had grown to football size.

Before she dialed again, she listened for the shower. The sound of rushing water reassured her. Quickly she pressed the numbers she remembered from Derek's letterhead stationery.

"Industrial Indemnity," a woman said.

"I'd like to talk to Mr. Archer about a claim." Still hoping against hope she was wrong, Susan clenched her hands so tightly the nails bit into the skin.

"Mr. Archer is out of town and won't be back until next week. If you'll leave your name and number, I'll have him call you sometime today."

A horrible suspicion raced through Susan's mind. "If Mr. Archer isn't there, let me talk to another agent."

"No one else is here."

"When will someone be in?"

"You'll have to talk to Mr. Archer, ma'am. If you'll leave your name and number, he'll get back to you today."

The woman's failure to give a direct answer convinced Susan her suspicion was correct. "Are you with an answering service?" She heard the faint thread of hysteria in her voice, but made no attempt to lower it. How could he do this to her? How could he?

"Yes," the woman replied without hesitation. "We're Mr. Archer's answering service." It was the final blow.

"Find out anything interesting?"

Susan jumped at the sound of his voice behind her. How long had he been standing there in the bathroom doorway, listening?

"You bet." She turned to face him. He wore nothing but a towel looped loosely around his waist. Somehow it looked smaller than the one she'd tied around herself.

Gathering her resolve around her like a protective radar screen, she looked him straight in the eye. "Isn't it about time you came clean, Captain—or rather—Mister Don Albright?"

DEREK STARED AT SUSAN from the bathroom doorway. She glared back with burning, reproachful eyes. A wave of anger swept through him at his terrible sense of loss. He'd known this moment had to come. Why was he letting it bother him?

"Don't act so surprised," he growled in his most dispassionate voice. "Haven't I warned you all along that I'm not a nice guy?"

"You should have told me you were Don Albright. Then I would have believed you." Though her eyes were accusing, she seemed more hurt than angry.

With the white towel wrapped around her and her curly blond hair still damp on her shoulders, she looked so innocent. Watching her, Derek felt a throbbing ache begin in his chest.

Don't trust her, he warned himself. She'd betray him, too, the way everybody else had. If he went soft now, he'd land back in jail and eventually on death row. The gnawing ache in his chest got worse.

"If I'd told you, you would have turned me in." He came around the bed and stood in front of her, daring her to dispute him. Her eyes, wide with dismay, followed him as he moved.

"What's to keep me from turning you in right

now?'' There was a husky tremor to her voice as her gaze swept to the phone. Derek stepped to one side, away from the nightstand where it sat. If she wanted to call the authorities, he wouldn't interfere, only try to talk her out of it.

Folding his arms, he planted himself in front of her like a sturdy oak. ''About an hour ago you said that what happened to me before we met would never affect how you feel. Was that a bare-faced lie, or did you really mean it?''

A blush like a shadow crept across her cheeks. ''What you've done is much worse than anything I could imagine when I said that. Not telling me you're Don Albright is—'' he could see her struggling for the right words ''—it's a hellish trick worthy of the devil.'' A glazed look of despair spread over her face. ''You've used me, Derek. Right from the very beginning. How could you, when you knew I trusted you?''

He resisted his unwelcome impulse to gather her close. ''What have I been telling you all along, honey? If you'll search that fantastic memory of yours, I think you'll remember me saying that I was helping you for the money.''

''I could understand that,'' she cried. ''Honest work for honest pay. But using me the way you did wasn't the same.''

''You were a tool,'' he agreed, wondering why it felt so disgusting to admit the truth. She started to get up, and Derek had the distinct impression that if she'd been wearing more than a towel, she would have leaped off the bed and slugged him. He could have handled that. But not the look of loathing in her lovely brown eyes.

"You used me to find out about my covert mission," she cried, her eyes flashing fire. "And about Brian's safe-deposit box. Now you're spying on everything I do to make sure I don't find out about this illegal smuggling ring you're running."

His jaw dropped. "What the hell are you talking about?"

She forged ahead without answering. "What are you really doing with me here in Seattle, Derek? Lining me up for a court martial for desertion so I won't get in your way anymore? Or are you going to polish me off, the way you did Brian, now that your lust's been satisfied?"

How could she possibly think he might kill her? He reached for her and she pulled away with a shudder. My God, what had he done with his lies? He opened his mouth to speak, but she wouldn't let him.

"No wonder you showed up at my condo two minutes after that terrible man did." She gave a choked, desperate laugh. "You'd planned the whole thing. That's why you let him go. Did you plan the mugging and the car bombing, too? So your *tool* would be scared into doing just what you wanted her to?"

"Whoa, there." Derek stared at her, appalled that his lies had led her to such awful misconceptions about him. "I'm bad but not that horrible. Listen to yourself, Susan. What you're saying doesn't add up. If I had any connection to the smugglers, why would I have told you about them?"

"Why? That's easy." She set her chin in a stubborn line. "So I'd trust you, and you could worm information out of me."

What she said might be all wrong, but it made a weird kind of sense, he realized. "And why would I explain the figures in your husband's notebook?"

"Oh, you were safe there. You knew I'd find out myself, eventually."

He sat down on the bed beside her. Pointedly she rose and went to the chair across from the bed. He couldn't help noticing her long slim legs, tanned to a silky golden color from her month in Hawaii. What an odd picture they made: the convicted murderer and the wife of an alleged victim, wrapped in nothing but towels, glaring at each other across what seemed like a mile of empty space. It should have struck him as humorous, but the last thing he wanted to do was laugh.

Leaning toward her, he put all the sincerity he could muster into his voice. "I used you, Susan. I admit that. But I did it so I could find out what's going on at Fairchild." He hesitated, wondering if he should tell her why. Even to himself, his desperate urge for revenge seemed a little irrational.

How strange, he thought. It had never appeared irrational to him before.

Chapter Twelve

Clutching her towel tightly around her, Susan leaned toward Derek in their shadowy hotel room. The gray light of a drizzly Seattle morning crept through the room's one window, mirroring the gray sinking feeling in her heart.

"Exactly why did you use me to find out what was going on at Fairchild," she asked, warning herself not to believe him.

"I wanted to get even with the men who betrayed me, and I thought you might help me—inadvertently, of course." He paused, his rugged face grim. "I needed information to ruin them, take away everything they hold dear, leave them penniless, without honor, for what they did to me."

"Kill them?" she asked abruptly.

"No. I wanted them to suffer for years." He had to force the words. "For the rest of their lives, the way I'm suffering." His scowling face reflected the bitterness in his voice.

Was he lying? He sounded so sincere. But he'd sounded honest before, when everything he'd said was a lie.

"Did you risk your cover and come to Spokane because of Brian's death?" Maybe if she acted like she believed him, he'd talk more and trip himself up. She hated herself for pretending, but she had to find out the truth. Deliberately she kept her gaze trained on his face so she wouldn't be tempted to lower her eyes to his bare chest with its enticing mat of dark hair.

"Of the men who accused me, your husband was the third to die," he said. "Though the first two seemed to be accidental, they robbed me of my chance to even the score. When your husband was killed, I knew I had to find out what was going on at the base."

"Didn't it bother you that Don Albright might be a suspect in Brian's death?" She kept her gaze fixed on his face, watching for any sign he was lying. "Didn't you come to Spokane to prove your innocence?" Why hadn't he mentioned such an obvious goal?

"Not really," he said, shrugging her question off as though unimportant. "I've resigned myself to being someone else for the rest of my life. As far as I'm concerned, Don Albright died in a suicide leap from the Tacoma Narrows Bridge." Pain darkened his eyes, and he threw her a questioning glance. "Unless you decide to turn me in before I can get the hell out of here."

"I'm not going to turn you in," she assured him. *At least not right this minute,* she thought grimly. "Now, what's the story on the eyewitness to Brian's death? Who is he and what's his connection to Don Albright?"

His familiar cynical smile returned, the one that

never quite reached his eyes. "Don't tell me you think I'm behind that, too?"

"Maybe. Maybe not." Studying his face, she saw a small vein pulse in his throat.

"Forget the eyewitness," he returned shortly. "He was a middle-aged man who's got nothing to do with me."

The vein in his throat kept pulsing. Did it pulse when he lied? she wondered.

"Level with me, Derek," she said. "Obviously you know how to change your appearance. With a little makeup and different clothes, you could easily add fifteen, even twenty years. I think the eyewitness was you. If you're honest with me about that part, I might even decide to believe the rest of your story."

The vein stopped pulsing. "I hate to tell you this, Susan."

As she stiffened, alarmed by the foreboding in his voice, her towel drooped. Hastily she grabbed it and jerked it back into place. Across from her, Derek averted his eyes. She was sure he'd noticed, and grateful he hadn't embarrassed her by looking.

Lifting her chin, she pretended nothing had happened. "You might as well tell me the truth about everything. I'm going to find out sooner or later, anyhow—the way I found out who you really are." She forced her lips to part into a curved, stiff smile.

Still he didn't speak, just kept staring at her with a sardonic expression that suddenly struck her as infuriating.

"Give me a break, Derek. I already know it was you."

He hesitated only a moment longer. "Yes, I was the eyewitness."

I knew it, she told herself. But he'd been on the verge of lying when she'd forced the truth out of him. *Face it, Susan,* she told herself. *He simply isn't trustworthy.* With the thought, a slender shot of hope inside her withered back on itself.

"I made the appointment to meet your husband because of the two accidental deaths." He spoke slowly, deliberately. "I figured he'd think Don Albright was somehow responsible. His fear would loosen his tongue when he talked to me, and he'd tell the others about our meeting."

His piercing stare made her feel he could read her mind.

"Incidentally, I talked to you that Sunday I made the appointment with your husband," he said.

Forcing herself to meet his gaze, Susan nodded. "I thought your voice sounded familiar when you called from the Riverfront Hotel. Lucky for you I didn't place it."

Something inside her trembled when she saw his frozen expression. Though he was playing tough guy, she saw through his veneer to the man who had soothed and comforted her last night. Somewhere inside this convicted killer was a kernel of goodness.

"Yeah, lucky for me," he growled. "If you'd recognized my voice I'd be back in jail now."

Susan ignored his comment. "Was there any other reason you wanted to see Brian? Other than telling him about the accidental deaths of the two witnesses?"

EYEING SUSAN FROM THE BED, Derek could read the doubt in her eyes, and damned himself for causing it. He rose from the bed and went to the window.

Don't be a fool, Archer, he told himself, yanking open the curtains. What had he thought she'd do? Leap into his arms the minute she realized he was the man she most despised on the face of the earth?

Outside, the morning was a gray, damp reflection of his own dark mood. Ten stories below, Seattle had come to life. Vehicles inched bumper to bumper along the one-way street, hard-shelled bugs in a towering concrete maze.

Breathing deeply, he turned back toward her. "I already told you. By talking to your husband I hoped to find out something, anything, that would help me even the score with him and the remaining four witnesses who framed me for a murder I didn't commit."

"And did you find out anything?"

Leaving the curtains open, he picked up his shorts and undershirt. "We'd barely started to talk when your husband got shot."

He slipped his undershirt over his head. Then, with his back to her, he unknotted the towel and threw it on the bed. He could feel her eyes on him as he pulled on his shorts. That damned scar on his butt. Wade must have told her about it. That's how she'd figured out who he was. Turning to face her, he noticed that she hadn't moved.

She regarded him with cool equanimity. "Did you shoot Brian?"

Quickly he buttoned his sport shirt over his undershirt. "If you think the eyewitness killed him, you haven't been reading the papers. The shot came from the street, not from two feet away."

Her eyes narrowed. "You're wrong about that being in the papers, Derek. The police never said anything about the distance, at least not in the newspapers I read. How did you know? Did you see the killer?"

Zipping his pants, he dropped to the end of the bed and pulled on his socks. Dammit, he was going to have to tell her what he'd seen and hurt her even more. If he didn't, she'd think he was still lying.

"Yes, I saw the killer." He watched her eyes widen.

Her towel drooped again when she leaned forward, making her seem even more unprotected and vulnerable. The ache in his chest spread and he despised himself for it, knowing it meant he loved her. How had he let this happen?

"For God's sake, Derek, who was it?"

He could no longer postpone telling her. "I thought it was you."

He watched her carefully as she sat huddled in the chair, stunned. "You've got to be kidding."

"I only got a glimpse of her through the open car window, but she had blond hair like yours." He cleared his throat to conceal his awareness of Susan's obvious distress. "I was certain you'd killed your husband, but I couldn't figure out what part you played in the murder I'm accused of. That's the main reason I came to Spokane last Monday. To find out."

Susan swallowed hard. He could tell she was struggling to get control of herself.

"After I'd met you and we'd talked," he continued, "and the police hauled you in, I realized you were being framed, the same way I had been. That's when I figured maybe we could help each other.''

He paused, watching her closely. She seemed to have a better grip on herself so he went on with his story. ''Somebody went to an awful lot of trouble to make sure an eyewitness saw a killer that looked like you. When I didn't show up to identify you, they even printed my picture in the paper to force my hand.''

''How could they know about your appointment with Brian when I didn't even know about it myself? I thought he was at the squadron conducting a preflight inspection.'' Her voice, though shaky, sounded more normal. The skepticism he'd seen in her eyes had disappeared.

''He must have told someone.'' Then suddenly Derek knew that wasn't the answer. ''No, I'll bet they bugged your phone.'' He jumped to his feet and paced back and forth in front of her. ''Why didn't I see it sooner? They probably did it while they were tinkering around with your alarm system last December.''

''What do you mean?'' The skepticism was back in her voice.

He sprawled on the floor beside her chair. ''Yesterday while you were at work I called your alarm company. They didn't send a technician last December, the way you said.''

Susan expelled her breath in a huge sigh. ''So that's why the panic button didn't work.''

Only inches from her long, tanned legs, he smelled the apricot fragrance of her body lotion and felt warmth building in his loins. He'd just gotten out of bed with this woman for God's sake, and now he felt his fingers itching to remove her towel and make long, hot, passionate love to her again.

"Exactly." He forced himself to concentrate on the flickering television screen—anything but on her beautiful body. "The bug also explains why muggers were waiting outside the bank."

"And how they knew we had reservations at the Blue Boar the night before," she added, staring down at him. "You know what that bug means, Derek?" In her excitement she stood, hurrying to pick up her bra and panties off the floor.

To his fascinated amazement, she unwrapped her towel with as little seeming concern as Derek himself had felt. Tossing it on the bed next to his, she stepped into her panties. For an exhilarating moment, he viewed her firm, well-rounded backside and narrow waist, and struggled with an almost irrepressible urge to feel her silky skin beneath his fingertips. This time he didn't even consider looking away.

Pulling on her slacks, she glanced over her shoulder at him. "If the bug was in place last January, that means we were right. Somebody was spying on Brian."

"The smugglers," he said, answering her unspoken question. "Your husband must have had his hand in the cookie jar. That's why he had the secret Swiss bank account, the passport in somebody else's name, the property in South America. When he'd stolen enough, he planned to disappear and live happily ever after on the smugglers' riches."

Rising, Derek dropped into the chair Susan had left. "There was only one problem. The smugglers found out what he was up to. That must be why he was killed.'' It was all starting to fall into place.

She eased her sweater over her head. "Why are they going to so much trouble to blame me for his murder? Why not just shoot him and be done with it?''

"That's a good question." As he watched her sit down on the foot of the bed and put on her socks, he wondered if she had the remotest idea how much he wanted her. "I think your husband's murder is linked to the crime I was convicted of last year. The smuggling organization doesn't want the authorities to make the connection so they contrived to blame you. Unfortunately for them, the eyewitness they were sure would identify you—that's me, of course—dropped out of sight.''

Derek let a touch of pride creep into his voice. "Even with a full-face picture on the front page of the paper, it's pretty hard to locate a man who doesn't exist.''

"You should know," she said, eyeing him with a calculating expression. Then, right before his eyes, her bitterness vanished and she changed back into the excited, upbeat woman she'd been only a short time before. "Don't just sit there, Derek. It's after ten and we're meeting Mr. Lindsey at eleven. Let's get going.''

She thinks I made up the story about seeing the woman, he thought, watching her deceptively bright smile.

Well, he couldn't blame her after all the lies he'd told her. He prayed their visit with Ted Lindsey would provide something—anything—to change her mind.

COULD SHE BELIEVE HIM?

The question kept repeating itself in Susan's mind as they hurried along the wet sidewalks of the Seattle waterfront. Though she'd pretended to accept Derek's story about seeing a blond woman, lingering doubts remained. Maybe he'd made the whole thing up so she'd think she was as much a victim as he claimed to be.

And now she was depending on him in a way she hadn't before. Without him by her side, she wasn't certain she'd have the nerve to meet Ted Lindsey, who might well be tied into the smuggling ring. His name and phone number were included in the contents of Brian's safe-deposit box, a depository that contained details about the ring's activities. It was only logical to assume Lindsey had some connection with the smugglers.

Since they were a few minutes early, Derek told the cabdriver to let them off at the Washington State Ferry Dock at Pier 52, about a block from Ye Olde Curiosity Shop where they were meeting Lindsey.

"We'll be sitting ducks if we stand around in front waiting for him," he told Susan after the cab had left.

What were they getting into? A thrill of frightened anticipation touched her spine. She breathed deeply of the damp, salty air with its fresh seaweed smell. "You don't really think someone would shoot us?"

He gave an impatient shrug. "They've already threatened us three times. If Lindsey's one of theirs…"

Susan's breath seemed to have caught in her throat.

She swallowed hard. "There must be some precaution we can take."

He slowed his fast pace. "One thing we can do is wait inside. If he doesn't show in fifteen minutes, we'll get out of there and call his number from the ferry dock."

All around them were the muffled sounds of a March morning when the city was smothered in drizzle: the honking of a ferry leaving its slip, the dull rumble of vehicles on the viaduct overhead, the raucous cries of sea gulls. These ordinary sounds seemed oddly ominous as Susan thought about meeting this stranger.

"How about splitting up?" she suggested. "He said he knows me from a picture, but presumably not you."

Stopping, he leaned over the concrete barrier that paralleled the sidewalk. Below, the incoming tide lapped against algae-covered pilings. "If he's part of the ring, he already knows what I look like. They've seen me with you. But it's still a good idea. Can't do any harm for me to stay out of sight until he shows up."

As always, Susan felt new energy at his compliment. Then she saw him glance at his watch and her heart plummeted. It must be nearly eleven. Without speaking, they hurried the rest of the way to the shop.

No one was waiting near the tall Indian totem poles in front. Derek yanked the door open and they went inside. The smell of old wood and spices enveloped them. Above, fluorescent lights shone down on shelves piled high with everything from touristy cloth bags to jars containing shrunken heads preserved in formal-

226   *The Eyes of Derek Archer*

dehyde. With a nod, Derek disappeared behind the nearest row of shelves. Susan could feel him behind her, watching her every move. Instinctively she knew he'd let no one harm her.

The tourist crowd seemed light for a Saturday morning. Anxiously Susan glanced around the interior, searching for a man by himself. She saw lots of couples, but no single men. Perhaps Lindsey was waiting behind a row of shelves like Derek, watching her. Or perhaps he was only Brian's drinking buddy, just as he claimed, and had decided not to show up.

Her logical mind told her he was more than a drinking buddy—much more. A shiver of dread spiraled down her spine, and she realized how much she'd been counting on Lindsey to provide some answers. If he failed to appear, where would they go from here?

Then the shop's front door opened and a man entered. Brown-haired, tanned and attractive, he wore a dark suit and conservative tie under a plastic raincoat. The absence of an umbrella marked him as a local resident, not a tourist. Catching Susan's eye, he smiled and started toward her with the superb self-confidence of a well-educated professional. When he reached her side, he stuck out his hand.

"Good morning, Mrs. Wade," he said. "I'm Ted Lindsey."

She shook his hand, and he took off his raincoat, holding it over one arm.

"Where's Mr. Ellis?" he asked, glancing over Susan's shoulder. "I thought you said your private investigator would be with you."

Watching him peer around the shop, she suspected

that he'd come to see *Stephen Ellis,* not her. So the name *did* mean something to him. Good for Derek for suggesting they use it.

"Have you heard of Mr. Ellis?" she asked, acting innocent.

Lindsey focused light blue eyes on Susan and smiled congenially. "No, but I assumed you wanted your private investigator in on our discussion."

In his conservative dark suit and polished black oxfords, Lindsey looked more like a banker than a smuggler. But his well-groomed appearance didn't stop Susan's stomach from churning with anxiety. Lindsey's interest in meeting *Mr. Ellis* suggested he might be involved with the ring. And if the ring knew where they were, she and Derek were in real danger.

"Mr. Ellis will join us in a moment." She moved closer to Derek's shelf so he could hear.

To Susan, Lindsey's delighted chuckle sounded out of place, like laughter at a funeral. "Checking me out, is he?" He lifted both hands with the palms facing out in a mock gesture of surrender.

Watching his brief movement, Susan saw a suspicious bulge on one side of his coat. She stiffened, her breath frozen in her throat. As he lowered his hands, the bulge disappeared. But from her intelligence training, she knew what she'd seen: a gun in a shoulder holster.

Now she was sure. Lindsey was connected to the smugglers. Swallowing hard, she managed a smile. "Thank you for coming, Mr. Lindsey." Her voice sounded reasonably strong. "I'm sure you can help me with my investigation into my husband's murder."

A frown marred his handsome face. "I doubt it, Mrs. Wade. I met Brian last year when he came to my firm for some legal advice about a will, and I've seen him a few times since. But I know nothing about his death."

"You're a lawyer?" She forced herself not to tremble. Didn't organized crime use clever young attorneys like Ted Lindsey appeared to be? Not daring to stoop and peer through the shelf, she held her breath, listening for any sign of Derek on the other side. Why was he waiting so long to join them?

"Yes," Lindsey replied. "After we met at the office, Brian and I discovered we were both Seahawks fans. We went to a couple of games at the Dome when he was in town—watched some others on TV." Shrugging, he leaned nonchalantly against Derek's shelf. "But that's the extent of our relationship. I know none of his friends or associates and have no idea why he was killed."

Impatiently, Lindsey glanced around—apparently still looking for *Mr. Ellis*—then gazed back at Susan. "Why don't you let the police find the murderer, Mrs. Wade? That's what they're getting paid for."

"Because they don't know what they're doing." Her anxious fear veered sharply to anger. "The only two suspects they've come up with so far are me and a man who doesn't exist."

Lindsey's eyes widened, his nonchalance turning to alert interest. "*A man who doesn't exist?* Do you mean the eyewitness whose picture was in the paper?"

Susan heard movement behind her. Then Derek appeared at her side. "I'm Stephen Ellis," he said.

The two men shook hands.

"I'm sure you were listening," Lindsey said to Derek, "so you heard Mrs. Wade call the eyewitness *a man who doesn't exist.*" He gazed at Susan. "That's an odd way to describe somebody who was photographed. What did you mean?"

Susan felt her cheeks burning. She'd put her foot into it this time. By referring to the eyewitness as nonexistent, she'd inferred he was someone in disguise, someone pretending to be who he wasn't. No wonder Lindsey was curious.

Both men stared at her: Lindsey quizzically, Derek with a warning frown creasing his brow. Taking a deep breath she lifted her chin and met Lindsey's gaze head-on.

"It's been two months and the police still haven't found him," she declared haughtily, as if any fool would know what she meant. "As far as they're concerned he doesn't exist. So that leaves me as prime suspect, Mr. Lindsey. You can see why I hired a private investigator."

The alert expression left Lindsey's face. "I'm sorry I can't help." She was certain he believed her explanation.

Derek touched Susan's arm, reassuring her. "Mrs. Wade found your name with some of her husband's important records. You must have some idea why he put it there."

Lindsey shook his head. "Sorry, I don't. But tell me where you're staying, and I'll call if I think of anything."

Before Susan could open her mouth, Derek had supplied the name of a hotel in the University District, miles from theirs. *Thank God, he's suspicious,* she thought gratefully.

Lindsey turned to go. With Susan and Derek following, he walked toward the open area near the shop's front door. Then, reaching in his pocket, he swung around and handed a card to Susan, another to Derek. "If you think of anything I can do to help, please call."

She glanced at it. It was a simple business card. Noting the phone number was different from the one Brian had listed on the card with Lindsey's name, she shoved it in her purse.

STANDING BEHIND SUSAN, Derek thrust Lindsey's card in his coat pocket without looking at it.

The attorney gave Derek his hand. "I'm sorry I couldn't be of more help."

Frowning, Derek met the other man's eyes. Deliberately Lindsey looked at the coat pocket where Derek had put the card. Still holding Derek's gaze, Lindsey dropped his hand. In that split second, Derek knew something was written on the business card he had just stuck in his pocket, something Lindsey did not want Susan to see.

With an almost imperceptible nod, Derek watched Lindsey turn and walk away. The door had barely closed behind him when he heard Susan's excited whisper.

"Is there a back way out of here?"

"Probably, but an emergency exit only." He shoved his hand into his pocket and fingered the card. What was written on it? "This place is built on a pier over the water."

"We can't leave through the front door." Her voice was low, breathy. "He'll be waiting for us."

Puzzled, Derek examined her face. Obviously upset, her cheeks were flushed, her eyes wide. Had he missed something? He glanced around them. Nearby a couple examined some Eskimo carvings in a glass case by the door. They were close enough to eavesdrop.

"Let's go back into that corner, and you can tell me what's bothering you." He nodded across a line of shelves.

She glanced at the couple and at the other people milling around near the door. Unlike the more secluded shelf area where they'd talked to Lindsey, this part of the shop was open and exposed. Quickly she followed him to the back.

The rear part of the shop featured oddities from around the world—grotesque masks, two-headed animals preserved in formaldehyde, shrunken heads. Susan glanced at the gruesome display without a sign of squeamishness.

"Lindsey was wearing a gun," she said, a sharp edge of excitement in her voice.

Derek stiffened. "How do you know?"

"I saw the bulge in his coat. That's one of the things we learned at intelligence school—how to spot someone wearing a hand weapon in a shoulder holster."

His internal alarm system flashed red alert. Why would a man carrying a gun pass him a secret message? "Looks like we need to do some legwork to find out exactly what kind of business Lindsey's firm is involved in.''

''I already know.'' From the way her voice trembled, he could tell she was scared, but determined not to show it. ''Lindsey and the smugglers are with organized crime, Derek. That's what we've been dealing with.''

Seeing the dread on her beautiful face, he wished he could assure her that she was wrong, but he couldn't. He knew something about organized crime. Maybe the smugglers *were* involved with it. Everything that had happened at Fairchild fit the mold.

''They're going to kill us, Derek.'' He heard excitement mingled with desperation in her words. ''We've got to get out of Seattle.''

Leaning toward her, he squeezed her arm with both hands. ''Later,'' he said. ''Since I told Lindsey we're staying at the University Towers Hotel, that's where we'll go first.''

''In case they're following us,'' she whispered, stepping closer to him. ''But first we've got to get out of this store without getting shot.''

At first he thought she was kidding. But when she reached out and caught his hands, he realized she was dead serious. Putting his arm around her shoulders, he hugged her close, oddly pleased when he felt some of the tension leave her.

''He's not going to shoot us anywhere near here, Susan.'' He kept his voice even to reassure her. ''Too many people saw him with us just now.'' *And a man who delivers a secret message doesn't shoot the re-*

cipient before he has a chance to read it, he added to himself, itching to see what was on the card.

"If he and his buddies are as interested in us as we think," Derek went on, "they've probably already called the University Towers to see if we're registered. When they realize we're not, and we go directly there, they'll wonder what the hell is up."

"Good idea," she said thoughtfully. "Since we've got to take a roundabout route back to our own hotel to be sure we're not followed, we might as well head out to the University District and keep 'em guessing."

"Now you've got the idea," he said, hugging her again. She didn't object when they left through the front door and hurried to the taxi stand near the ferry terminal.

"Be careful what you say in the cab," he warned, opening the door for her. He knew the taxi might have been sent by Lindsey and his associates.

The short ride through the downtown traffic and then out the interstate to the University District seemed to take an eternity. The message from Lindsey burned in his pocket. She'd never trust him if she thought he was hiding something from her. But he didn't want to show her the card until he'd assured himself nothing in the message could cause her more pain.

As soon as they entered the lobby, he excused himself and found the men's restroom. In the privacy of one of the stalls, he withdrew the card from his pocket and read the message on the reverse side.

Chapter Thirteen

You have questions. We have answers. Noon. The Space Needle. Come alone.

Exultant after reading the message, Derek tore up the card and dropped the pieces in the toilet. This was the chance he'd been waiting for, the opportunity to talk to someone who knew the score. The scent of victory burned hot in his nostrils. Once he knew what really happened, he'd nail the men who'd betrayed him.

The outside door opened and someone entered the next stall. Engrossed in what he'd read, Derek paid scant attention. He stuck out his foot, ready to flush the remains of the card down the sewer.

"Stephen Ellis?" The voice whispered from the next stall.

Derek froze. Now he knew for sure. He and Susan had been under surveillance from the time they'd left the waterfront.

A sudden spurt of adrenaline sent his nervous system into overdrive. With frightening clarity he smelled the room's strong lemon odor, heard the drip-drip of a leaky faucet and wished he'd purchased another handgun when they'd gotten off the plane. The one he'd bought in Spokane was lying under his mattress at the hotel where he'd hidden it.

"Who are you?"

"A friend." The voice was not Ted Lindsey's. "Have you read the message?"

Derek didn't look over the top of the stall and risk a bullet. "Yes."

"Ditch the woman and be there."

"What if I don't show?"

"You're both as good as dead."

SUSAN WAITED IMPATIENTLY for Derek to emerge from the hall leading to the men's room. At last she spotted him.

As he walked toward her, he kept glancing back at the hall entrance as if watching for someone. Something about his posture made her think of a coiled spring, about to snap. His head was cocked to one side, his hand dangerously near the pocket where he kept his gun. Had he managed to get hold of another one without her knowing it?

He slid into the chair next to hers, giving her a quick smile. "Everything okay?"

At her nod, he relaxed. "We need to decide where we go from here," he said, glancing again at the hall to the men's room.

"Shouldn't we leave this hotel?" She felt her stomach clench and told herself to relax. "If they followed us, they could be watching us right this minute."

"We're safer here than outside," Derek said. "I

doubt they'll try anything here in the lobby. It's the perfect place to make plans.''

Silently Susan followed his gaze to the men's room door. "Who do you expect to come out of there?" she asked.

He responded with a bland half smile. "Some jerk in the next stall made an offensive remark. I'd like to get a look at him.''

"What kind of remark?"

"You don't want to know."

Susan clamped her lips shut. For a moment she was silent, glancing around the lobby. It looked so ordinary, just like any other hotel lobby. But could an assassin be lurking somewhere nearby, behind a newspaper or on the other side of a door? Lord, what were they doing here, when assassins were after them?

"We've got to get out of town," she cried.

Derek laid his hand on her arm. "We can't leave until we do some checking into that firm on Lindsey's card.''

"But why?" She felt her panic moving into her throat, and swallowed hard, trying to control it. "I want to get out of here—go back to our room—but that's not safe, either, is it."

"Don't worry, honey," Derek said. He favored her with a reassuring smile, his eyes still on the restroom door. "We just have to be certain nobody follows us there. When we get downtown, we'll split up and take roundabout routes back to our hotel. That'll give me a chance to pick up some disguises.''

So he'd already worked out a plan. *Splitting up.*

That's what she didn't like. How could she love a man and not trust him?

"Why don't we get the disguises together?" She plastered on an innocent smile. "I hate to think of separating."

Such a warm expression came over his face that she hated herself for mistrusting him. He reached out and took her hand, lifting it to his lips. A feeling of joy pulsed through Susan as his breath warmed her fingers.

"I don't want the clerks to connect me with you." For a few brief moments his attention was focused on her instead of on the hall to the restroom. "I won't be gone long. A couple of hours at most." His eyes were open and sincere. "I care about you, Susan. Nothing can keep me away from you for very long."

She wanted to believe him, but she sensed he was hiding something from her again.

"Okay, let's go," she said finally. "That man's never coming out."

Tensing, he squeezed her hand. "There he is."

A tall, gaunt man wearing a dark business suit emerged from the hall entrance. Looking neither to the right nor left, he passed directly in front of them on his way through the lobby. With his well-trimmed beard, Susan thought he looked rather distinguished, more like Abraham Lincoln than someone who made lewd remarks in a hotel bathroom.

"Are you sure that's him?" she whispered, keeping her voice low.

"Positive. Everybody else who's come out of that restroom went in during the ten minutes I've been sitting here." Derek's brow furrowed. "Too bad I didn't get a look at him inside. It would have saved us some time.''

"But why *was* it so important to see him?'' Eyeing Derek's dark face, she saw a hard expression that made her draw back.

He stood and took her hand, helping her to her feet. "I like to know who I'm talking to, Susan. That way I'll recognize him if I ever run into him again.''

"But why does it matter?'' she persisted, an uneasy knot forming in her stomach. Was he really this vindictive?

Frowning with exasperation, he started toward the lobby's rear door. "When you've been on the run for a while, you learn some basic facts about survival. Rule number one. Know your enemy, and make sure he always gets what's coming to him.''

Something about the cold way he spoke caused anxiety to race through her. "Why are you calling that man an enemy, Derek? Do you know something I don't? Tell me.''

They reached the outside door and he pulled it open for her. His expression softened. "Anybody who makes offensive remarks in the latrine—or anywhere else—is an enemy.''

"Then you don't think he's got something to do with this mess we're in?'' Anxiously she searched his face.

"No, of course not. I hope I didn't scare you.''

Her gaze dropped from his face to his throat where a small vein pulsed with the regularity of a ticking clock. *The same way it pulsed in the room this morning, when he was lying.*

"Ever since I was framed, I've made it my business to get even with anybody who crossed me." He took her arm as they left the hotel. "It's the one thing that's kept me going. If I ever see that SOB again, I want to recognize him."

Under her short coat, Susan shuddered. "You're starting to sound like someone out of *The Godfather*."

Giving her an enigmatic look, he started toward the taxi stand in front of the hotel. "I never pretended to be perfect."

THEY SEPARATED at Westlake Center in downtown Seattle, promising to meet at their room in three hours. Derek waited until Susan had disappeared inside the cavernous building, then headed toward the elevated platform to catch the monorail train.

Would she be all right? They'd obviously been followed to the University Towers Hotel. Even now someone might be tracking her through the maze of shops inside Westlake Center.

Taking a deep breath, he stepped aboard the sleek car. Susan was a trained professional, probably better at eluding pursuers than he himself. As the elevated train sped the mile and a quarter to the Seattle Center, Derek warned himself not to waste precious energy worrying about her. But he couldn't seem to help himself. When the train lurched to a stop and he joined the cluster of passengers headed for the Space Needle, he found himself searching for her face.

What the hell was wrong with him? He reassured himself that she wasn't here. She was safe back at Westlake Center. But, illogically, still he searched.

Once he thought he saw her. But the woman, her back to him, was walking hand in hand with a young boy and another woman. The three of them disappeared inside the gift shop before he got a good look at her face.

Susan's not here and not in immediate danger, he assured himself grimly. *If Lindsey and his buddies want us dead, they've already had plenty of opportunity.*

Just the same, the quicker he got back to her, the better. He checked his watch. Just past twelve. He'd wait fifteen minutes, no longer.

Pacing around the base of the soaring Space Needle, an alarming new thought struck him. What if the message was a ruse to separate him from Susan so they could get at her more easily? He spun around and started back toward the monorail. He should never have left her alone.

Two men detached themselves from the crowd waiting to go up the Needle on the outside elevators. One was Ted Lindsey, the other the bearded man from the hotel restroom. The bearded man pulled a badge from his pocket and flashed it in front of Derek's startled eyes.

"FBI, Mr. Ellis. Would you please come with us."

"What the hell's going on?" Angrily Derek jerked his arm free of the man's restraining grip. He spun toward Ted Lindsey on his other side, prepared to bolt through a small group of tourists.

Lindsey's calm voice stopped him. "Don't be a fool, Archer. We can help each other."

Derek stiffened at the sound of his alias. How much

did the FBI know about him and what had happened at Fairchild?

He had to find out.

SENSING THAT DEREK was hiding something from her, Susan darted after him as soon as he walked away from Westlake Center. Not for an instant did she think he'd do anything to hurt her. Just the opposite. He was probably trying to protect her. That's why he hadn't told her what he was up to.

But Susan didn't want protection. She wanted to know who was trying to kill her and why. So she felt no guilt at spying on him.

Once she almost lost him. Obviously trying to elude pursuit, he went in the front door of a men's haberdashery and exited to the alley in back. She didn't realize what he'd done until crucial minutes later, when he didn't come out of the store. Running to the alley, she spotted him turning north on Pine and guessed he was heading for the monorail station.

Now, standing behind a display rack in the Space Needle gift shop, she thanked the woman who had helped her trick Derek. She'd felt his eyes on her back, had known he recognized her hair and clothing. In desperation she'd told this stranger he was an old boyfriend who'd cause trouble if he saw her.

How easily the lies come, she thought. And how much she'd changed in the few days since Derek Archer had shoved his way into her life. What had happened to the bereaved widow who prided herself on her honesty? She'd been accused by the police of murdering her husband. And she'd fallen in love with a convicted killer who now seemed her only friend. A warm glow swept over her at the memory of Derek's eager passion. Thanks to him she was still alive and determined to stay that way, no matter how many lies she had to tell.

"We'd be glad to walk you to the bus stop," the woman offered, interrupting her wayward thoughts. "Are you sure you'll be all right?"

Smiling, Susan nodded. "I'll be fine. I'm sure he didn't recognize me."

After mother and son had left, she slipped outside into the drizzly noon grayness. Derek was nowhere to be seen. Had she lost him?

Stepping away from the covered walkway near the gift shop, she glanced up the Needle's steel elevator shaft where a sleek gold car whooshed toward the posh restaurant on top. The mere sight made her dizzy. Had Derek gone up there? If she didn't spot him in the next five minutes, she'd have to take the elevator and check for herself.

Light-headed, she sank to a concrete bench. The elevator nauseated her. In her mind's eye she could see the ground dropping away beneath her, could feel her stomach's sickening lurch as the car soared skyward.

But she shouldn't dare assume he'd gone up and wait for him to come down. Even now he might be heading back to the hotel. If she didn't spot him soon, she'd simply have to get control of herself and go on up to check. Sighing, she glanced around the area again.

Thank God, there he was, pacing back and forth in

front of the elevators like a caged lion. She drew in a relieved breath. He was waiting for someone. But who? And why hadn't he told her about this meeting? She'd been so sure he wanted to protect her. But was that the only reason he hadn't told her?

Head down, Susan rose and shrank back against the gift shop wall, partially hidden by the people milling around in front of her and by the massive iron work supporting the distinctive Space Needle. When she looked up again, something had changed. Derek had stopped pacing, his attention riveted on two men hurrying toward him.

Instantly she recognized them. *Ted Lindsey and the bearded man who came out of the restroom at the University Towers Hotel.* She already knew Lindsey was with the smugglers. The bearded man must be, too. She wanted to burst into tears—everything had become so painfully clear.

Derek had been working with the smugglers all along. She felt a nauseating despair even worse than vertigo. How could she have let herself forget her dark suspicions that Albright was behind the smuggling at Fairchild? Or her knowledge that Albright was a killer? A stab of guilt pierced her heart. When she discovered Derek and Don Albright were one and the same, she should have known. The proof was right in front of her. He must have arranged this secret meeting with his fellow smugglers to decide what to do with her.

Shaken to the core, she leaned against the Needle's massive steel structure, struggling to keep her legs from collapsing. When Derek discovered she was missing from their hotel room, he'd come after her. Horror mingled with her despair. She had to get away from Seattle before he realized she'd gone.

But where could she go? Not to friends or relatives. She couldn't expose them to such danger. And not to the local police. When they found she was a suspect in her husband's death, they'd return her to Spokane to be exposed to the smugglers' assassins.

Derek must have arranged for the earlier attempts on her life so he could rescue her and get her to trust him. Bereft and desolate, she felt a terrible sense of bitterness. Now that he'd taken everything she had to give, now that he knew all her secrets, would he let her be killed? She closed her eyes, her heart aching with pain. Lord, she wasn't sure…of anything anymore. Only that she had to get away from Seattle.

SUSAN CALLED Colonel Tinnerman from Seattle-Tacoma Airport. As commander of the security police squadron, he represented law and order, something she desperately needed. And he'd shown a fatherly interest. He was someone she could depend on.

The colonel answered on the first ring.

"Susan?" Just hearing his voice brought tears of relief to her eyes.

"Thank God!" he said. "Are you okay? I was afraid you'd been involved in that car bombing at the mall. The police traced the vehicle to your friend, the insurance agent."

"I'm sorry, sir. I should have called before I left for Seattle, but I've been so scared. When I saw that car blow up, all I could think about was getting away.''

''Is that where you are? In Seattle?'' She felt his concern over the miles separating them.

''Yes. I'm at the airport.''

''Get to Spokane as fast as you can. I'll send someone to meet you. Have you checked the schedules?''

''There's a commuter flight at 1400 hours.''

''Don't worry about a thing. You're in safe hands now.''

Susan hung up feeling a hundred pounds lighter. Since Derek had most of their cash, she paid for her ticket with a credit card. He'd be able to trace her, but she didn't let that bother her. With luck, she'd be in Spokane before he even realized she was gone.

When the two o'clock commuter flight took off across the Cascades, Susan was aboard.

''WHY DID YOU CLAIM to be Stephen Ellis?'' the FBI agent asked Derek.

Hunching down in his chair, Derek eyed him without speaking. If these people wanted answers, they'd have to provide some of their own before he said a word. They'd brought him to the local FBI office. In the room where they sat, practicality took precedence over luxury. The leather chairs were worn; the desk, scarred.

''Look here, Archer,'' Lindsey broke in. ''You need something. So do we. If you won't talk, we're not going to accomplish anything.''

Derek shrugged. ''You want to talk? Then you go

first. Tell me who Ellis is, and I'll tell you why I picked that name.''

The two agents stared at each other. Derek didn't miss the bearded man's slow nod. Apparently he was the senior officer.

"Stephen Ellis is the code name for one of our agents," Lindsey said.

"Sure it is. And I'm the reincarnation of Elvis." Derek rose from the beat-up old leather chair where he was sitting. "Since you haven't read me my rights, I assume I'm not under arrest, so I'll be on my way." He started for the door.

Ted Lindsey jumped in front of him. "Hold on, Archer. I'm telling you the honest truth. Since you obviously got the name from Brian Wade's papers, by now you should have figured out who *Ellis* was the code name for."

Derek paused, momentarily stunned by Lindsey's implication. "Are you saying Mrs. Wade's husband worked for the bureau?"

"That's exactly what I'm saying."

"Since when?" Astounded by this development, Derek sank back to his chair.

"We recruited him less than a year ago, only a couple of months before he married."

Derek's brain was flooded with images of what Susan had told him about her days with Wade, about how he seemed to have an ulterior motive for rushing her to the altar. "That damned SOB married her just to make himself look like a dependable family man to the FBI." Derek spit out the words without thinking. "He didn't care for her at all."

"You didn't like Captain Wade very much, did you, Archer?"

As soon as Lindsey asked the question, Derek knew he'd made a mistake. He should have taken off while he was at the Needle. "I didn't know him well, only the way an insurance agent knows a client."

"That brings us to another question." Lindsey smiled smugly. "You say you're an insurance agent. With what company, Mr. Archer?"

"Industrial Indemnity in San Francisco." His heart sinking, Derek remembered Susan's call to Ted Lindsey yesterday. It had undoubtedly been traced to her room. From the hotel staff, the FBI would have had no problem learning an insurance agent named Derek Archer had been with her when she checked in early that morning.

The bearded man—Bob Brown—moved to Lindsey's side. Now there were two armed FBI agents between him and freedom. A terrible tension gripped his body. Was this where it would all end, his glorious quest for revenge, here in this dingy little office? His heart gave a painful twinge. If they arrested him, what would happen to Susan? Alone in a hostile world, she'd be totally exposed to the assassins out to kill her.

"Industrial Indemnity has no agent named Derek Archer," Bob Brown said, his voice cool, impersonal. Derek clenched his fists at his sides, afraid of what was coming.

"Just who the hell are you, Mr. Archer?" He examined Derek's face with such intensity that every line must have been etched into his brain. "We think we know, but we'd like you to level with us. You help us and we'll help you. Maybe we're all chasing the same fox.''

Derek stared at the two men opposite. Did he dare trust them? Had his options—and Susan's—just run out?

Spokane

FROM THE AIR, Spokane looked like a fairy-tale city, its buildings sparking in the sunshine. After Seattle's gray drizzle, the brightness beckoned to Susan with the lure of safety, and a normal life. As if her life could ever be sane again after the deep wound Derek had inflicted. She knew she would never heal completely, that she'd never fully recover from the pain. Her heart still ached from the blow. But that didn't mean she intended to give up. Her hands tightened into fists. If Derek wanted a fight, by heaven she'd give him one.

Staring out the cabin window, she should have felt relieved and happy. In a few minutes she'd be under Colonel Tinnerman's protection. He'd know how to deal with the criminals who were after her.

But Susan felt no relief. She closed her eyes as a sensation of desolation swept over her. Derek's betrayal seared her heart like a branding iron. Deep in her soul, she knew she could never forgive him for what he'd done. Still, she couldn't force herself to hate him. The memories of what they'd shared were still too fresh. His lusty male scent lingered in her nostrils. She could feel the warm touch of his lips kissing her flesh, his hands stroking her hair.

Angrily she thrust the memories aside. This man had betrayed her. He wasn't worth remembering. But her angry thoughts didn't relieve her pain—or her yearning.

A sergeant came up to Susan as she left the plane. A beefy man with the longest chin she'd ever seen, he was someone she'd never run into around the squadron. But she'd only been there a few days and didn't know everyone.

Saluting, he introduced himself. "Sergeant Bollman, ma'am. Colonel Tinnerman sent me to pick you up. Do you have bags?"

"No," she said, her suspicious nature emerging again. "Just out of curiosity, how did you recognize me? I'm sure I've never seen you before."

He grinned at her like the farm boy he'd probably been before he joined the service. "Maybe you've never seen me, but I've caught a glimpse of you a time or two, ma'am. A blond lady lieutenant sort of sticks out, if you know what I mean."

In spite of herself, Susan had to smile. "Exactly."

He led her to a van in the parking lot and helped her climb in. It was Colonel Tinnerman's personal vehicle.

"The colonel got the paddy wagon back, I see," she commented, fastening her seat belt.

"Yes, ma'am. They never did catch the bas...guys who stole it."

Settling back in the passenger seat, Susan let herself relax. She hadn't felt so peaceful since early this morning when...an image of her lying next to Derek on the bed, holding his hand, flashed through her mind. Angrily she forced herself to erase it. Why couldn't she forget?

"Where are we going, Sergeant Bollman?" she asked as they turned out of the airport lot.

"Wherever you want to, ma'am," he said, glancing at her. A gap between his front teeth made him seem even more the country boy. "The colonel said to take you to your quarters or the hotel if you wanted to change, just so long as I stayed nearby."

"The hotel, then," Susan said. Her cosmetics and uniform were there. "Is he waiting for me at the office?"

"He's at home," the sergeant said, his eyes on the road. "He said you needn't wear your uniform."

How thoughtful of Colonel Tinnerman. Maybe putting on fresh clothes would remove some of her soiled, used feeling. For an instant she remembered Derek's warning that an appearance at the hotel would let the smugglers know she was still alive. Then, annoyed, she shrugged off her apprehension. As long as Derek knew she hadn't been killed in the car bombing, all the smugglers must know.

At the Riverfront Hotel, the desk clerk glanced at the sergeant, then back at Susan. "When you checked in, you said you wanted the adjoining room to Mr. Archer's. It became available yesterday afternoon, so we moved your things when we couldn't reach you. I hope that was all right."

How dare they do such a thing? Squaring her shoulders, Susan forced herself not to protest. This wasn't the time to call attention to herself by railing at a hotel clerk. "Fine, thank you." At least the adjoining rooms meant Sergeant Bollman wouldn't have to wait in the hall while she changed.

In her room, she put on her favorite outfit—the same pleated cinnamon-colored dress she'd worn the afternoon Brian had been killed. The dress had been too nice to give away. Not until she was back in the van headed toward the colonel's quarters, did she realize this was the first time she'd worn it since Brian's death. A foreboding sense of déjà vu swept over her. Would someone die tonight?

Chapter Fourteen

"Before we do any more talking, I need to call Mrs. Wade at the hotel." Derek made the statement flatly, so the agents would know he meant business. He stood up and started for the corner of the room where a plain black phone sat on a scarred, round table.

Special Agent Brown motioned him back to his chair. "Before you call, you need to know a few things about Mrs. Wade." He settled himself on a leather couch as worn as Derek's chair.

Reluctantly, Derek returned to his seat. "Make it quick, Brown. I've been gone nearly three hours. Somebody's trying to kill her and she's scared to death. No telling what she'll do if I don't show pretty soon."

"Is that what she says?" Brown's mouth spread into a thin-lipped smile. "That somebody's trying to kill her?"

From Brown's mocking tone, Derek could tell he thought she was making up the whole story. And that

Derek, being a gullible fool, had swallowed it hook, line and sinker.

"That's what I know," Derek said grimly. "An assassin with a knife broke into her condo night before last. And last night somebody blew up my car only minutes before we reached it. Check with the Spokane police. By now they'll have found out I rented the car." He permitted himself a sarcastic smile. "They probably think we're both dead."

Glancing at Lindsey, Derek saw him scribbling on a yellow tablet.

"This puts a different light on things," Lindsey said. "We thought she found out her husband was working for us and squealed to the smugglers. He was killed because of his FBI connection."

"We don't trust her," Brown added. "That's why we told you to come alone."

"You can't be serious!" Derek sprang to his feet. "If you boys had done your homework, you'd realize Mrs. Wade's an agent just like you. She was sent by the Pentagon Intelligence Agency to smoke out the smugglers."

"She told you this?" Brown's expression was incredulous.

"Damned right. She was a desperate lady, and I was the only one there to help. She heard a few rumors about smuggling on the base, but couldn't get the goods on the guys involved, so the operation was canceled."

"Damn!" Brown exclaimed, his gaunt face flushing. "Why wasn't the FBI informed about this?"

"Who knows?" Derek shrugged, enjoying the

agent's anger. "Maybe the Pentagon doesn't trust you guys at the bureau. But you can get your hush-hush people in Washington to check with their military counterparts across the river. The Pentagon will confirm everything I've said. She called it Operation Macula."

"Get on it," Brown snapped to Lindsey. After the agent had hurried from the room, Brown focused on Derek. "Before you talk to Mrs. Wade, there's something else you need to know, Archer. I've been trying to tell you ever since we walked in."

Frowning, Derek glanced toward the phone. "It'll have to wait. This call comes first." Quickly Derek punched in the hotel number and asked for their room. There was no answer. Derek transferred to the front desk and asked if his wife had returned. To his dismay, both room keys were still in the box.

"Something's wrong." Derek dropped the receiver back on its cradle. "I never should've left her." Mixed anger and guilt coursed through him as he pictured her tense expression when he'd turned away from her at Westlake Center.

"Don't worry, Archer," Brown said, heading for the door. "If she's in Seattle, we'll find her."

Spokane

"DEREK WILL SEND SOMEONE here looking for me." Anxiously, Susan brushed a strand of hair off her forehead and studied Colonel Tinnerman's face. It was wreathed in a smile of reassurance.

"I don't think he'll be that foolish." Though the

colonel had told her to be comfortable in civilian clothes, he was decked out in his blue service uniform.

"You don't understand, Colonel. This is organized crime with lawyers, thugs and assassins hiding under every rock. I met their lawyer in Seattle. And later on I saw Derek—Mr. Archer—with him." Susan couldn't repress a shudder. "They're obviously the ones behind the smuggling on the base."

The colonel leaned back against the sofa cushions. The late-afternoon sun filtered through the window blinds to cast shadows on his face. For the first time Susan noticed that his face was almost free of wrinkles.

"You say you went to Seattle to follow up on some of your husband's papers?" he said.

"Yes." Susan had already told him what she and Derek had found in Brian's safe-deposit box. The one thing she hadn't told him was that Derek was really Don Albright. Somehow, she couldn't bring herself to betray him.

"Did Captain Wade's papers say anything about the smuggling?"

Nodding, she turned toward him. "Brian kept a notebook with a list of shipping dates. At least that's what we—I—think they are. Apparently he had an account in a Swiss bank. The deposits were listed in the same notebook and correlate with the shipping dates. A considerable amount of money was siphoned off each shipment and deposited in the account."

The colonel's eyes widened. "Really." An instant later he got up from the sofa and paced to the window. "The more you tell me about Captain Wade's papers, the more I think they should be kept in a safe place, under lock and key. We'll need them as evidence when we bring these people to trial."

"They *are* in a safe place," Susan said. "They're locked up at the Riverfront Hotel." A troubling new thought hit her. "Derek—Mr. Archer—has access to them."

The colonel wheeled around so quickly he knocked over a Chinese vase next to the window. Cushioned by the plush Oriental carpet, it didn't break. "We've got to get those papers and lock them up at the squadron where Archer can't get them."

"Of course." Her heart in her throat, Susan started for the door.

Seattle

"HAVE YOU FOUND her yet?" Derek stopped his pacing long enough to confront the gaunt Bob Brown, who had just burst into the dingy little office with a tray containing hamburgers and coffee.

"Patience, man." Brown set the tray on the room's one desk, and handed Derek a foam cup of black coffee. "We've only been looking half an hour. Not even the FBI can work miracles."

Derek lifted the plastic top from the cup and resumed his pacing. "I should have shown her your message and brought her with me to the Needle."

This is all my fault, he thought, watching Brown unwrap a hamburger and take a huge bite. *If anything's happened to her...* He steeled himself against the tightness in his throat.

"If she'd been with you, we'd have arranged to meet you somewhere else." Brown dropped into a chair. "I've already told you, we didn't trust her."

"So why the hell did you trust me?" Derek stopped pacing long enough to take a swallow of coffee.

"Like I said before, Archer, we know who you really are." Brown's eyes narrowed and he motioned toward the chair opposite him. "You might as well sit down and hear me out."

Had Brown guessed he was Don Albright, or was he stabbing around in the dark? Uneasily, Derek edged toward the door.

Undismayed, Brown went on speaking. "We suspected who you were after we ran a check on Derek Archer and found out you had no past beyond last year. Now there's no doubt. We've got a perfect match from your prints off that doorknob in the hotel restroom."

They knew he was Don Albright. Stunned, Derek glanced at the closed door behind him, figuring his chances to escape. Who was he kidding?

"Don't leave until you hear what I've got to say." Brown took another huge bite of his hamburger.

"Have I got a choice?" Derek lowered himself to the chair.

"I'm not going to arrest you, if that's what you're asking."

"Why not?" Derek asked through clenched teeth.

Brown swallowed before he spoke. "Because it isn't a crime to change one's identity."

Had he heard right? Surely the FBI knew Don Albright was a convicted killer. Derek was barely able to control his gulp of surprise. "I beg your pardon?"

"We know you aren't guilty of murder, Albright."

Speechless, unable to make sense of the agent's words, Derek stared at Brown's face. The agent stared back with an apologetic smile.

"Wade killed your squadron commander. Of course, we didn't know that when we recruited him. We knew he'd been involved in the smuggling, and we recruited him as an informant. But we still thought you'd committed the murder."

A crazy weightless sensation swept over Derek as the agent's words struck home. After this year of shame and toil, could he be free? Really free?

"But why?" he asked, finding his voice. "Why would Wade kill the commander?"

"The commander found out about the smuggling operation. Apparently Wade, who never knew the identity of the person in charge, was ordered to shoot the commander and arrange for you to be blamed."

Taking another bite of his burger, Brown chewed it thoroughly before he went on. "We suspect Wade had a hand in killing the two witnesses in that case, too, the ones who died in so-called *accidents,* but we'll probably never be able to prove it. We think they're the only ones who knew for sure that Wade murdered the commander."

Derek lurched to his feet. "They were sitting closest to Wade and me in the tavern."

"That's right," Brown said. "Wade must have been worried that they'd squeal on him and ruin his nice little arrangement with the bureau involving the witness protection program and a juicy little piece of property in Paraguay.''

Floored by the enormity of Brown's revelations, Derek sank to the sofa next to the agent. Was he really free or could the FBI have made a terrible mistake? "How the hell did you find out Wade killed the commander?''

"We found the woman who turned out the lights in the tavern just before the commander was murdered. You remember the case? The lights went out, the shot was fired, you ended up with the gun—''

But Derek's mind had clicked off as Brown repeated the familiar details. Free. Free to be himself again. And free to love Susan. The thought jumped into his mind unbidden. But now she was gone. Had he lost her at the very moment he'd been unshackled?

He shot an accusing glare at Brown. "Why the devil didn't you tell somebody about this new evidence? I've been going through hell this past year. If I'd known, I could have had the case against me thrown out of court.''

"You were officially dead, Albright.'' Brown shrugged his shoulders. "A suicide off the Tacoma Narrows Bridge. Wade was dead, too. The woman who turned off the lights was an old girlfriend of Wade who came to us voluntarily after he was murdered. In exchange for her cooperation, we decided not to prosecute.''

Unable to sit still longer, Derek resumed his pacing. "So we had no reason to reopen the case against you," Brown said. "By keeping the new evidence on the QT, we figured we'd have a better chance at catching whoever's masterminding this operation. Like I said, Wade didn't know so he couldn't tell us.''

"Then that's why the FBI was called in? To catch the smugglers?'' Suddenly Brown's hamburger looked and smelled like a gourmet dinner. Grabbing one of the three remaining on the tray, Derek unwrapped it and bit into it.

"Technically, no. Catching smugglers is a job for the Customs people. Their Operation Exodus handles illegal exports. We were called in because the smuggled equipment was first stolen and then transported over state lines to Fairchild.'' Brown shook his head in irritation. "Damn the Pentagon brass. They should have told us what they were up to.''

Tensing, Derek watched the agent devour the rest of his hamburger and reach for another. "Then the smuggling was *out* of the country, not *into* it?'' No wonder Susan never uncovered anything. She'd been checking the incoming squadron planes, not the outgoing.

Brown took a long swallow of coffee. "I thought you knew that.''

"What the hell were they smuggling?''

"High-tech equipment—the kind of stuff that will be used against us if we don't stop this damned techno-smuggling. In one shipment, we think somebody got enough gear to intercept classified communications from U.S. and Russian satellites. If they know how to build the system, that is.''

Brown went on talking, but Derek didn't listen. His attention was focused on Lindsey, who'd just entered the room.

"Have you found her?" he said, interrupting Brown who swung around toward the door.

"Horizon Air. A commuter flight to Spokane." Lindsey grabbed the last hamburger on the tray. "She charged the ticket on her Visa."

Derek leaped to his feet and faced the two agents. "You've got to stop the plane."

"Slow down, Albright," Brown said. "Whoever's running this smuggling operation thinks she died in that car bombing, so she'll be safe for a while."

Tossing the remains of his hamburger on the tray, Derek flung the door open. "As soon as she gets there she'll go to the hotel for her husband's papers. Then they'll know she's still alive. I've got to get to her first."

Spokane

WITH COLONEL TINNERMAN beside her, Susan hurried to the end of the registration desk where the hotel safe was located.

Will Brian's papers still be here? She glanced around anxiously as she waited for the clerk to finish with another customer. Though there wasn't one chance in a hundred that Derek had somehow managed to get to the hotel ahead of her, she couldn't rid herself of the notion that he'd already come and taken them. Or hired someone else—maybe a crooked hotel employee—to remove them.

Finally the clerk was free. Heart pounding, Susan signed the register and watched him open the box with her key. He took out the contents and handed them to her.

"Is everything there?" The colonel eyed the unassuming bundle as if he couldn't wait to get his hands on it. His face displayed an unusual eagerness that made her uneasy.

Don't start suspecting the only person you can count on, she warned herself. Slipping off the rubber band, she leafed through the documents. "Yes, everything's here, and all the pages are in the notebook." Feeling the tension drain out of her, she replaced the band and dropped the bundle in her bag.

"Now, let's get them out to the base." The colonel edged her away from the counter.

"Oh, Mrs. Wade," the clerk called after her. "Will you be checking out tomorrow as planned?"

"Yes...no..." In confusion she stared at Colonel Tinnerman. "I don't dare spend another night in this hotel, and I can't stay at my condo."

He patted her arm. "Of course not. I've arranged for you to stay with one of our people—Lieutenant Carla Drew. Half the people in the squadron have already volunteered for special guard duty while you're there. I guarantee you won't be bothered."

"You're too good to me, Colonel." She held back tears of gratitude. Suddenly all she wanted was to get away from this place. It had too many memories of Derek. Now she'd probably never see him again, never feel the touch of his hand on her skin. She could hardly bear the thought of how he'd betrayed her.

Turning, Susan met the clerk's eyes. "I won't be coming back. I'll sign for the charges right now."

"Shall I have a bellhop pick up your bags in your room?"

My things. With a sinking feeling Susan visualized her cosmetics neatly laid out on the bathroom counter, her clothes hung in the closet—including her one tailored uniform. She couldn't simply walk away and leave them.

"I'll send someone from the squadron to pack your suitcase and bring it to you," the colonel offered quickly. "Right now we need to get out to the base ASAP with Captain Wade's papers."

Susan had been ready to agree, but the eagerness in the colonel's voice stopped her. Why was he so anxious to get his hands on Brian's papers?

"No, we won't need a bellhop," he said to the clerk without consulting Susan. His hand tightened on her arm and she winced.

But she didn't budge. Derek had wanted to see Brian's papers, too. And Derek had used her and betrayed her, as he'd always warned he would. Could the colonel be planning to betray her, too, as soon as Brian's notebook and other papers were firmly in his grasp? A chill shot through her.

Defiantly she stood her ground. "I don't want some stranger pawing through my things, Colonel Tinnerman. Since we're here, it'll take only a minute for me to throw them in my suitcase." She turned toward the clerk. "I'll check out after I pack my bags."

"That's not a good idea," the colonel warned, frowning. But his grip on her arm relaxed. "We need to get this material out to the base ASAP." The same eager expression flashed across his face, making Susan even more uneasy.

"Another ten or fifteen minutes won't matter." Avoiding the colonel's eyes, she turned to the clerk again. "Please call my room if Mr. Archer picks up his key. I don't want to see him."

"No problem, Mrs. Wade," the clerk said.

"Well, if that's what you really want," Colonel Tinnerman conceded reluctantly. "I guess you'll be all right as long as I'm there with you."

Susan didn't realize he meant to watch her pack until he strode into her room behind her. His move hit a raw nerve. Was he there to protect her or to keep an eye on Brian's papers?

Laying her coat on the bed, she turned to face him. "I'd rather you waited in the room next door, Colonel." After all he'd done for her, she felt guilty asking him to leave. But she couldn't afford to make another costly mistake.

His scarecrowish figure dropped into a chair. "I'll watch the news on your TV. You won't even know I'm here."

Disguising her annoyance, she opened the adjoining door to Derek's room. Though the sergeant had waited there for her to change, Derek's essence still filled the place. Swallowing hard, she focused on the colonel. "Why don't you watch TV in here? Then you'll be near and I'll still have my privacy."

"Is that Mr. Archer's room?"

"Yes." She offered no explanation, felt no embarrassment.

"Call if you need anything," said the colonel as he

disappeared into the adjoining room. A moment later Susan heard the familiar voice of a TV announcer broadcasting the evening news. She let out her breath. *Good. If he's watching TV, he won't be as aware of what I'm doing or how long I'm taking.*

Her suspicions about the colonel might be paranoid, but Susan was taking no more chances. She had let her guard down with Derek, and now she was paying the price in pain and suffering. Her next mistake might mean her death. What she needed—and fast—was a way to buy time, something to deceive the colonel until she was certain he was one hundred percent trustworthy.

Rummaging through the drawers of the desk, she found hotel stationery—business-size envelopes with matching paper. After addressing three envelopes to herself, she stuffed pages from a hotel magazine in one so it would look as though a small notepad was inside, and two sheets of plain paper in the other two. Then she went to the adjoining door.

"I'm ordering some coffee from room service to keep me going while I finish packing. Do you want anything?"

His skinny angular form appeared in the doorway. "You don't have to order anything, Susan. I thought we could stop somewhere for dinner after we lock up the papers."

"I've had a hard day, Colonel. I need something now."

He smiled his considerate crooked smile. "Of course you do. I'll have coffee, too, and get a snack. That'll tide us over until dinner. Oh, and Susan?"

What now? Holding her breath, Susan stared at his unlined, gnomelike face. "Yes, sir?"

"Have room service bring the coffee to my door. That way you won't be disturbed, and I can take care of the bill."

"That's nice of you, sir," Susan said, intending to do no such thing. When she called room service, she repeated her room number twice to be sure the operator got it straight.

After she'd hung up, she stuck Brian's two credit cards and the Paraguayan property title into the false bottom of her suitcase. The notebook she shoved under her panty hose. Thanks to the pleated skirt of her dress, she could detect no bulges that might reveal its presence.

The three sealed envelopes waited on the desk. Since she had no stamps, she'd have to ask the room service waiter to buy them before he mailed the letters for her. Colonel Tinnerman would be listening and would be sure to overhear.

She took a deep breath to control the sudden tightening in her stomach. Was this the fatal flaw in her plan? There was no way she could whisper to the waiter.

Still, maybe it would be best if the colonel did overhear her request. Then he'd be more likely to believe her when she said she'd mailed Brian's papers to herself from the hotel. She'd explain that she intended to protect the papers from a possible thief.

Was this elaborate scheme of hers a big waste of time? Remembering how generous the colonel had been, she could hardly imagine him doing anything to hurt her. Still, he'd been almost too nice. Maybe he had an ulterior motive for his generosity.

She'd almost finished packing when she heard a knock on the colonel's door. Damn. In spite of her emphasis on the room number, the waiter had gone to the wrong door. Sure enough, when the colonel said, "Yes?" a man's voice replied, "Room service." Did she dare to stalk boldly into the room with the three envelopes? Yes, she decided. She had no alternative. Darting to the desk, she snatched them up.

Next door, the subdued clink of dishes was barely audible over the chatter of the television. But before she could reach the partly open door, the colonel's voice stopped her.

"What the hell do you think you're doing?" His words ended in an alarmed snarl.

Ready to push the door open, Susan stopped with her hand on the knob. Her feet were rooted to the carpeting beneath her. What was going on? From the adjoining room came scuffling noises, then a door banged.

The phone. Turning, she flew to the bedside table and pressed the number for the front desk. Nobody answered.

The adjoining door swung open. The receiver crashed to the nightstand. As she stared at the open door, Susan felt her heart leap into her throat.

Derek stood there, dressed in a waiter's jacket. "Susan," he whispered.

Chapter Fifteen

Susan's first instinct was to run. But the bed lay between her and the hall door. Yanking up her dress, she scrambled across the bed and bolted toward the hall door. She had to get away from Derek. He meant pain and betrayal. Maybe, death. Mindlessly she fled, knowing only that she had to escape from this room before he caught her.

But he grabbed her arm before she could yank the door open. Thrusting himself in front of her, he stood between her and the hall. "Susan, listen."

She jerked her arm free. "No," she screamed. "I know what you are. I saw you at the Needle with the smugglers."

He took a step toward her and she backed away from him, knowing she couldn't let him get close or she'd never get away.

"It's not what you think," he said, holding his arms out to her. "Those men at the Space Needle weren't criminals. They were FBI agents."

"You lying bastard." Trembling with fright and anger, Susan kept backing away. "Haven't you figured it out yet? Your lies won't work anymore."

He shortened the distance between them. "It's not a lie. It's the truth. You've got to believe me."

Susan felt the bed against the back of her legs. She'd re treated as far as she could go. Where was Colonel Tinnerman? Why didn't he help her?

Slowly Derek moved toward her. In another instant he'd be close enough to grab her. Already she could smell the male scent of his body. He came a step closer. Without thinking, she reached out and slapped him with such force that her palm tingled. He didn't flinch.

"You warned me you were bad," she cried. "Now I know it's true. Please go away and leave me alone."

He grabbed her hands, holding them so she couldn't slap him again. "No, I won't go away. I love you, Susan. I want to marry you." His all-seeing indigo eyes probed to her very soul.

"More lies." She laughed shrilly, hysterically. "What do you want this time? Another roll in the hay? How you must have laughed when the gullible widow practically insisted you take her to bed this morning."

He pulled her to him. "Shut up, Susan."

Struggling against him, she fought his embrace. "How could you hurt me like this? I loved you, damn you. In spite of everything, I loved you."

Slowly, tenderly, his mouth descended on hers. Susan wanted to lash out at him. To bite him, kick him, pummel him with her fists. But she couldn't. When she felt his tough, hard body against her, his moist mouth caressing her lips, all the fight went out of her. He released her hands, and she raised them to his neck, clinging to him with a longing so great she wanted to drown in his kiss.

"Why do you keep lying to me?" she whispered when he finally released her.

"This time I'm not lying, Susan. I swear I'll never lie to you again about anything." He kissed her a second time then, so lovingly she almost believed him. On his face was an expression of such tenderness that her heart cried out for him.

"Ted Lindsey isn't a criminal," he said. "He's an FBI agent." His words rang with sincerity and truth.

"If he's an FBI agent, why didn't he say so up front?" she asked weakly. How she wanted to believe him.

Derek hesitated as though afraid to tell her. "Well, since I've sworn never to lie to you again—he thought you were part of the smuggling ring."

Her mouth dropped open. "Me?"

A grunt from the next room stopped her short.

"What did you do to Colonel Tinnerman?" She couldn't keep the accusation from her voice.

"He's fine." Derek shrugged. "When he refused to listen to me, I put some tape on his mouth, tied his hands loosely and locked him in the bathroom so I'd have a chance to talk to you. He's trying to get out. That's the noise you hear."

"You've got to let him go." Her suspicion of the colonel had been tenuous at best. Remembering his generosity, she couldn't stand knowing he was locked up.

"There are still some important things I need to tell you about your husband, and about me, too."

"That can wait." She started for the inside door. "We've got to let him out, Derek. Right now."

Putting a hand on her arm, he thrust himself in front of her. "Once he's out of there, we won't have a chance to talk, and you really need to know these things, Susan."

She eyed him suspiciously. Here he was in front of her again, putting himself between her and where she wanted to go. Was she letting her love blind her to serious problems?

"Is there something in that room you don't want me to see?"

"Hell, no. Be my guest." He stepped aside, and she swept past him.

In the flickering light from the television screen, she couldn't make sense of what she saw. A tray containing coffee and snacks sat on the dresser. A chair was tipped over, and the bedding was snarled, as though someone had yanked off a blanket and tossed the spread aside.

Though her view was partly blocked by the bed, at its foot was what appeared to be a crumpled pile of clothes. Behind her she heard Derek's voice, ruthless in its urgency. "Come back into your room, Susan. We need to talk."

She didn't obey. Instead, she ran to the hall door and flicked the light switch. Automatically, two bed-side bulbs and a floor lamp switched on, flooding the room with brightness.

At the foot of the bed, his blue uniform soaked with blood, lay Colonel Tinnerman. The tape covering his mouth slashed an obscene line across his round, gnomelike face. A length of rope hung from one wrist. From what she could see of his body, the poor man hadn't had a chance.

Frozen with shock, Susan couldn't move, couldn't breathe. Derek must have done this awful thing. Somewhere in the dim recesses of her mind she thought she heard him yell ''Run.'' Or was she imagining it? She could hardly get her lungs to work, let alone her legs.

On the other side of the bed, the bathroom door opened. A hulking form appeared.

Krakow, her attacker at the condo. He'd been working with Derek all along.

All hope vanished. Derek had lied again.

Krakow started around the bed toward her just as Derek leaped for the hall doorway where she stood. A sudden burst of adrenaline shot through her. She had to get out of here.

Flinging open the door, she burst into the hall and glanced wildly in both directions. No one was there. Frantically, she ran toward the exit stairs. Yanking the heavy fire door open, she ran into the concrete stairwell.

Forcing her tired legs to keep moving, she pounded down the bare metal stairs. At the first landing she paused to glance back. Nobody. Why weren't they after her? No sound broke the silence except her own harsh gasps.

Panting, she sprinted downward. Nearing the next landing, the heel of one pump broke with a sickening crunch. She stopped only long enough to strip off both shoes. In her stockings, she continued her mad flight.

By this time she was running on pure adrenaline,

barely conscious of the racking pain in her lungs, or the screaming insults to her feet as she flew down the rough stairs. Like a wild creature racing for its life, she moved on instinct, with no guarantee that her next step wouldn't mean her death.

After what seemed an eternity, she reached the first floor. The metal door with the Exit sign over it read For Emergency Use Only. If she opened it, an alarm might sound, and they'd know where she was. After a moment's hesitation, she yanked the door open. Silence.

Thankfully she stepped through, breathing in the cold night air. Not until the metal door clanged shut behind her did she realize it had no outside knobs or levers, no way to get in from outside. But it didn't matter. She'd gotten away.

Quickly she glanced around, taking stock of where she was. Overhead a single light burned above the concrete platform she stood on. She was at one end of the hotel near the covered swimming pool. A walkway between the building and the pool led to a small parking area. Beyond, the lawn sloped down to the river.

Was her car still where she'd left it? Not that it would do her much good. Her keys were in her bag upstairs in her room.

At that moment she knew how vulnerable she was. She had no ID, no money, no credit cards and, she realized as her flimsy dress blew in the cold night wind, no coat or shoes. She needed help, and Derek was the last person in the world she could count on to rescue her.

Much as she hated the idea, she'd have to go to

Detective MacElroy at police headquarters. He'd never believe a weird story like hers, but if she was lucky he'd provide refuge until she could get assistance from the Pentagon.

But how could she reach the police? She couldn't call from the lobby. The smugglers would surely spot her. She'd have to walk, she decided. Headquarters was across the river, only a couple of blocks beyond the park. If she used the pedestrian bridges she should make it in less than an hour.

Suddenly Susan realized how conspicuous she was, standing in a pool of light on the concrete pad outside the emergency exit. Quickly she darted into the shadows beside the building, the small rocks sending pinpricks of pain into her stocking feet.

She didn't see the man hiding in the bushes until he grabbed her. Striking silently, like a cobra, he caught her arm and twisted it. The shock sent stabbing pain through her arm and shoulder. Already unsteady on her stocking feet, she was flung completely around until he held her tightly against his chest.

When she opened her mouth to scream, a meaty hand closed over her face. Vainly she twisted and kicked, her shoeless feet stinging from each blow.

She felt a bag come down on her head.

Chloroform.

Her captor's voice came from far off. "She must have gotten away from Krakow."

"Yes." It was a different voice, a woman's voice. "How nice of her to use his exit route."

They were the last words Susan heard.

DEREK SLAMMED THE DOOR closed as Susan dashed into the hall. Thank God she'd gotten away. Then he turned to face the hulking figure opposite him. The assassin was at least four inches taller and a hundred pounds heavier. In his bloody hand was a ten-inch knife with a blade that looked razor sharp. He'd already used it once—on Colonel Tinnerman. Derek knew he was itching to use it again.

"Not so tough without your gun, huh, mister?" Krakow taunted.

Derek eyed the man across the king-size bed without saying anything. How fast could Krakow move? he wondered. All he needed was an instant to yank his gun from under the mattress where he'd hidden it yesterday.

If it's still there, he thought, his breath tight in his chest. Nothing looked disturbed, but the police might have searched his room after the car bombing and confiscated his gun.

"Tough guys like you should be careful who they mess with," the assassin jeered. In the brightly lit room, his head seemed smaller than Derek remembered it. A pinhead on a hulking body. Smiling broadly, he jabbed at Derek with the knife.

Good, he wants to toy with me before he finishes me off. A few seconds was all Derek needed. He had to get out of here and find Susan.

"Sorry about taking your shoe the other night," he said, trying to sound humble. "I'd be happy to buy you a new pair."

"I'll bet you would." Krakow stabbed the air again. This time Derek ducked.

Krakow laughed. "Knife making you nervous? Well, you're not half as nervous as you're gonna be." He drew back his arm as though to toss the knife.

Derek knew he'd never throw it and risk losing his weapon. But he ducked, anyway, below the top of the bed, knowing this might be his last chance to grab his gun. Quickly, he thrust his hand under the mattress.

To his shocked surprise, the knife whizzed over his head. With a roar, Krakow started around the bed toward him. He clutched another knife, the twin of the one he'd thrown. Jumping over the colonel's body, he lunged at Derek.

On the floor with his back against the nightstand, Derek groped for the gun, but his fingers encountered nothing. He thrust again, and this time he touched cold steel. He jerked the weapon out and rolled to one side. The assassin's knife stabbed at the empty space where Derek had sprawled only an instant before.

Taking aim quickly, he fired at Krakow's foot. The bullet found its mark, and the assassin howled in pain.

Derek scrambled to his feet. "Drop the knife, you bastard." It clattered to the floor. "Now, put your hands on top of your head and sit in that chair so we can talk."

SUSAN WOKE TO THE SMELL of rubber and faint gas fumes. Not a sliver of light penetrated her prison. She had no idea where she was. Only that she was chilled to the bone, curled on her side in some sort of uncomfortable box. At least the bag over her head was gone and she could breathe again.

Beneath her, she felt a coarse carpet. God, she was

cold, so cold. Wrapping her arms around herself, she tried to warm her body by rubbing her upper arms with her hands through the flimsy dress fabric. It did no good. Her teeth began to chatter.

She heard the subtle whine of an engine and felt vague vibrations. When she reached up, her fingers touched bare metal.

A car trunk. They'd locked her inside. And now they were taking her somewhere, probably to kill her.

Derek couldn't do this to me, she thought miserably. He might be in league with the smugglers, but he'd never permit her to be chloroformed and thrown in the trunk of a car. Susan knew that beyond any doubt. No, somebody had done this without him knowing. And now they were going to kill her.

So if they're going to kill me, why not back at the hotel? her logical mind asked.

Because they wanted something from her. *The contents of Brian's safe-deposit box.* That's what they'd wanted all along.

Well, they'd have the cards and property deed as soon as they searched her room. The false bottom in her suitcase might fool them for a few minutes, but no longer. They wouldn't find the notebook, though. She felt for it. It was still there, thank God. She could feel its smooth cardboard cover lying flat against her belly.

Then a puzzling thought hit her. Why did the smugglers need Brian's papers, when Derek had seen them and knew exactly what they contained? The question stopped her.

Maybe he couldn't remember the figures in the notebook. But the answer didn't satisfy her.

What if he hadn't been lying about the FBI? She forced her mind back to the bloody scene in his room. The colonel's body at the foot of the bed, and Krakow on one side with Derek on the other. Had Derek been as shocked as she was by the assassin's appearance? Perhaps it had been Derek she'd heard, telling her to run.

A suffocating pain tightened her throat as she remembered the leer on the ugly face of the assassin. What if Derek had been telling the truth about the FBI, and she'd jumped to the wrong conclusion? She might be responsible for both their deaths.

Dear God, let him be safe, she prayed.

The car jerked to a stop, its motor still throbbing. Curled in a tight ball, Susan held her breath. She heard familiar noises.

Aircraft engines. The sound gave her new hope. Were they near the base? A second later the car moved forward at a slower speed. She had to do something to protect herself.

Frantically she felt around, searching for a tire iron or some other weapon to strike out with. Her groping fingers felt the spare tire and the coarse cloth of the bag they'd put over her head. There was nothing else in the trunk.

But she had to get rid of the notebook. She reached around the spare tire, searching for a loose place in the carpet. After a moment's yanking, she'd pulled a small section free. Quickly she thrust the notebook under it and smoothed it down.

The noise of aircraft engines was much louder now. The car slowed and stopped. The motor was turned off.

For Susan, time had just run out.

"THE LINCOLN'S PASSED through the main gate at Fairchild." Lindsey repeated what Derek had already heard over the car radio. "The duty SP got a good look at the back seat. The only people inside are the driver and a woman passenger, both dressed in flight suits."

"Dammit, Lindsey, you've got to stop that car and check the trunk." Scared half witless, Derek yelled the same demand he'd shouted at least ten times since they left the hotel. "We found Susan's shoes on the exit stairs Krakow intended to use. It's only common sense that his buddies grabbed her when she came out the door."

Alone with Colonel Tinnerman's murderer, Derek had needed only a few minutes to force information out of Krakow. He and his two cohorts had intended to abduct Susan. To surprise her, Krakow had entered through Derek's room, but had himself been surprised by Colonel Tinnerman escaping from the bathroom. When Tinnerman tried to stop him, Krakow had killed him.

Agents parked near the hotel lobby had tailed the Lincoln driven by Krakow's associates since it left Riverfront Park. Now Derek and Special Agent Lindsey were following the first government car, a mile or so behind.

"I keep telling you, we don't even know she's in

the Lincoln," Lindsey retorted. "Try to relax, Albright. We'll find her."

"Like you found the smugglers at the base?" Derek gritted his teeth to keep himself from shouting an oath. At this moment everything about Lindsey irritated him, even the agent's strong cologne. "You've been after them for a year, and you still don't know who's in charge."

"We have a pretty good idea."

Derek stared at the special agent with unbridled skepticism. "Who the hell is it?"

"I'll let you know when we have some positive evidence."

"When will that be?"

Lindsey stared at the road. "Later tonight, if things work out right."

A nasty suspicion leaped into Derek's mind. For a long moment he didn't say anything. Fighting to keep from blurting out something he'd be sorry for, he clutched the middle-seat armrest. "So that's why you haven't stopped the Lincoln."

"What do you mean?"

"You think they're taking Susan to the mastermind behind this smuggling scheme." Derek's fingers ached from his tight grip on the armrest.

"You bet we do." Lindsey's voice rose in jubilation. "This time we've got him. Maybe we can never prove the robbery and smuggling charges, but as soon as she's delivered to him, we can nail him for kidnapping."

"Or maybe murder," Derek growled. "You bastards! You're risking her life to get your hands on some tinhorn military smuggler.''

"He's not exactly a tinhorn smuggler." Lindsey glanced soberly at Derek. "He ordered the murders of at least two people—Wade and the man you were accused of killing. His assassin just killed Colonel Tinnerman because the poor man made the mistake of escaping from the bathroom where you'd locked him up.''

"Dammit, that's all the more reason—"

"Hear me out," Lindsey interrupted. "The man we're after has smuggled high-tech equipment out of this country that can be used to attack the United States. He's a murderer and a traitor. Isn't it worth some risk to a trained intelligence agent like Mrs. Wade to put a man like that behind bars?''

Without thinking, Derek spit out the answer. "No, dammit. Nothing's worth that risk." A week ago he would never have made that statement. A week ago he was ready to sacrifice his future—and anybody else's who got in the way—to get even with the men who had testified against him. He cared for nothing and nobody else. Now, with Susan's life at stake, his crusade for revenge seemed hollow. Without her, nothing made sense.

"If she's locked in that trunk, she's nothing more than a sacrificial lamb." Derek's gut wrenched with fear. "Stop playing God and get her out of there."

Turning, Lindsey frowned at Derek and then stared back at the road. "Wasn't this her objective when she was assigned to Fairchild? To stop the smuggling?''

"It's been stopped," Derek growled. "There's been

no smuggling for months now." But some of the heat left him. Would Susan want to be rescued if it meant a traitor and murderer might never be caught? In his heart, Derek knew she wouldn't. But that didn't stop the fear eating away at him.

"That's not the point and you know it," Lindsey said, his expression sober. "The point is, Mrs. Wade is doing what she was assigned to do. She's helping us put this SOB behind bars."

He glanced at Derek again with a questioning expression. "Say, I just thought of something. Don't you military people have to have ID on your vehicles to get on base?"

"On Fairchild, you do," Derek said, tensing. "Why?"

"The Lincoln must have had a base sticker. The SP at the main gate didn't pull it over."

"It was probably stolen from somebody who works on base," Derek said. Colonel Tinnerman's van had been stolen, too, he remembered. By stealing the security police commander's vehicle, the smugglers had found a perfect way to thumb their noses at the military.

The number one man must be a real sociopath, Derek thought, more frightened than he'd ever been in his life. If Lindsey was right, this man was now holding Susan captive.

Chapter Sixteen

The trunk lid swung open, and cold night air struck her body. Dark human shapes were silhouetted in the dim light that flooded the area. In the distance Susan heard the dull roar of aircraft engines.

An instant later, the beam from a flashlight pierced the semidarkness. Wincing, she shut her eyes and covered her face with her hands.

"Douse the light," said a woman's voice. "You crazy or something?"

So Susan hadn't been wrong when she'd heard a woman at the hotel just before the chloroform knocked her out. Was this the woman Derek had seen when Brian was shot? Was she the one who had impersonated Susan at Cavanaugh's that awful afternoon?

The beam flicked off, and fiery images danced before Susan's eyes. What were they going to do to her? Panic welled in her throat. Would she ever see Derek again? Would she ever tell him she loved him?

Rough hands grabbed her arms. Half dragged, half under her own power, Susan scrambled onto solid ground. She would have fallen, but her captor held her upright, clutching her around the waist like a sack of potatoes.

The woman shoved a flight suit at her. "Here, put this on." She was about Susan's height but thinner. Or maybe her baggy flight suit just made her seem that way. In the dim light Susan could see her clearly. With her square face, dark hair and bushy black eyebrows, she needed only a pointed hat and a broom to turn her into a witch.

The man released Susan, and her legs cramped. She sank to the ground. From the weedy dirt beneath her, she knew they weren't on a paved parking strip. Turning her head, she peered under the car. About half a block away was a chain-link fence. At that point the ground gave way to a smooth surface, probably asphalt, lit by floodlights. The back glow from the floods provided the dim illumination around the car.

The flight line. That's where she was. The car was parked parallel to the part of the operations area where the aircraft were serviced. On a nearby apron, Susan saw a C-130, its large cargo door open. A forklift carrying a crate headed toward the plane's ramp. She tensed. Did they plan to take her aboard?

Her mind shifted into overdrive. Once they got her on an airborne plane, she'd have no way to escape. She had to get away now. But how? She had no weapons, nothing but her numb feet and tired legs. She'd have to pretend she couldn't walk. Anything to throw them off guard so she could run.

The woman prodded Susan's hip with the pointed toe of her boot. "Put on this flight suit."

"I'm sorry, I can't stand." She whispered the words.

"Then put it on sitting down." There was no sympathy in the woman's husky voice.

"Come on, Marta," the man whined. "If she can't walk, I'll have to carry her again." He wasn't much taller than the woman, though much broader.

"We'll have to drag her between us," the woman said, "so it looks like she's walking."

Without removing her dress, Susan forced her stiff hands to pull the flight suit over her freezing feet. By now they were so cold she couldn't even feel them. Teeth chattering uncontrollably, she yanked the suit up the rest of the way and closed the front zipper. Protected by the heavy fabric, she felt warmer. When she started to stand, she pretended her legs wouldn't work and sank back to the ground.

"We'll have to help her, Burt." Stooping, the woman grabbed one of Susan's arms. The man grabbed the other. Between them, they dragged her to her feet.

"Now, hold her while I tape her mouth."

"Do you have to do that?" Susan cried between her chattering teeth. "I promise I won't yell."

"Sorry, Wade." The woman laughed unsympathetically. The sound was high and grating, a radical change from her whiskey-flavored speaking voice. "We were ordered to tape your mouth, and around here we do what we're told." She produced a roll of tape.

Susan's heart sank. Now she wouldn't be able to cry out for help. Wincing, she felt pressure on her lips as the woman plastered a piece of the tape on her mouth. The stuff felt strong enough to tear skin when it was removed. She glared at the woman, who only laughed and slapped on more tape.

With Susan between them, the abductors started for the flight line. A six-foot-high chain-link gate with barbed wire on top, like the fence, opened with a push.

Somebody's unlocked it, Susan thought, dragging her feet so her captors would have to support all her weight. Her kidnapping had been planned in advance and, unknowingly, she'd walked right into her captors' arms. Who was behind this? The two civilians holding her captive must be working with someone in the air force, someone with access to the Hercs.

Once they were through the gate, the brilliant glare from the floodlights burst around them. Now she saw where they were headed—to the aircraft parked on the apron. About halfway there, they stopped as another forklift headed toward the C-130's cargo bay, its crate strapped to a wooden pallet.

The woman muttered an oath. "They should be finished by now. He said not to bring her aboard until the cargo was loaded. The aircrew won't talk. They're with us. The ground crew isn't."

"They'll be done loading in a few minutes," said the man. "Nobody'll notice us in our flight suits."

Susan's heart leaped at their conversation. If only the man driving the forklift would look in their direction. Maybe she could break free and run toward him.

But the forklift driver's attention was focused on maneuvering his equipment. Carefully he lowered the pallet and its crate onto the ramp, which had been adjusted to the level of the aircraft floor. Two load-masters dressed in flight suits rolled the cargo inside on rollers built into the ramp and aircraft floor.

This was the best chance she'd have to escape. Tensing, Susan jerked her arms free and shifted her weight to her numb feet. Caught by surprise, her captors released her.

She started to run. But she'd taken only a few steps when the man's hand closed on her arm. "Thought you'd fool us, did you?" he said with a sneer. "For somebody who can't walk, you run mighty good, lady."

Susan stared wildly after the forklift driver. Had he seen her? No. He didn't so much as glance toward them. With mounting despair, Susan watched the fork-lift rumble away from the ramp and toward the build-ings.

"That should be the last," Marta said, eyeing the loading area. No other forklifts were headed toward the plane. With a firm grip on Susan's arms, she and Burt approached to within earshot of the ramp.

From inside the cavernous C-130, a man appeared. At first his face was in shadow, and Susan thought he was a loadmaster. Dressed in a flight suit, he was indistinguishable from the other crewmen. Short and wiry, he seemed to be in charge. When the two load-masters appeared from inside the aircraft, he spoke to one in an authoritarian tone.

"I'll take care of the passengers, Sergeant Sim-mons." His voice seemed familiar, but Susan couldn't identify it over the engine noise on the nearby runway.

"Go check the loading platform to be sure everything's aboard," he said. Since he was giving orders, he must be an officer, probably the aircraft commander. Could he be in on this dreadful scheme to kidnap her?

Then he walked across the ramp and stepped into the glare of the floods lighting the apron.

Susan took a quick breath of pure astonishment. His hawklike face was almost as familiar as her own. Not ready to believe her own eyes, she stared so long she finally had to blink.

It was her old boss, Major Savage.

Major Savage. What was he doing here? Obviously commanding this aircraft.

Thank God, she thought, weak with relief. She tried to hold her arms out to him, but her two captors kept them pinned firmly by her side.

Major Savage. Rescue was at hand. He'd know what to do with these people holding her captive—and with whomever was trying to commandeer this aircraft.

As the major strode down the ramp and turned toward Susan, she felt a chill of foreboding race down her spine. Now that the loadmasters had left, her two captors rushed toward him. In their eagerness, they moved as fast as they could, forcing her to run. The major intercepted them a few feet from the ramp.

Unfazed by her taped mouth and shoeless feet, he eyed her up and down. "Lieutenant Wade," he said. His voice was raspy and cold, just the way she remembered it. "When we're airborne, we'll talk." He shifted his gaze to the woman beside Susan. "Bring her on board."

Susan wanted to scream out her terror and disappointment, wanted to tell the world this man was a traitor. A suffocating sensation tightened her throat as she watched him turn and walk away.

THE AIRCRAFT accelerated quickly down the runway for takeoff, its four turboprop engines at full throttle. Inside, the noise was deafening.

The woman, Marta, sat on one side of Susan on a seat with a webbed canvas back along the metal side of the C-130. The man sat on Susan's other side.

With a sudden quick movement, Marta turned toward Susan and stripped the tape from her mouth. She felt the skin rip from her lips and bit her tongue to keep from screaming. Running her tongue over her lips, she tasted blood.

With the tape in her hand, Marta grinned and mouthed the words "Too bad," her eyes as hard as granite. The intense engine noise made normal conversation impossible.

Deliberately Susan turned her head so the woman wouldn't see the brightness in her eyes. The stinging on her lips was matched by aching twinges in her feet. After she buckled her seat belt, she'd rubbed her feet and pulled down the legs of the too-large flight suit to cover them. Now feeling was returning to them with a vengeance.

On her other side, the man was toying with something in the leg pocket of his flight suit. *Probably a gun.* Why had he brought it? She was as helpless as a newborn. Shuddering, she tried not to think about what they were going to do to her.

Where was Derek now? How could she have thought he was in league with these people? Right from the beginning she'd sensed something strong and good in him. Why hadn't she trusted her intuition? If she had, maybe she wouldn't be in this mess.

But even if he was okay, he couldn't help her now that the C-130 was airborne. She was beyond anybody's help. As soon as they found out what they wanted to know, they were going to kill her. Nothing she could do or say would stop them.

Now that she knew Major Savage was running the smuggling ring, he couldn't let her live. She might prolong her life a few minutes by refusing to answer his questions, but that would only make him angry and her death more unpleasant.

Well, she'd tell him everything written in the notebook. Brian's figures couldn't hurt anybody, now that he was dead. The major probably guessed he'd been skimming off the top. That must be why he'd been killed. The figures in the notebook would tell him exactly how much.

But she wouldn't reveal Derek's real identity. If Major Savage didn't already know who Derek was, he'd never find out from her.

She stiffened as the aircraft leveled out. He had said they'd talk when the plane got airborne. That meant he'd be coming soon. Every cell in her body seemed to freeze at the thought.

From her troop seat along the side of the plane, Susan was only a few steps from the bulkhead separating the cargo bay from the crew area. Even as she stared, the curtain in the bulkhead opened, and she smelled fresh coffee. The odor reminded her of the big office coffeepot and Colonel Tinnerman's many kindnesses. How could she have thought he might be involved with this awful gang? And how could she have imagined Derek had anything to do with his murder?

Heart thumping madly, she stared at the parted curtain. Major Savage stepped down into the cargo bay, pulling the curtain closed behind him. In spite of herself, Susan cringed. Though small and wiry, he had always been intimidating with his hawklike features. Now, knowing what she did about him, he terrified her. With the dim light in the cargo bay, he looked even more menacing.

He focused on her two abductors. "Get some coffee. I want to talk to her alone." He had to shout over the roar of the engines. Though the aircraft had leveled out, there was no discernible difference in the noise level.

Abruptly her captors scrambled out of their seats and disappeared through the curtain into the darkness behind it. He stood before Susan with his arms folded.

"Lieutenant Wade," he shouted. "You have me at a disadvantage. Now you know who I am, but I have no idea who you are."

Her jaw dropped. What was he saying? With the engines roaring in her ears, could she have misunderstood him?

"Please enlighten me," he said with a humorless grin. His eye teeth looked like fangs. "Who are you and what were you doing at Fairchild?"

"I'm...I'm Susan Campbell," she stammered, thinking he meant her maiden name.

His eyes narrowed, and he examined her the way a swooping falcon studies a mouse a thousand feet below it. "We both know that's your cover name, Lieutenant. Whom are you working for?"

She took a deep breath and tried to keep her voice from trembling. "The Pentagon."

"Don't get smart with me," he snarled. "You're working for the FBI and Customs, just like your stinking husband. And so is your friend, Archer."

Floored, Susan stared at him tongue-tied. Finally she found her voice and blurted out her astonishment. "Did you say Brian worked for the FBI?"

"As if you didn't know." Savage dropped to the bucket seat next to Susan. "Your husband did a very stupid thing when he double-crossed me and turned FBI informant. But I didn't suspect *you* until Archer showed up."

He leaned toward Susan, his mouth so close to her ear that she could smell garlic on his breath. She forced herself not to back away.

"The FBI didn't do its usual professional job when they established Archer's cover," Savage said. "Unlike yours, which is beautiful. But his stinks. He's a man without a past."

"He's just an insurance agent," she insisted. "And I'm an air force lieutenant. Nothing more."

He gripped her shoulders. "Stop lying and tell me how much the FBI knows about my smuggling operation."

She forced herself to look him straight in the eye, hoping he'd see her anger, not her fear. "I'm not lying. I know nothing about the FBI."

He leaped to his feet. "All right, then, come with me. I want to show you the paratroop door. That's how you'll be leaving this plane if you don't stop lying." Grabbing her arm, he yanked her up.

"The paratroop doors?" she cried. There were two, one on each side of the aircraft under the wings. Was the major serious about forcing her to jump? Her insides froze into a lump of solid concrete as she pictured her falling body.

"I'll bet you've never seen a paratroop door open at fifteen thousand feet." Eyes narrow, he glared at her. "Get moving, Lieutenant, or I'll blow your head off right here."

Susan felt the unmistakable pressure of cold steel at the back of her neck.

THE METAL DECKING stabbed her feet with a thousand tiny needles. Grimly, Susan forced her shaky legs to plod toward the back of the aircraft.

She'd gone only a few steps when she stubbed her toe on the rollers used to shift cargo in the dimly lit bay. Excruciating pain shot up her leg. By biting her tongue she managed to keep from crying out. Major Savage would enjoy this sign of weakness. She was determined not to give him the satisfaction.

Hobbling as slowly as she dared, she maneuvered around the first of the big rectangular crates tied down the center of the C-130. Space wide enough for a man to walk had been left between the crates, and she swung abruptly to her right around the first. For an instant she was out of Savage's sight. In that brief instant she felt the air stir and smelled a tiny whiff of tobacco—the same odor she'd smelled on Brian's leather bomber jacket *and on Derek's*. Could he be near? Impossible. She was so desperate, she was imagining things.

Behind her, Savage prodded her in the neck again with the gun. "Go to the door on the right side," he yelled in her ear. "Don't go between the crates."

Was there any way to get his gun? Susan resisted the urge to glance at him over her shoulder. She felt his eyes piercing the middle of her back like a white-hot poker but didn't turn her head. She sniffed, hoping to smell tobacco. Instead, Savage's garlic breath hung in the air. But she smelled something else, too.

Cologne. The odor was too strong to be in her imagination. Was a loadmaster working back here somewhere, hidden by the cargo? Anxiously she glanced around. She'd thought they were alone. Another crewman meant another enemy.

She saw no one, but ahead loomed the right paratroop door. The cargo bay swirled dizzily around her.

Shoving her up against a crate, Major Savage pushed past her to the door, then swung around to face her. "What's the matter, Lieutenant? You look green. That door make you nervous?" His mouth took on an unpleasant twist. "Better tell me how much the FBI knows, or you've got a long drop ahead of you."

She was going to be sick. She felt bile rise in her throat and struggled to control it. Grabbing a corner of the nearest crate, she leaned against it for support.

Tell him what he wants to hear, she thought frantically. "You're right about my working for the FBI, sir.'' She shouted as loud as she could. ''They know all about you.''

His lips drew back showing his pointed eye teeth. ''You're lying again, Lieutenant. If they know all about me, why haven't they arrested me?'' He stepped toward the heavy metal door. ''Maybe if you get a good look at the mountains through an open troop door, you'll start telling the truth.''

For a moment his back was to her. In that split second, a tall figure jumped from behind a crate and knocked the gun from the major's hand. Savage lunged for it, but his assailant caught his arm and jerked him flat against the C-130's side.

Stiff with shock, Susan caught a glimpse of the man's face. *Ted Lindsey!* How had he gotten aboard this plane?

Run! her brain screamed. But before she could move, a strong arm grabbed her waist. She was lifted off her feet and jerked behind a crate. Her heart skipped a beat. Powerless in his grasp, she froze.

''I'm going to let you go,'' a voice yelled in her ear. ''But stay behind this crate.''

Derek! She spun around to face him. ''Is it really you?'' Tears sprang to her eyes.

He hauled her to him. ''I love you, Susan.'' Though he shouted, his voice was so filled with emotion she could barely hear him over the engine noise.

''Major Savage is the smuggler,'' she cried in his ear.

''I know.'' He held her close and kissed her in a way that was more tender than passionate. Finally he let her go, but caught her arm when she tried to peer around the crate. "By now Special Agent Lindsey should have him in handcuffs," he said. "But let's not take chances."

"Special Agent Lindsey?" She could hardly believe her ears.

"FBI," Derek replied, grinning. "Three agents and yours truly came aboard in the last two crates. By now they should have arrested the others. But we couldn't get Savage until he took the gun off you."

Derek peered around the corner of the crate, and then stepped from behind it. Susan followed.

Major Savage was in handcuffs. She and Derek joined Lindsey in front of the closed paratroop door.

Savage sneered at them, his lips a hard, thin line. "If you don't let us land in Colombia and walk away from this aircraft, the copilot will crash it, and you'll all be killed."

"Go to hell, Savage," Lindsey said, smiling back. "We don't need him—or you—to fly this plane."

"What do you mean?" A frown appeared on Savage's face.

"Have you heard of Don Albright?" Lindsey nodded toward Derek. "He's a qualified C-130 pilot."

Eyeing Derek, Savage muttered an obscene oath. "So the rumors were true. You faked your suicide."

"You bet," Derek replied. "And I've been looking forward to this day ever since." Catching Susan's eye, he reached for her hand.

Gazing at his face, Susan saw only love for her and relief that she was safe. Tonight there was no cynical smile that failed to reach his eyes. Instead, they shone with a luminous glow that seemed to light up the whole cargo bay. She was so proud of him she thought her heart would burst.

"IF THE FBI KNEW Major Savage was the mastermind behind the smuggling, why didn't they arrest him?"

Wrapped in blankets, Susan had rested on a crew bunk while Derek flew the C-130 back to Fairchild. Now, wide awake in her own living room, she was bursting with questions. Derek sat beside her on the couch, his arm around her shoulders. A fire blazed warmly in the fireplace.

"No evidence," he said. "When Savage found out your husband had turned FBI informer, he had him killed. Then Savage stopped smuggling the stolen high-tech equipment out of the country."

"I still can't believe Brian really worked for the FBI." She gazed at Derek, shaking her head in wonder. "Why do you suppose he didn't tell them who Savage was?"

"He didn't know," Derek said. "Savage organized the operation from the Pentagon. Then he arranged to have himself transferred to Fairchild to replace the squadron commander your husband killed. Savage ran the show with the woman, Marta, as his front. So he remained unknown to the men who worked with him."

The blazing fire spit a glowing spark onto the carpet. Rising, Derek flicked it back in the fireplace and drew the screen across the opening.

When he returned to the sofa, his face was troubled. "Marta was an assassin, like Krakow." He slid his arm across her shoulders, and Susan felt his fingers gently stroking her arm. "The FBI thinks Marta's the one who killed your husband."

Susan let her breath out in a huge sigh. "Then we know the whole story. Thank God it's over."

"Not quite the entire story," Derek said, obviously relieved that she had accepted the truth about Brian's death with equanimity. "I still can't figure out why Savage tried so hard to kill us."

"That's easy," she said. "He told me he thought we were working for the FBI, like Brian." She couldn't help smiling at the preposterous notion. "When we opened Brian's safe-deposit box, he figured we were getting too close."

Derek whistled softly. "So he guessed we were both undercover. He just came up with the wrong reason."

She nodded. "He said you were a man without a past. That's what made him suspicious. Then he must have remembered all my snooping around the C-130s, and that cinched it for him."

For a moment they sat quietly, watching the crackling fire, thankful they were together.

"The FBI thinks it can help me get my past back with only a slap on the wrist for jumping bail." Derek spoke quietly. "I wouldn't blame you if you walked away after the way I lied to you—but I love you, Susan. I want to spend the rest of my life with you, if you'll let me." There was an uncertain note in his voice.

Her heart leaped at the devotion in his eyes, void of vengeance and now brimming with affection. How she wanted to say yes. "I love you, too," she said, snuggling against him. "But we've only known each other a week. Let's wait till Christmas to make permanent plans.''

When Derek took her in his arms and kissed her, he prayed with his heart and soul that she'd never leave him.

''There's only one problem,'' he said hesitantly, after he'd released her. Dammit, he didn't want to talk about this now, but he couldn't afford to put it off.

''What's that?''

''You're the only person who knows I was the eyewitness to your husband's murder. If the FBI finds out, they might think I was gunning for him, that Savage's assassin just beat me to it. A notion like that could affect the way they handle my case.''

Watching her expressive face in the firelight, he caught an elfin sparkle in her brown eyes.

''That eyewitness had a lust for revenge,'' she said, snuggling closer. ''There's no connection between him and the man I love.''

For the rest of his life, Derek would remember the vote of confidence in her silken voice. His heart swelling with joy, he drew her close and whispered, ''I'll be counting the days until Christmas.''

HARLEQUIN *Super* ROMANCE®

...there's more to the story!

Superromance.
A *big* satisfying read about unforgettable
characters. Each month we offer *six* very different
stories that range from family drama to adventure
and mystery, from highly emotional stories to
romantic comedies—and much more! Stories
about people you'll believe in and care about.
Stories too compelling to put down....

Our authors are among today's *best* romance
writers. You'll find familiar names and talented
newcomers. Many of them are award winners—
and you'll see why!

If you want the biggest and best
in romance fiction, you'll get it
from Superromance!

Emotional, Exciting, Unexpected...

HARLEQUIN®
Makes any time special ®

HARLEQUIN®
INTRIGUE

WE'LL LEAVE YOU BREATHLESS!

If you've been looking for thrilling tales of
contemporary passion and sensuous love stories
with taut, edge-of-the-seat suspense—then
you'll love Harlequin Intrigue!

Every month, you'll meet four new heroes
who are guaranteed to make your spine tingle
and your pulse pound. With them you'll enter
into the exciting world of Harlequin Intrigue—
where your life is on the line
and so is your heart!

THAT'S INTRIGUE—
ROMANTIC SUSPENSE
AT ITS BEST!

HARLEQUIN®
Makes any time special ®